Something
She's
Not
Telling
Us

ALSO BY DARCEY BELL

A Simple Favor

Something She's Not Telling Us

A Novel

Darcey Bell

HARPER LARGE PRINT

An Imprint of HarperCollinsPublishers

HarperCollins books may be purchased for educational, business, or sales promotional use. For information, please e-mail the Special Markets Department at SPsales@harpercollins.com.

FIRST HARPER LARGE PRINT EDITION

ISBN: 978-0-06-297935-3

Library of Congress Cataloging-in-Publication Data is available upon request.

20 21 22 23 24   LSC   10 9 8 7 6 5 4 3 2 1

Something
She's
Not
Telling
Us

PART ONE

The Purple Jacket

1

April 19

Charlotte

The one thing they need to remember is the one thing they can't recall.

What was Daisy wearing when she left for school this morning?

It had been one of those mornings. An underwatery wake-up after a very late night.

Charlotte and Eli and Daisy were supposed to land at JFK by seven. But their plane was delayed in Mexico City. They didn't get back to their East Village loft until well after eleven.

Unforgivable on a school night. But what else could they do? Charlotte tells herself that the wooziness she feels has nothing to do with the two bottles of red wine she and Eli drank last night to celebrate getting back from Mexico in one piece.

Well, not exactly in one piece. In one piece if you discount the fact that they'd had to leave Charlotte's brother, Rocco, behind in Oaxaca.

Rocco's girlfriend, Ruth, lost her US passport.

Charlotte hears herself groan.

"What's the matter?" Eli asks.

"Nothing." The first lie of the morning.

She doesn't want to think about what happened to Ruth's passport. She doesn't want to think about Ruth.

Anyhow, Rocco is safe. In the taxi back from JFK, Charlotte had gotten a text from him:

Boarding plane home. All good. Talk tomorrow.

Thank God he's okay. And thank God that Charlotte doesn't have to feel guilty about leaving him in Mexico, with Ruth.

Now, the first morning they're back, Charlotte tries to convince herself that the goofy disorientation she feels has nothing to do with the fact that, buzzed out of her mind from drinking all that celebratory red wine with Eli, she took Ambien to fall asleep. How much? Enough that now, when she turns her head toward

Daisy's voice, her brain doesn't seem to be turning along with the rest of her.

Probably that sloshy brain is why she and Eli didn't hear the alarm on her phone, or the backup alarm on *his* phone, why they didn't open their eyes until Daisy ran into their bedroom.

"Mom! Dad! Don't I have school today?"

Yes, sweetheart. You have school.

So now the problem of Daisy's breakfast. Charlotte can do it, even though she'll probably be late for her nine o'clock meeting.

The event planners have to understand—Charlotte has a school-age child!

They don't have to understand *anything*. There are dozens of hungry, creative floral designers in New York who can take meetings at dawn because they don't have to pack their kid's lunch.

The milk is sour, and someone (no one's perfect, not even Eli!) put an empty Cheerios box in the refrigerator. What else is there? A banana. A massive Sub-Zero with nothing inside but spoiled milk and one dead banana. Daisy hates bananas, even when they aren't mottled with gray-green splotches.

Eli can buy Daisy a doughnut on the way to school. It's not the ideal breakfast, nothing Charlotte would admit to when the mothers get together, not even when everyone's bitching about what their kids won't eat. But it's better than nothing. Better than Daisy going to kindergarten with an empty stomach on her first day back after spring break. And Daisy will love it. Charlotte worries about how much her daughter likes sugar. Most kids do, she knows, but she can't help thinking that sweets might really pose a danger to her daughter's fragile health.

At eight in the morning, the loft is already bright, with a view of the pinkish, early-spring sun warming the beautiful bridges—Brooklyn, Manhattan, Williamsburg. Charlotte counts them—one, two, three—as if she's afraid they might have vanished while she was out of the country.

Eli says, In this city you pay for sunlight. Whenever Charlotte thinks about how much the loft cost, she has to knock off $400,000 from its terrifying price.

Charlotte smells smoke. Dear God, is the building on fire? Welcome home.

Last month, the city fire marshals came to warn them that they have six months to replace the old wooden staircase in the hall with metal, or the building will be condemned. The marshals don't care if Charlotte and Eli own their loft, or how beautiful they've made it.

All that money, all that costly, painstaking renovation—so their home can smell like an ashtray.

Charlotte's pretty sure that the building's not on fire. Her downstairs neighbor, Ariane, the stubborn, difficult widow of a famous painter, refuses to stop smoking. One spark, and all her late husband's canvases will go up in a flash.

Charlotte's family house in upstate New York burned down when she was in high school. So she's sensitive about fire. Not obsessed or phobic, but definitely aware.

The last holdout when the building went co-op, Ariane is why the staircase *hasn't* been replaced. She refused to sign the release, even when Eli offered to pay for the project. When the co-op (Eli is president of the tiny board) banned smoking, Ariane responded by switching to expensive black cigarettes, as smelly as cigars.

In her charitable moments, Charlotte thinks: Who can blame her? Ariane has no money. And her crazy middle-aged son, Drew, moved back in with her a few months ago. Charlotte knows that Ariane resents her for her privilege, her money, for the beauty of their loft, for Charlotte's easy life. For what Ariane *thinks* is easy. But what can Charlotte do? She can't think of a way to defuse the ill will between herself and her downstairs neighbors.

Charlotte has heard Ariane and Drew shouting and

slamming doors, sometimes all night long. Fighting and smoking and fighting.

The smoke would be less upsetting if Daisy weren't asthmatic.

Every puff Ariane and Drew exhale up through the floor terrifies Charlotte. So far cigarette smoke isn't among Daisy's triggers, but there's always the chance that smoke could bring on an attack. Sometimes Charlotte lies awake at night, smelling smoke or maybe just *thinking* she smells smoke, feeling scared and enraged, waiting to hear that first horrifying wheeze and rasp from Daisy's room.

If that happens, if Daisy has an attack, they'll have to sue Ariane or move . . . or something.

Actually, Drew scares Charlotte even more than the smoking. Charlotte doesn't like the twitchy smile on his face when he sees Daisy and pats her on the head. Who pats five-year-old girls on the head? Charlotte hates to think this way, but with his furtive little face, his steel-rimmed glasses dirty with fingerprints, his brush of short gray hair, stiff with excessive product that is probably natural grease, Drew looks like a serial child molester on *Law & Order: Special Victims Unit.*

One especially paranoid night, Charlotte woke Eli and made him look up Drew in the online sex offender registry. But Drew wasn't on the list. Not yet.

It makes Charlotte super vigilant, as if she weren't already vigilant enough. What will they do when Daisy is old enough to go up and down the stairs—to pass Drew's door—on her own?

Charlotte's shrink, Ted, is helping her work on not worrying quite so much. Not living in fear. Not worrying about Drew, or about anything, until something happens. Until something is *about* to happen. It's a subject that she and Ted talk about, a lot.

She says that every mother is as bad as she is. And Ted oh-so-gently says she's wrong. There are mothers less plagued by fear and able to enjoy their lives more of the time. If only Charlotte were one of them! She can't stop worrying about what Daisy eats and doesn't eat, why she doesn't have more friends, why she seems so shy. Why she always seems so . . . worried. Like me, Charlotte thinks guiltily.

Charlotte can't explain how it works, but after fifty minutes in Ted's sunlit office looking down on Madison Square Park, she feels braver. More comfortable out in the world. More in control. Not that therapy isn't hard, not that she doesn't cry sometimes. But Ted knows what to say, or *not* say, to help her get through it—and get over the past. He's helping her forgive herself for the things she's done—well, for *one* thing she's done—that she can't seem to get over.

At the same time, Charlotte feels confident that she's handling her life so well that sometimes therapy almost seems like an indulgence. Except she has to watch out for the lasting damage done by crazy neglectful Mom, who became a normal person only after a stay in a facility—and really only after Charlotte and Rocco were out of the house.

Ted says that Charlotte needs to remember that her fantasies aren't real. She's too quick to imagine catastrophe and disaster.

By the time Daisy's old enough to come home on her own . . . who knows? Maybe they'll live someplace else. Maybe—better option—Drew will live somewhere else.

Eli goes into Daisy's room to help her pick out clothes for school. Charlotte hears the first sounds of a disagreement likely to escalate between her daughter and her husband. Charlotte needs to shower and get dressed, but she pauses outside Daisy's door.

Daisy is insisting on wearing the gauzy shirt, embroidered with flowers, that her grandmother—Charlotte's mother—bought her in Oaxaca. It's great that she wants to wear Grandma's present. But it's still very cold outside. And she's refusing to wear a coat.

The argument lasts until Eli throws open the window and says, "Not warm! It was warm in Mexico, but this is not that, here it's cold, cold, cold, *muñeca*." Charlotte likes when he calls Daisy "*muñeca*." It means *doll* in Spanish. Eli is half Panamanian.

Daisy says she doesn't care how cold it is, but finally she agrees to put on a blue cardigan over the flowered shirt. Her bright purple quilted jacket will go on top of that.

Charlotte would intervene if she had more energy, if she weren't hungover. Anyway, Daisy will shed the jacket the minute she gets to school. Her school is still so overheated—Charlotte has been in greenhouses colder than Daisy's school. She's had to stop herself from suggesting jungle plants that would thrive in the urban microclimate.

Charlotte wriggles into her navy Jil Sander power suit, wrestling with the zipper that seems to be saying: Sorry, girl! One too many tacos at Mom's house in Mexico!

A talking zipper means too much wine and too many sleeping pills. Charlotte changes shoes three times, ultimately deciding on a pair of Marc Jacobs heels, a bad idea if she plans to do any walking at all.

She keeps her favorite sneakers at the flower shop, where she'll go after her meeting, to catch up with her assistant, Alma. Charlotte will answer her emails, do some work, and chill until it's time to pick up Daisy from her after-school program at P.S. 131.

By that afternoon, Charlotte will wonder: What *was* Daisy wearing?

What did they finally settle on?

Was it the blue cardigan or the pink sweater? The purple jacket or the puffy white vest?

She won't remember. Eli won't remember.

Their whole lives will be on the line.

How could they not know?

Just as Charlotte is getting out of the taxi at 39th Street and Eleventh Avenue—at the entrance to one of those brand-new skyscrapers that have popped up overnight while everyone's back was turned, like forty-story steel-and-glass mushrooms—her phone beeps.

Her nine o'clock meeting is now a four o'clock meeting.

Sorry! Scheduling conflict! Let us know if you can't make it!

Now Charlotte has a problem. Daisy's after-school program ends at five.

Standing on the windy corner, shielding her phone from the glare and trying to keep the Hudson River wind from wrecking her hair completely, she types: RESCHEDULE?

Then she erases the text. In her experience, by the time a meeting is rescheduled—New York being the dog-eat-dog struggle that it is—someone else will have been hired.

Charlotte desperately wants this job, not so much because of the money, which is good, but mostly because it represents a career move up to a whole nother level—a level to which she has aspired, one that will call on all her skill, creativity, imagination, everything she's learned about the way that flowers and plants and living things can transform a space.

They're asking her to design the floral arrangements for a benefit dinner at Cipriani. A dinner for eight hundred. Eight hundred! She's never worked on this scale, with this budget.

Just yesterday—was it really *yesterday?*—she'd been stuck in the Mexico City airport lounge when two emails came in.

The first was from Daisy's school. Two second graders have head lice. The risk to other grades is minimal, but . . . Charlotte skims . . . Watch and wait. It's the school's duty to inform parents. Sorry for any inconvenience.

The second message was from Alma at her florist

shop and floral-arrangement business, Buddenbrooks and Gladiola.

The header said: Good News!

"What's that?" Eli was reading over her shoulder, not a habit she loves.

Charlotte tried to focus. When she travels, a delay always means: head to the business lounge and drink as much free liquor as she can. She can always sleep on the plane, and no one—except, she hopes, the pilot—is driving.

"It says 'good news,'" Eli said. "That would seem to mean: good news."

"So it seems," said Charlotte.

The good news is: There is going to be a huge benefit dinner, in Manhattan, for hurricane relief in the Caribbean. An emergency response. A gala at Cipriani. They want to talk to Charlotte about the floral arrangements. Can she come in for a meeting at nine . . . tomorrow morning?

Tomorrow? Either the benefit really is an emergency response to an emergency situation, or—more likely—they'd hired someone else, and it hadn't worked out. All of which sharpens Charlotte's desire to show them what she can do.

She emailed back: Could they give her *some* idea of what they had in mind? No need to say she was in another country, relying on Aeromexico to get her back that night.

The organizers wanted something stark—maybe just bare branches—to reference how much land has been deforested. Maybe they could do something to suggest palm trees blown over.

The costs need to be low because they want the money to go to the islands, not the dinner. Charlotte (they said) has a reputation for thinking out of the box. They hope that the exposure will compensate for the modest fee.

If not for the margaritas, she would never have emailed back: WHAT'S "MODEST"?

It was twice what she'd ever been paid for any job. And the list of celebrities on the benefit committee was long and growing daily.

In the taxi home from the airport, Charlotte was already making sketches on the back of her boarding pass.

This morning, in the cab ride from the East Village to Hudson Yards, where the meeting is being held, she'd rehearsed how she would communicate her enthusiasm and her ideas for the project.

But now that the meeting has been postponed . . . She's still determined to go. If it threatens to run late, she has all day to find someone to pick up Daisy.

Eli has to leave the theater. It's as simple as that. Or she can ask Alma.

PERFECT, she texts, though it isn't perfect at all.

It could hardly be less perfect. SEE YOU AT 4.

Charlotte has loved flowers ever since she was little. Not a day goes by when she isn't grateful for having flowers in her life. They *are* her life. Though she's worked at the business six days a week for over a decade, she still loves opening the shop.

Alma would be happy to do it. But Charlotte loves waking up early, leaving Eli and Daisy asleep, and walking—even in winter—all the way from the East Village to the Meatpacking District.

Some blocks are darker, emptier, windier, but she never feels cold or lonely or scared. The word she thinks is: *private.* As if the city were made for her. Every morning, she buys coffee from Ali or Felipe at the all-night bodega and brings it to the store. The warmth and smell of the coffee is happiness in a cup printed with Christmas holly all year.

She loves turning on the lights, seeing the flowers, and thinking (though she knows it's ridiculous) that the flowers are happy to see her. She loves the everyday details: signing for the deliveries, talking to the drivers who take such pride in their fragile cargo. She knows the names of their wives and kids. She gives them huge tips at Christmas.

She even loves reading her email. More job offers are coming in, charity dinners and weddings. When she clicks on her business account, she feels as if a stranger is going to give her a present: money—and something to think about, a fun problem to solve.

Charlotte was high on weed—that was pre-Daisy—when she came up with the name for her shop: Buddenbrooks and Gladiola. It seems a little twee to her now, but there's a story that a certain kind of reporter likes to tell. She leaves out the weed when she explains that she named her shop after a novel she'd never understood and a flower she'd never liked—until one day she realized how amazing they both are. It's the perfect early-midlife lesson: a second shot at wisdom.

That story, which was true, got her a write-up and a photo in O, The Oprah Magazine.

Charlotte has gotten some lucky press, a helpful interview in W in which she said that her influences were the Victorian language of flowers, punk rock, and 1960s science fiction. The people who run charity benefits like her brand, a little edgy and modern instead of old and stodgy, and she charges less than people who have been in the business longer, though her fees are increasing.

When the commissions began coming in, Charlotte opened a studio in Bushwick and hired more help: smart kids who know and care about flowers. She pays decent wages with benefits, and she arranges cars when her workers need to go home late.

She keeps the Gansevoort Street shop open, though the rent has skyrocketed and it barely breaks even, because that's where she started. That's where she still likes to be. She loves opening boxes of perfect pink roses, each wrapped in white tissue paper and cellophane. She loves the birds-of-paradise, cleomes, zinnias, cosmos, and bachelor buttons, which are basically weeds but look stunning in masses. She loves the smell of flowers, living, dying, on the edge, even the chemical spice of the fungicide she sometimes has to use, though she tries to stay green.

Today Alma's opened up the store and taken care of the deliveries and tended the flowers in the chilled space behind the wall of glass. Alma could run the business—maybe she will someday. She took over when Charlotte was in Mexico, and as far as Charlotte can tell, everything's shipshape.

Everything, that is, but Alma, who's been in tears—or on the edge of tears—for weeks, ever since her boyfriend left her for a twenty-one-year-old: a woman precisely half Alma's age.

Charlotte's feet hurt. She'd taken her shoes off in the cab going downtown to the shop from Hudson Yards. She might have liked to walk if she'd been smarter about footwear. They're still a little puffy from the airplane ride from Mexico, and they swelled even more in the taxi. Just to get from the cab to the store, she had to stuff her feet back into the high heels.

Charlotte and Alma hug. She's family. They're always happy to see each other, even now, when so little makes Alma happy.

Alma says, "We've been selling tons of daffodils." That happens every spring, and now the thought of the bright clumps of white and yellow remind Charlotte of how many springs she and Alma have spent in this shop. "I forwarded you that email about the benefit. How was the meeting?" She looks at her watch. "It couldn't have taken very long. That's not a good sign."

"It's postponed till this afternoon. Listen, if I get stuck, can you pick up Daisy . . ."

Several times, in semi-emergencies, when Charlotte has been held up, Alma has picked up Daisy. She's on the pickup list at Daisy's school.

Daisy loves it when Alma comes for her because Alma always takes her out for ice cream, which Charlotte only rarely does. No one can eat ice cream every day!

Alma mumbles so softly that Charlotte can hardly

hear: "Therapy appointment." She pulls away from Charlotte's hug, and Charlotte sees tears on her face. Sometimes Alma sighs so loudly that their customers look alarmed, and often Charlotte catches her staring blankly into space.

"Never mind," says Charlotte. "I'll figure it out. I think Eli has a rehearsal, but maybe he can get out. Maybe I'll be done in time. I'll just have to play it by ear."

Charlotte tries to sound relaxed, but she hates being late to pick up her daughter.

She hates the thought of Daisy nervously watching the doorway to the gym where they have the after-school program. More than anything, she hates the idea that Daisy might feel anxious. In fact Charlotte has never once got there to find Daisy watching the door. She's always been busy doing the fun projects that the after-school teachers dream up.

Alma goes back to making a floral arrangement for a customer to send his wife for their fiftieth anniversary. Charlotte goes back to trying to call and text and email Eli, who keeps not answering. Maddening! She knows that Eli is having a hard time, but still . . . He *is* Daisy's father.

A decade ago, Eli did so well—first in real estate for foreign investment firms, then buying and selling domain names—that he was able to retire from finance and do what he loves, which is working in the theater. Right now he's the set designer/stage manager on a production of *Macbeth*, in a theater on the Lower East Side. Charlotte has to remind herself that he's earned the right—that is, the money—to do what he loves.

There's a crisis every day, and Eli's usually right in the middle. Several times, he hasn't taken her calls, and he and Charlotte argued about it. They have a child! Charlotte needs to reach him! He promised to do better, but he sometimes forgets his promises.

She texts Eli one more time, punching question marks into the phone. Again he doesn't answer. Is something wrong? How many bad things can happen at once?

She sends another message: NEED YOU TO PICK UP DAISY.

Let Eli be okay. Let Eli be okay and she'll never again pressure him into doing something he doesn't want to (or can't) do. He already does so much.

Charlotte closes her eyes and seems to hear her therapist's calming voice:

Don't worry till something happens. Don't imagine the worst. Don't obsess about the past—and about things you can't change.

Who else can she call? Rocco has been on Daisy's

pickup list ever since—against her better judgment—
she let Rocco and Ruth take Daisy to the circus. She'd
felt sure she'd made a terrible mistake, but they'd all
had a good time. Charlotte has admitted to Ted—and
no one else—that one of the things she distrusts about
Ruth is the fact that she and Daisy seem to like each
other.

She texts Rocco: CAN U GET DAISY IF I NEED U?

Rocco's the only person she lets herself text in that
dopey millennial shorthand.

Rocco doesn't answer. The last she heard he was on
his way back from Mexico.

Let Rocco be all right too. I'll give up drinking. Rocco
has! And I'll never get impatient with Daisy, no matter
how crazy she drives me. I'll never yell at her, never—

She considers asking Alma if she could please cancel
her shrink appointment, but she's afraid that Alma will
dissolve in a puddle. Alma takes a long look at Charlotte and reaches into her multipocketed, multizippered
purse and extracts a bottle of pills. Alma's discovered
muscle relaxants since her breakup.

The Xanax might not be the best idea after last
night's wine and sleeping pills. But Charlotte takes it
anyway, except that it doesn't relax her. It just makes
her sleepy and anxious at the same time, an uncomfort-

able combination. Still . . .

The pill helps Charlotte get through the next few hours, helps her decide to wing it. And . . . oh, yes, it lulls her into what's probably a false sense of security. Everything will be all right. At worst, she'll be half an hour late. The school will just charge her extra. One of the teachers will stay with Daisy. They're definitely not going to throw her out on the street. At least she hopes not. Why is it so hard for her to trust people to take good care of Daisy?

By the time Charlotte needs to leave for the meeting, the pill has worn off, in a particularly unhelpful way. She feels awful. Anxious. On edge.

She looks out the window. Her Uber's arrived, as if by magic. For the first time in history, the driver has arrived *sooner* than the app predicted. She can tell by the way the driver is looking at his phone that he's not a patient guy.

Okay. Showtime.

She runs into the back room and looks in the mirror. Not bad. Only a little worse for wear. In her mind, she goes over—one more time—what she has to say. And she practices her most confident, competent professional smile.

Then she rushes out of the shop, forgetting to say

goodbye to Alma, hearing Alma's wan "good luck" trailing her out the door.

Charlotte passes through two sets of metal detectors and takes two elevators to the conference room. The space might seem less intimidating were the leather swivel chairs occupied by more than the three people who look like little dolls at the gargantuan table that dwarfs them.

They rise to shake hands—a man in a Hollywood-blue suit and two women, both blond, both in their early thirties, both wearing little black dresses. The women could almost pass for mirror images—or fraternal twins except that one is wearing lush false eyelashes and twice as much makeup as her coworker.

They say their names, but Charlotte is too distracted to catch them. Now she may never learn them. What if she has to call the office and ask for one of them by name? She should never have taken Alma's pill. Or drunk so much wine last night, or those margaritas in the airport.

She sneaks a look at her watch.

Four ten.

A minute later, she looks again.

Four fifteen.

How is that even possible?

The man motions for her to sit down and clears his throat in a way that says, We're too busy for small talk. "Okay, Charlene, show us what you've got."

"It's Charlotte."

Less Makeup seems embarrassed by her boss's rudeness, or just his businesslike-ness. "So how did you first get interested in flowers?"

Charlotte wishes she'd let her boss be as rude or brusque as he wanted. She's all for any approach that will speed this up.

"I meant *Charlotte*. Humble apologies. I haven't had my fifth cup of coffee. Or my first cocktail. And the crazy thing is, I can't ask one of you to get it. Not unless I feel like having a long heart-to-heart with human resources about mistreating my female employees. Oops. I mean . . . coworkers." He waits for the laughs that don't come.

"No worries," Charlotte says. A phrase she despises. To be alive at this moment and not to be worried would be clinically insane. And she's always worried, no matter what her therapist says.

She produces her portfolio, and they riffle through the sketches that look like what they are: drawings she made in a taxi. Charlotte sees the sketches through their eyes: palm trees drawn by insomniac toddlers.

The man and More Makeup nod. Their faces are

masks of pure nothing. Less Makeup (Charlotte wishes she'd registered their names—how *will* they stay in contact if she gets this job, which she probably won't) says, "Well . . . I guess we can work with these."

Charlotte says, "I was thinking about long black and red stems, vaguely . . . ikebana. Though no one will *think* ikebana unless they're thinking harder than anyone's ever thinking when they walk into a party space."

"Not me," says the man. "Me, I'm thinking like crazy. I'm thinking, How soon can I blow this clam shack and get home in time to watch the game?"

"Now that's inappropriate," says More Makeup. "And not funny."

Less Makeup mimes being deep in thought. "You know, the ikebana meme might not be so bad. Let's not forget the tsunami. Not a major tsunami this time, not a headline grabber. But a wall of water, nonetheless."

The man says, "I'm going to guess that no one has forgotten the tsunami."

The women turn back to Charlotte. It's the women against the man now, three against one, though it's just a game. At the end of the day—this *is* the end of the day, Charlotte thinks, fighting down a mini-surge of panic—he's the boss.

Charlotte says, "We'll keep with just a few red

leaves and blackened palm trees, a combination of real and artificial, ghostly and vital. I know a guy who can do wonders with bare branches. I'm thinking something . . ." (Charlotte also hates that phrase, *I'm thinking something*, so much that she says it twice.) "I'm thinking something . . . a little Halloweenish, postapocalyptic, not ugly or depressing but still perfect for this time of catastrophic weather events."

"Now we're heating up," says the man. "I'm beginning to get excited. Am I even allowed to say that these days? That I'm getting . . . *excited*?"

"You can't be too careful," Less Makeup says mirthlessly.

Eager, helpless Charlotte smiles. She steals another glance at her watch.

Four thirty.

This is taking forever. She'd assumed they were busy people. But they (the guy, anyway) are enjoying this. As if they have all the time in the world.

Just then she gets two texts in a row. *Bing bing.*

"I need to check this." Her voice is almost a moan.

"Kids?" says Less Makeup, with a patient little frown.

"One child," Charlotte corrects her, sounding like the grade school teacher she has no desire to sound like.

First text from Eli: Stuck in theater.

Second, from Eli again: Can't get Daisy. Sorry.

So at least Eli's alive. That's good news. The bad news: He can't pick up Daisy.

Now he decides to tell her.

Pick up. Charlotte thinks of a news clip she saw last night in which a pickup truck was being swept by water down a California street. Wall of water. This is not *that!* She's just worried and feeling sorry for herself because there's no one to help her. Everyone's told her to hire a nanny. This is the price she pays for her ridiculous pride in being a hands-on mom. But why must the buck always stop with her? She could write a book entitled *Mommy Buckstop.* Who would read it? Lots of women. Mothers. They'd understand right away.

She texts Eli back: I CAN'T! HELP!

He doesn't answer. Infuriating. It's up to Mommy Buckstop to figure out what to do next.

More Makeup says, "We'll send you a slide show of images of the hurricane. We just want you to see what we're thinking. Just for inspiration."

"Not just '*thinking*' but '*doing*,'" the man corrects her, hanging air quotes around her mistake. "This is what we're *doing* here. What gets us out of bed in the morning."

"That's what I mean," says the woman. "What we are thinking and *doing.*"

The man presses a button, then a switch. The lights dim, a screen descends behind him, and Charlotte sees destroyed homes, floating vehicles, anguished children, people waiting on food lines, Red Cross workers distributing water. It's obscene to use these people's suffering for inspiration, but she's not going to say that. And they're raising money for them. *Good cause, good cause, good cause.* She thinks those two words, like a mantra, until she can look at them without fearing that her face has turned into a Medusa mask of don't-speak-to-me, don't-come-near-me, I'm-late-to-pick-up-my-daughter.

The slide show is taking a thousand years. She's trapped here by good manners and by her desire to work for them. The minutes are flying by. What now? What now? What now?

They could stop at any point. She needs to pick up Daisy!

"Right," she says. "I've got this."

It takes all of Charlotte's self-control not to look at her watch and look again ten seconds later.

"Yes, well," says the man, "one more detail before we break up the party. It's a bit of a delicate question, but . . . can we assume your business includes employees of color? It's not a question I'd ask, but there are other voices in the mix, voices I have to listen to."

"You can," Charlotte says. "It does. I do." Though she'll be damned if she'll pimp out—by name—the Mexican, black, and Asian kids at her Bushwick studio. Plus she needs to leave. Now.

"Then let's go forward," Boss Man says. All three shake Charlotte's hand. By the time she leaves—thank you, got to run!—she has twenty minutes to get Daisy before the end of after-school.

It's seems she's got the job. But she's too nervous to process that, too anxious to feel happy.

The assistant who shows Charlotte to the elevator is wobbling so perilously on painful-looking Louboutin heels that Charlotte lurches forward to catch her. The young woman shoots her a filthy look.

"Thanks." What is she thanking her for?

"No problem. Have a good one." The young woman says it like a curse. That's probably just Charlotte's own anxiety and paranoia.

Have a good what? A good *what*?

It's just money. Charlotte will just have to pay extra— the late fine—and the fine is not all that much. But Daisy will be alarmed. That's what Charlotte wants to avoid.

The minute she leaves the building, she gets a text from Rocco: Home.

Great. Too late now.

Another text from Rocco. Going to sleep. Don't call.

Great again. Why *would* she call at this point? Charlotte's probably being unreasonable . . . but she can't shake the certainty that Ruth has sent the text. Rocco would never say, Don't call, not even if he was exhausted.

Well, they're safely home from Mexico. One less thing to worry about.

Then she begins to run.

At least she had the wherewithal to bring along her sneakers.

When you race down the street without being chased, it's as if you're surrounded by a cocoon of stress and pain. People move out of your way, like drivers moving over for an ambulance with its siren wailing. Beneath everything, humans are animals. They recognize animal fear.

Don't worry until something actually happens. She tries to hear Ted's sensible voice.

There's nothing to be afraid of. Five dollars for every ten minutes you're late. So that's . . . she's too freaked to do the math.

She runs down the block, crossing diagonally against the light, weaving between cars. How awful if she were killed on her way to pick up her daughter. Daisy would never get over it. No matter how much of a hurry Charlotte's in, she has to wait for the light, look both ways.

She tries hailing a cab, but there are no cabs. There never are when you need them. Finally, a rogue limo slows down.

The driver leans out his window.

"Where you going?"

"First Avenue and Twelfth Street."

"Thirty dollars." He must see the panic on her face.

It's an outrageous price, but she'll pay. If he'd said a hundred dollars, a million dollars, she would have paid that too. Well, maybe not a million. She can hardly breathe.

"Can you hurry?" she says.

"My favorite words," the driver says, and zooms off down the street.

Twenty minutes later, Charlotte rushes into the cafeteria, hoping she looks as anxious and breathless as she feels so that the after-school teachers will know she's made every effort—every painful, superhuman attempt—to get there on time.

There are at least ten kids still there, so Charlotte's not the last, which is a relief. They're all slurping something out of a paper cup, and when she passes, one of the kids says, "Microwave pizza!"

"Cool," says Charlotte. "Delicious."

She doesn't see Daisy, but that happens. Sometimes her group stays behind in the classroom or goes to the library.

Charlotte's anxious, but she always is. She never once comes to pick up Daisy—and she does it every day—without feeling that twinge of absurd, irrational fear that her daughter won't be there. It only makes her happier to see her sweet little face.

Right away she can tell that something's wrong. The supercompetent after-school teachers—Tanya, Edditha, and Michelle—are trying not to look confused. Clustered around the sign-out book, they scrutinize the final page.

"What's going on?" Charlotte asks.

What she wants to hear is: Nothing. But she senses that's not what she's about to hear.

Tanya says, "I guess there's been a little mix-up. She's already been picked up."

Maybe Eli changed his mind and left rehearsal—how grateful Charlotte will be! She feels guilty for having been annoyed with him. She'll make it up to him somehow. She'll be extra nice this evening, and then tonight, in bed . . .

"Her dad?" Charlotte says.

Tanya and Michelle look at each other.

"No," says Michelle. "Her aunt."

"Her aunt?" says Charlotte. "What aunt? She doesn't have an aunt!"

Her anxiety has gone from zero to sixty in under five seconds. She tells herself: Calm down. It's a mistake. They'll figure this out and get Daisy from her classroom, and that will be that. Problem solved.

She reaches for the sign-out book.

"Can I see?" A jagged vibrato shakes her voice, though it's too early for panic. Unless it isn't. Before she can look at the list of names of the parents and caretakers happily going home with their children, the women gently repossess it and call the head of after-school, Mrs. Hernandez.

"Hello, Charlotte," Mrs. Hernandez says, proving that, like her employees, she remembers everyone's name. "There must be some misunderstanding. Your sister-in-law signed Daisy out at three—that's over two hours ago." She shows Charlotte the line on which it says:

3:00. Ruth Seagram

"She's not my sister-in-law!" It's not what Charlotte means to say. What she wants to say is: I need this to be fixed! I need this not to have happened! Why does Ruth have my daughter? Someone needs to make this right! Now!

Michelle says, "She was very nicely dressed, in a suit and little heels and this big fuzzy vest."

What does Charlotte care what her daughter's kidnapper was wearing?

Actually, she cares a lot. What Ruth's wearing might be the most important fact in the world, second only to what Daisy has on.

What was Daisy wearing this morning? Why can't Charlotte remember?

Maybe Rocco and Ruth came for Daisy. Maybe Eli reached Rocco.

"Was she alone?"

"No," says Michelle. "There was a guy with her."

So it was Rocco. Thank God.

"Big guy? Six four? Dark curly hair? Two-day stubble, probably? Three-day stubble, maybe." Charlotte laughs. "My brother."

Tanya and Michelle aren't laughing.

"No . . . ," Michelle says. "This guy was short. Kind of slight. Glasses. Graying hair."

"Heavily gelled," says Tanya. "I remember thinking that the guy used an awful lot of product."

It sounds like someone Charlotte knows, but who? Where is Daisy? Why has Ruth taken her daughter? Who was Ruth with?

They wait several minutes for two school officials, a

man and a woman Charlotte has never met. She doesn't want to meet them, doesn't want to know who they are or what their position is. She doesn't want to watch them calmly and professionally dealing with the question of who might have taken her daughter by mistake. Mixed signals, confusion, whatever. Who has stolen Daisy?

With her permission is what these strangers seem to be saying. They show her Ruth's name. On the pickup list. There it is. Right there.

Then she remembers: The circus. Rocco and Ruth took Daisy to the circus. She should have taken Ruth off the list. But it didn't seem important. And she'd had so many more urgent things that she had to do.

Charlotte is going to wake up, and this will be a normal afternoon. Daisy will appear in the doorway and burst into smiles when she sees her mom, and she'll run across the cafeteria, swinging her lunch box in circles.

Mrs. Hernandez says, "We have it on record . . . Ruth Seagram is right here on the list . . . We can only do what you tell us."

Charlotte should have taken Ruth off the list. She had other things on her mind. She'd been focused on the Mexico trip. And now her daughter has been kidnapped by a woman claiming to be her sister-in-law. Rocco and Ruth aren't married. Daisy doesn't have an aunt!

Once more she thinks: Calm down. There's probably some logical explanation. Maybe Ruth just wants to spend the afternoon with Daisy. Maybe Rocco got Charlotte's text and asked Ruth to pick Daisy up, since he couldn't or wouldn't. Maybe this isn't a problem. But why didn't Ruth ask her—or tell her? Why didn't anyone bother to inform her?

She knows in her heart and in the pit of her stomach that it *is* a problem. That something is not right. That something is very, *very* wrong. And this time—she doesn't know how she knows, but she does—it's not just her overactive imagination.

Who was the man with Ruth?

"Where is she?" Charlotte says. "Where the fuck is my daughter?"

The whole cafeteria goes quiet. Everyone is looking at them. Even the kids, especially the kids, know something's going on. They stop playing and yelling and eating their microwave pizza—and stare. How lucky they are, how safe. None of those children have been kidnapped. Only Charlotte's child. She has never felt so lonely than she does here, surrounded by teachers and kids.

"Please," says Mrs. Hernandez. "We understand that you're upset. But you're upsetting the children. I'm sure we can figure this out. We'll clear this up in no time."

Charlotte looks at the clock. It's five thirty.

Daisy's been gone for two and a half hours.

She's gasping. Someone brings her a paper cup of brackish water. She takes a sip.

Disgusting.

"Daisy's asthmatic."

Whatever warm, cooperative fellow feeling flowing between her and the others cools in an instant. They are *not* all in this together. She is in this alone.

"We *do* know she's asthmatic," says Michelle. "Believe me, we are fully aware of the children's health issues."

Just as Charlotte is growing enraged by the thought that the person she loves most in the world has become a "child with health issues," Tanya says, "We know that Daisy's inhaler is in her backpack."

"Did she take her backpack?" Let the answer to that one question be yes, and Charlotte can cope with everything else.

"Yes," says Tanya. "I remember. We're careful . . . because of your daughter's health issues . . ."

They look toward the corner where the backpacks are piled in a heap. Even from a distance Charlotte can tell that Daisy's pack—a lurid purple, decorated with black and white piano keys—isn't there.

Daisy was wearing her purple jacket.

Daisy's inhaler! Charlotte has the GPS tracker on

her phone that lets her locate the inhaler. If Daisy has the inhaler, she can find out where Daisy is.

The app was a present from Ruth. Best not to think about that now.

Charlotte whips out her phone. "There's an app. So we can find her inhaler . . . it's a tracking device . . . it's . . ."

She's tapping her phone as she says this, trying, even in her panic, to show these strangers that she is a responsible mother. She's figured out how never to lose her daughter's rescue inhaler. Meanwhile they are the ones who have lost *her child*.

She finds the app and presses LOCATE. Her screen goes blue, and a brighter blue doughnut circles and circles and circles. The children in the cafeteria have lost interest in her and resumed making noise. Charlotte hopes someone is looking after those kids. The people around her are watching her phone.

In tiny yellow letters against the blue background, it reads:

Oops! Service interrupted, please try again later.

Oops. She's gotten used to Oops! when online service breaks down. Oops! Her daughter has been kidnapped.

She feels her heart plummet in her chest. She feels like she's swallowed an egg. She wants to sit down. She can't sit down. She will get stuck there forever and never find Daisy.

She wants to throw her phone against the wall. But that's the last thing she can do. She needs the phone now more than ever. She tries again, presses LOCATE again, and the same thing happens. Oops!

"Turn it off and on," suggests Tanya.

"I will," says Charlotte.

"The reception's not great down here," says Michelle.

It was always fine before.

Charlotte says, "Are you sure she didn't leave her backpack here?" This makes no sense, she knows. If the inhaler was in her backpack, and if her backpack was in the gym, that familiar, comforting beep would be audible across the room.

"Yes," says Tanya. "Your sister-in-law was clear about that."

"Let me say this one more time, okay? *I don't have a sister-in-law.*"

"Her name was on the list," repeats Mrs. Hernandez, as if Charlotte is Daisy's age. "And 'sister-in-law' was how she self-identified." She looks to the others for confirmation, and all of them nod.

Michelle says, "She told us that she was Daisy's aunt, and Daisy looked happy to see her Auntie Ruth."

Tanya says, "That's what we look for. The response of the child."

"And the guy?" says Charlotte. "Did my daughter respond to this man . . . this stranger?"

Tanya and Michelle look at each other and shrug.

How safe these women used to make her feel. And now they've become her enemies. How could they let this happen? Charlotte let it happen. Nothing was ever safe.

"Legally," says Mrs. Hernandez, "she was—"

"On the list," says Charlotte. Oops again! She sounds curt and ungrateful. But don't you get cut some etiquette slack when your child is missing? "Did they happen to say where they might be going?"

Tanya, Edditha, and Michelle—they all have photographic memories, but they're having a hard time with this.

Charlotte is texting Rocco and talking to them at the same time.

CALL ME! NOW!!!!!!

There aren't enough exclamation points for how urgent this is.

"Can you call the police?" Charlotte asks.

"You would have to make that call," says Mrs. Hernandez. "Because nothing illegal has happened."

"Call the police," says Charlotte. "I'm begging you."

"Let's give it a few hours," says Mrs. Hernandez. She smiles, as if to reassure Charlotte that this problem will be cleared up soon. They deal with these things all the time. Custodial parents, nannies, confusion. In fact this little problem is probably not a problem at all.

"We don't *have* a few hours," says Charlotte.

She runs outside with no idea where she's going. She just needs air, light, space, and to be away from people who want to help her, who say they want to help her, but who can't and won't do one single thing to help her. She'd loved those women until now. Now she hates them all, even though she knows that this isn't their fault.

Ruth was on the list.

Parents walk by, hand in hand with their children. Each loving, chattering pair is a knife in Charlotte's heart.

She texts Rocco and Eli separately.

RUTH HAS DAISY. SHE TOOK HER FROM SCHOOL.

Rocco texts back right away. Jesus X.

A second text, moments later, also from Rocco: Ruth will come here. Soon. Trust me.

Trust me. At this point Charlotte will trust anyone who says *trust me.*

Bing bing. Eli texts: Rocco says meet him at Ruth's. Wait there.

Seconds later Charlotte's phone rings. Her ringtone is a spooky theremin *woo woo woo* she downloaded from the internet. She's always been amused by its weird, ghostly sound, but now it terrifies her. It's strange how your favorite jokes can turn into bad jokes. Warnings you should have heeded.

It's Eli. Charlotte explains what's happened, trying to speak slowly, comprehensibly, to not hyperventilate. For Eli's sake. For Daisy's. For her own. She can hear, in Eli's voice, that he also is trying to stay calm. Charlotte loves Eli—she always has. She always will. No matter what.

"*Should* we meet at Ruth's?" he asks.

"There was a man with her—"

"What man?"

"I don't know. Not Rocco. That's what scares me."

"You want me to send a car to take you out to meet Rocco?"

"Subway's faster," Charlotte says. "I'll call you from there."

She calls Rocco, and miraculously, he picks up.

Charlotte says, "Is Ruth there? Is she back yet? Where's Daisy?"

"No . . . I don't think . . . I was sleeping . . ."

There's a funny rhythm in Rocco's voice. A slight drag and the hint of a slur. It reminds her of . . . when he was drinking.

Oh, no, please no. Not that too.

Has Rocco gotten drunk and done or said something to Ruth that set her off? Or has Ruth gotten Rocco drunk so she could leave him passed out—and she could go steal Daisy?

"Don't move," she tells her brother. "I'll be there as soon as I can."

2

Six Months Earlier

Charlotte

Early Saturday morning, Eli and Charlotte lie in bed drinking coffee, enjoying what grainy sunlight the park allows into their window. Their silence is so companionable, each other's presence so soothing, that they can listen, in perfect contentment, to the noises outside their loft. Traffic, car horns, parents packing to leave for the weekend, shouting at kids, slamming car trunks.

They talk about Daisy, who's begun kindergarten at the local public school and seems happy. They talk a little about their work.

It's only when they get to the question of what to have for dinner that Charlotte says what she's avoided saying too soon after Eli wakes up.

"You do remember that Rocco's bringing his new girlfriend for dinner?" How could Eli remember when she hasn't told him?

She's never sure why her brother always wants them to meet his girlfriends, most of whom have turned out to be seriously unbalanced. He wants to see if they approve, but it's never clear how, or if, their feelings influence his.

Eli says, "Great. Hide the valuables and don't cook anything too delicious."

Charlotte laughs, a giggle she makes when someone (usually Eli) kills a hope that she knows is unrealistic. Each time Rocco brings over a girlfriend, Charlotte hopes she's *the one*, though she hates the idea of *the one*. She wants her younger brother to be happy, to have someone to love him and help him, someone kind and decent and conscious. Or at least *sane*.

In therapy, Charlotte and Ted have discussed the possibility that Charlotte might be ever so slightly possessive and territorial about her brother—the way she is about her daughter. And maybe that's why she's so critical—hypercritical—of Rocco's women.

But Charlotte didn't imagine what those women actually did. Mae-Lynn came to dinner with a bag of organic broccoli crowns and a beaker of distilled water in which she insisted they steam them. The girlfriend after that, Kathy, stole from them, never anything expensive, but always something treasured, which was the point. Daisy's beloved stuffed giraffe, Eli's favorite fountain pen, a business card from a man who told Charlotte he'd developed a solution that made cut flowers last longer. Each time there was a frantic search, especially for Raffi, the giraffe. Kathy is out of Rocco's life, but Charlotte will never forgive her for pretending to look for the toy when she had it all along. Charlotte had been so afraid that the dust kicked up by their search would bring on one of Daisy's asthma attacks.

Rocco has trouble breaking up with these women. Underneath his surface toughness is a good guy who can't bear to hurt anyone and has that male terror of women's tears. He refused to believe Charlotte when she suggested that Kathy was a kleptomaniac. He didn't end the relationship until he found, in her tote bag, a framed photo of him and Charlotte, on the steps of their childhood farmhouse in the Hudson Valley. The photo must have been taken not long before their mother burned down the house and got sent away.

Rocco couldn't look at Charlotte when he returned the photo. She didn't need to see his face. She knew that his expression (detached or dreamy, depending on what you wanted to see) would be just like the look on twelve-year-old Rocco in the picture.

Before Klepto Kathy, he dated a woman who ripped out her hair in clumps, and before her the cutter, and before her the nudist, and before her the one who locked herself in their bathroom and swallowed a fistful of antibiotics from the medicine chest.

The stable ones never last long. Boring, Rocco says. He jokes about his love life. But he doesn't learn from his mistakes.

Why should Charlotte feel responsible? If she wants someone to blame (and who doesn't?), it should be their mother, who, acting on some selfish childish romantic impulse, named them after Charlotte Brontë and Mr. Rochester. Mom should have been a character in a nineteenth-century novel; that's how she imagined her life until Dad took off and moved to the city to live with an intellectual property lawyer who consulted for his law firm.

That stress must have been too much for him. He died two years later, of a heart attack.

Mom survived, more or less. After Dad left, she evicted their tenant, who taught at a college nearby and lived in the attic rental apartment in their family home—on the farm they'd inherited from Mom's parents and rented out to local farmers.

Mom moved into the apartment and left the house—and Rocco—to Charlotte. When that failed to bring Dad back, Mom really went off the rails. After she burned down the house, a fire that almost killed Rocco, she had a choice: either jail or a stay at a hospital, the latter of which she agreed to because its inmates included movie stars. After a while she was released, more or less cured. For a short time she lived with Rocco in an apartment in Hudson while Charlotte went to college. Neither Mom nor Rocco did well, and Rocco got into trouble, drinking and doing stuff that Charlotte doesn't like to think about now.

Not long after Rocco left home, Mom moved to Mexico. Now she's living in Oaxaca, still partly on the money from the family farm, which they sold to Andrew John, the Argentine billionaire hobby farmer for whom Rocco works now, trucking perfect vegetables to the Greenmarket in the city.

When Rocco first went to work for Andrew John, he had been drinking heavily. He'd been twice in and out of rehab, for which Charlotte and Eli paid. At the beginning Charlotte feared that her brother might resent working for the owner of the farm *they* used to own, but Rocco seems to like it.

He's been sober ever since.

Eli has asked a question that Charlotte is supposed to have heard.

"What's this woman's name?"

"We shouldn't think of her as 'this one.' It's Ruby. No, wait. Ruth. Rachel. Robin—"

"Don't worry, he'll introduce us. Hush. Daisy's awake."

Their daughter stands in the doorway, clutching the battered, pouchy giraffe she hasn't let out of her sight since Klepto Kathy returned it. Daisy took it to kindergarten and over the summer took it to day camp in her backpack. Five seems borderline old for that, but Eli and Charlotte let it go. They feel guilty for exposing her to an adult who would steal a toy.

Inch by inch, Daisy materializes in a white nightgown and a silver headband with two glittery kitty-cat ears.

"Have you guys been smoking?"

"Of course not," says Charlotte. "You know Daddy and I don't smoke. You know who it is." She points down at the floor—at Ariane's loft, beneath theirs— then puts her finger to her lips, as if Ariane and Drew could hear them talking.

"Right," says Daisy. "It's the bad people downstairs."

Without looking at Eli, Charlotte can feel him looking at her. He's asked her not to make Daisy so frightened of their downstairs neighbors, who so far haven't actually done anything wrong—except smoke.

Charlotte has told Daisy to never *ever* let Drew get her alone, no matter what he offers her, no matter what he says. All right, Eli's said. It's probably a good thing to warn Daisy about. But Charlotte doesn't have to remind Daisy every few days.

"They're not bad," says Eli. "They're just . . . unhappy."

Daisy looks from her father to her mother and back. Whom should she believe? Charlotte notices, as she often does, that Daisy looks nothing like her. She takes after Eli's Panamanian mother. When Charlotte and Daisy are alone, strangers assume she's adopted, but when Eli's there, they remark on how much she resembles her father.

As always, Charlotte wonders: Who *is* that beautiful child? Then comes the rush of feeling, the pressure in her chest, the shock of a love for which she has no words. She loves Daisy more than anyone. Even Eli, Charlotte secretly thinks, a secret even from herself.

"Climb on board, little. Cuddle up."

"*Pasa, amor,*" says Eli.

Daisy approaches cautiously, as if she hardly knows them, as if her real parents have been replaced by actors. She lies down on Charlotte's side of the bed, stiffly, on the far edge. Charlotte pulls her closer, and Daisy leans into her mother.

Should Charlotte tell her that Rocco is coming? Daisy adores her uncle, but when she finds out he's bringing someone, she might worry all day. Like Charlotte, she's a worrier. Both hate surprises. It's possible that when Rocco and Rachel or Ruby or Ruth arrives, Daisy won't leave her room, which will cast an awkward pall on the new-girlfriend welcome dinner.

The asthma is the most serious but only one of the things Charlotte frets about. Daisy is too formal, too polite for a little girl. And Klepto Kathy did nothing to lessen Daisy's distrust of strangers.

This week, in therapy, Charlotte will tell Ted how anxious she was about how Daisy was going to react to Rocco's new girlfriend.

"Your Uncle Rocco's coming for dinner."

Silence. "Just him?"

"No," Eli says. "He's got a new girlfriend."

"What's her name?" says Daisy.

"Something with an *R*. Definitely not Kathy."

Charlotte can feel her daughter's relief.

Even better news, for Daisy, is that she won't have to clean up her toys. Charlotte fears that Rocco's women will be intimidated by the tasteful perfection of their loft. But she doesn't like feeling apologetic. So she lets Daisy make more of a mess than usual, to humanize things a little.

Still holding on to her giraffe's hoof, Daisy half surrenders Raffi to Charlotte.

"Hide him," Daisy says. "Please. Lock him up somewhere safe."

"It's not the same girlfriend," Charlotte says.

"I know that. You just told me. But I don't care," Daisy says. "Lock Raffi up, or I'll have to stay in my room and guard him."

"Fine," Eli weighs in. Finally! "I'll put Raffi in the safe."

"He's changed his name," says Daisy. "To Moses."

"Why 'Moses'?" Charlotte says.

"Because," Daisy says.

"Because he was found in the bulrushes?"

Daisy looks up at her mother: coolly, dead-eyed, appraising.

"Moses it is." Eli breaks their mini-standoff. "Moses is going to jail."

"Not jail," Daisy says. "We're protecting him, Daddy."

"He'll be safe in the safe," Eli says. "That's why they call it that."

When the intercom buzzes, Daisy runs to push the button. She likes to be in control. Eli and Charlotte converge at the door.

Rocco has never gone out with a woman who wasn't pretty, which may be part of the problem. This one (Ruth? Ruby?) has stylishly streaked red-blond hair and the startled expression of someone who has cultivated a perpetual air of surprise: intelligent, but still girlishly sweet and attentive. She's graceful, and looks even more slight beside Charlotte's tall, solid brother. But there's a tensile strength about her; she could defend herself if she had to. There's something doll-like about how her eyes blink: too fast and then too slowly—Charlotte finds it unsettling. Please, she prays. Not another lunatic. What exactly is she praying to? The god of her brother's love life?

There's no reason to think this one's crazy just because the others were. And her smile is friendly and (even Charlotte has to admit) genuine.

She wears a blue-and-white-striped T-shirt, cropped white cotton pants. A large straw tote bag completes the look of an early-autumn weekend guest.

"This is Ruth," says Rocco. "My friend Ruth Seagram. My sister, Charlotte; my brother-in-law, *mi hermano*, Eli. Where's Daisy?" Rocco pretends not to see Daisy pressed against the back of Eli's legs.

"I don't know," says Eli. "She was here a second ago. Daisy?"

Silence. Silence. A braver child would have giggled,

would have wanted to give herself away. It's likely that Daisy won't say a word to Ruth all evening. Charlotte hopes that Rocco has warned her: It's not personal.

When Charlotte hugs Rocco, he pats her back, a little too hard, but he means it as love. She hopes. Then she leans over to give Ruth the full-on big-sister open-hearted, open-armed welcome.

Ruth's embrace is light and relaxed. She neither freezes nor hangs on as if to keep from drowning, like some of Rocco's girlfriends had. Charlotte finds that reassuring.

For some reason no one seems capable of moving out of the doorway. Either Charlotte or Eli should step back and make some welcoming gesture, but neither does.

Ruth reaches into her tote bag and thrusts a package at Charlotte. Thinking of Mae-Lynn and her organic broccoli crowns, Charlotte flinches, even as she reminds herself that it's normal—polite!—to bring a hostess gift.

"Sticky buns," Ruth says. "Caramel butter walnut. My grandma baked them this afternoon. They're practically warm from the oven. They're delicious. Try one."

"Thank you," Charlotte says. "I will. We can have them with dessert—"

"I mean . . . try one now." Ruth means *now*.

Charlotte waves vaguely back into the loft, toward the kitchen, as if calling as her witness the delicious smell of frying potatoes. Potato pasta—pasta with tiny, deliciously browned potato cubes—is her fallback dish when someone (let's say her brother) is bringing a guest and doesn't tell her, or doesn't know, if the person is vegetarian.

"Smells delish," Ruth says.

Charlotte dislikes that word, *delish*—it sets her teeth on edge. And now she gets to dislike herself: her petty snobbishness about language.

"Potato pasta?" says Rocco.

"Duh." Charlotte regrets her impatience. Her poor brother! He was only trying to show . . . what? Belonging, familiarity. He knows what foods they eat. Around him, Charlotte often wants a do-over. It's not her fault if her life seems—*is*—easier than his. Maybe she has better luck.

Growing up in the country with a crazy mother, they were in a class of their own. But after Charlotte married Eli, it got harder to pretend that the differences between her life and Rocco's life don't matter. Charlotte wants to hug Rocco again, but doesn't want Ruth to think she's being possessive.

"Go ahead. Try them." Ruth brandishes the paper bag at Charlotte.

Insisting? Imploring? Both.

Charlotte can't help feeling annoyed. Extremely annoyed. Day after day, she struggles to keep her daughter from eating excessive amounts of sugar, and now their guest has brought a sugary dessert.

Charlotte looks at Rocco. From the corner of her eye she sees Eli silently asking his brother-in-law, *hermano*, Who have you brought us now?

Rocco smiles a dopey grin that Charlotte can't remember seeing before. A new expression. That must mean something, or maybe not. Maybe it's just new.

Eli says, "Why are we standing in the doorway? Please, come in." But he can't move without pushing Daisy, who's still behind him, clinging to his legs, taking baby steps backwards when he does.

Charlotte can't move, either. It's as if Ruth's parcel is casting a spell. Doing the wrong thing could ruin the entire evening. Their whole relationship with Ruth.

Ruth says, "I know this is crazy, but I really want you guys to try these." Crazy? *Now* she has their attention. She sets the bag down on the bare wooden floor.

There will be a grease spot! How can Ruth not know? How can Rocco not say anything? Charlotte almost moans. Rocco is watching Ruth. His gaze is approving, or at least not disapproving. In the past Charlotte and Eli noticed he hardly looked at his girlfriends. He didn't seem to see them. Okay, Charlotte can live with Ruth bullying them into trying her grandma's sticky buns if Rocco *looks* at her. If making them eat sweets before dinner is the worst thing she ever does. If Daisy tries a tiny piece and no more.

Ruth repeats, "I know this is crazy." She's talking to Charlotte now, the judgmental sister she needs to win over. Maybe she also intuits that Charlotte distrusts women who are overly friendly to Eli, her handsome husband.

"You know how they say that when you pick fresh corn, even if you bring it straight to the table, the sugar starts converting to starch? Well, that's how it is with my grandma's baking. They're best right out of the oven, and then they're still great but . . . less. Taste them. Every minute that passes, they're less perfect. Though they're still pretty good."

"Fine," Charlotte says, if only to make Ruth pick the bag up off the floor.

It would never occur to Charlotte to eat a sticky bun standing in the front hall. But Ruth makes it seem as if it would be hostile to refuse or even insist they wait for later. Ruth pries the gooey pastry from a corrugated plastic tray.

"Here. Take a whole one," says Ruth. "You need to

see how my grandma does the icing. It takes her hours and a lifetime of practice to get it right. She says she puts the sun on each one because she wants to bring light and warmth to everyone who eats them. She has this mystical spiritual thing about suns having eight rays. It's the number of infinity, or balance. I never remember. She knows magical stuff like that."

The buns are elaborately iced, each with a sugar starburst. It's the sort of thing that people did before they were working two jobs and raising kids. Charlotte is always touched by home skills passed through generations.

"It's great your grandma can do this," she says.

"Taste it," Ruth urges. "Come on. Just a little."

Daisy emerges from behind her father, unable to resist the spectacle of her mom and her uncle's girlfriend facing off about sugar.

"I want some too," Daisy says.

"That decides it," says Ruth, giving Daisy a double thumbs-up, as if to say: Let's stand up to your mom.

Ruth doesn't know that Daisy isn't so easily won over. Charlotte feels badly for enjoying the fact that Ruth has made a mistake with Daisy.

"Whatever you want, sweetheart," Ruth says.

Charlotte thinks: She's not your sweetheart.

"Please," says Daisy. "I *really* want some." This can

only go one way. Daisy rarely throws tantrums any-more, but there's no point pushing their luck.

Ruth tears off a feathery chunk and gives one to Eli. Then she pries off an even bigger piece and hands it to Daisy.

No, thinks Charlotte. No. Absolutely no!

Daisy tastes the pastry and breaks into an enormous grin. It's only a sticky bun, Charlotte knows, but she will never forgive Ruth for this.

She hears her voice shake with rage as she asks Rocco if he wants a sticky bun too.

Rocco says, "I ate one on the way over."

The older sister in Charlotte thinks a warning about ruining his dinner, even as the grown-up hostess eats the buttery pastry.

"Wow," says Eli. "This *is* excellent."

Charlotte savors the burnt sugar, licks icing off her fingers.

"It really is," she says.

The prickly moment is over. Sugar has beveled down the edges.

Sometimes Charlotte worries that she and Eli care too much about food, another aspect of privilege. Lots of people care about food. Rocco does too, and so, it seems, does Ruth.

"My grandmother is a genius cook."

"Obviously." She's nice, Charlotte thinks. She's open. She's just a little . . . jittery.

"Ruth can be bossy," Rocco says.

Ruth doesn't miss a beat. "You *could* call it bossy. Or you could say: Ruth knows when something is good and wants to share it."

"Nothing wrong with *that*," Charlotte says, at the same moment Rocco mumbles, "Touché." It's hard to tell if he's being glum or flirtatious. His girlfriends never challenge him. Maybe he'll like being with someone who shows a little spirit.

Ruth is the first who's ever brought something *good* to eat. That alone is endearing. Even if she's bullied them into eating it before dinner. Even if she's given Daisy more sugar than Charlotte normally lets her eat in a week.

Eli says, "Ruth, would you like a drink? White wine, red wine, beer, something stronger? Rocco, club soda?"

Charlotte holds her breath, even though Rocco has been sober since before Daisy was born.

"Sure," Rocco says. "Club soda would be great. Got any lemon?"

"You know we do. You got it," says Eli. "Ruth?"

"I'll take club soda too. With lemon."

"I'm hungry," Daisy says.

The ease with which Ruth glides onto her knees in front of Daisy reminds Charlotte that Ruth must be at least ten years younger than she is. Daisy shrinks back, as if from a scary dog, but Ruth keeps her in focus.

Ruth says, "Look." She puts her straw bag aside. Then she puts her hands up, palms out, as if she's being arrested and waiting to be cuffed.

"I'm not going to take anything," she says. Rocco must have told her about Klepto Kathy. Maybe this relationship is more serious than Charlotte thought.

Charlotte sees Daisy wondering how this stranger can read her mind. Daisy relaxes, a little. Anyway, Moses the giraffe is safely locked away.

"Watch," says Ruth. Charlotte has to bend down to see that Ruth is crossing her eyes and jiggling them in their sockets.

"Yuck," says Daisy.

Ruth bursts out laughing, and Daisy laughs too.

The sound of Daisy laughing with a stranger is as shocking as a scream.

"I *bet* you're starving, honey," says Ruth. "Your Uncle Rocco and his friend Ruth were almost an hour late. For which we're so sorry. The traffic, the—"

"*Are* you Uncle Rocco's friend?" The subject of friendship has been newly important since preschool, when Daisy noticed that some girls got more birthday invitations than she did. Daisy was mostly bewildered, but it had caused Charlotte pain, probably more than Daisy. Is there something she should be doing to help her daughter make friends? And what will she do when Daisy does have friends—and she asks to spend the night at a friend's house?

"I am," says Ruth. "Your uncle and I are friends."

"Are you his best friend?"

"I don't know about *that*."

Charlotte wants to hear what Ruth says next. But Daisy gives her mother a warning look. Stay out. This is her conversation. For just an instant, Charlotte feels almost breathless with shock.

Eli gestures at the couch and says, "Please. Everybody sit down."

In the kitchen, Charlotte slips the pasta into the boiling water. She sees Daisy streak past on the way to her room. Charlotte's relieved when no one comes in, offering to help.

Finally Eli looks in and says, "What do you need? Give me something to do. I'm begging."

"She seems nice," Charlotte says.

"You always think that. At first." He kisses her forehead, damp with steam.

"Well, *isn't* she? Nice?"

"So far so good," he says. "No special broccoli,

nothing stolen so far, no suicide threats, no . . . But the jury's still out. Let's say the jury has learned its lesson." Charlotte loves the faint traces of accent in Eli's speech, the way he says *yury* for jury.

Charlotte says, "I need everybody to sit down. Call Daisy."

By the time Charlotte brings in the platter of steaming pasta, everyone's at the table. They all applaud, even Daisy. Charlotte's mood improves. Her daughter glows in the candlelight. Daisy has parents who love her, good food, a comfortable home. A happier childhood than Charlotte's was. Isn't that what everyone wants for their kids?

Charlotte dishes out the pasta. Steam fogs her glasses, and Daisy gently removes them from her mother's face, wipes the lenses with a napkin, and tenderly replaces them.

"Thank you," Charlotte says, resenting how the sweetness of the moment is partly spoiled by her awareness of Ruth watching her and Daisy. It almost makes it seem as if they're performing for this outsider.

"You're welcome," says Daisy.

Eating keeps them quiet until Ruth says, "Charlotte, it's a miracle you can do this. Work all day, run a *hugely* successful business, and come home and cook something delicious. I mean . . . Rocco told me a little, plus

I Googled Buddenbrooks and Gladiola. I love how you said that you named the company after the flower and the novel you'd always overlooked until you understood how amazing they are. I'm so happy when something makes me wake up and smell the coffee. Of course I'd heard about you. Everybody has, if they live in New York and go to parties. Which I used to, all the time. Though not so much anymore."

Charlotte feels she's supposed to ask why Ruth doesn't go to so many parties anymore, but the moment passes.

Ruth says, "Gosh, I hope you don't think I'm your internet stalker."

"Not at all," Charlotte says. Charlotte looks up people, but sometimes she feels uneasy—violated—if people say they've looked *her* up, and at other times she's insulted if they clearly haven't. "And I don't know about 'hugely successful.' Everybody's working over-time and struggling."

Ruth says, "This pasta is fantastic."

"Thanks. It's really an everyday meal. Anyhow, I didn't work today. I make time for family. We don't have a nanny. I try to get out of work in time to pick Daisy up from after-school." Why is Charlotte trying to prove what a hands-on mom she is?

"Rocco tells me that Daisy's in public school."

"Yes, it's—"

"Admirable," says Ruth.

Charlotte's promised herself not to become one of those parents who ramble on about where their kids go to school and why. She likes Daisy's school; so does Daisy. It's nearby, the kids live in the neighborhood, the principal and teachers seem kind and smart and committed. She adores the after-school teachers, who always come up with interesting projects. Charlotte loves the women in charge. They're all memory prodigies who learn your name—and which child is yours—after meeting you only once.

She's lost the thread of what Ruth's saying.

"I wish this was *my* everyday meal. Though when I went to culinary school—"

"Culinary school?" Charlotte says.

"Those three Tuscan grandmas? Remember? They had quite a moment and then . . . Eli, Rocco tells me you made some genius business decisions."

"What I said was that my brother-in-law never has to work another day in his life. Go to sleep.com. Justthefood.com. Happytrails.com. That's *mi hermano*."

Rocco's fond of Eli, but around his girlfriends, he's critical, even dismissive, as if he fears they might prefer the handsome brother-in-law with the wife, the daughter, the money, the beautiful loft.

"That's awesome," says Ruth. "So are you like . . . retired?"

Why has she Googled Charlotte and not Eli? Unless she's pretending ignorance, the party trick some women learn to make men talk about themselves. Or maybe she's just being polite. There is always that chance.

Eli says, "The fact is . . . now I can do what I want . . ."

"Which *is* . . . ?"

"Set design. I'm working on a production of *Macbeth*."

"I love *Macbeth*. I played Lady Macbeth in high school. 'Out, out, damned spot. All the perfumes in Arabia . . .'" Ruth stares in mock horror at her hands as if they're covered with blood, then giggles. "I was good at it. I wanted to be an actress until my drama teacher told me that people would always be telling me to lose weight and fix my nose. And that was a total buzzkill."

Eli says, "Maybe Lady Macbeth ruined it for you. The bad-luck part, as you probably know. The role that ends a career."

"Maybe. Well . . . When does your play open? Where?"

"You've probably never heard of—"

"Try me," says Ruth.

"New Lights."

"That's amazing. I've been there a million times."

Charlotte thinks: Has she really?

"I love that you can bring cocktails from the lobby into the theater."

Maybe she has. Or maybe she *did* Google Eli.

"So how's it going?"

"Not great," Eli says. "The director is a maniac. He wants the witches to fly through the air on harnesses, even though the theater isn't insured. No one can talk him out of it—"

"Can I be excused?" Daisy has heard this before. "Look! I finished all my pasta."

"Good girl!" says Ruth. Charlotte shoots her a look that she hopes isn't as resentful as she feels. Who is this stranger to praise her daughter?

"Sure, sweetheart," Charlotte says. "I'll call you for dessert."

"See you later, alligator," Ruth says.

"In a while, crocodile," says Daisy.

Eli and Charlotte look at each other. What did their daughter just say? If Daisy has so readily accepted Ruth, maybe she senses something positive. Sometimes Charlotte thinks that her daughter is better at reading people than she is. And maybe it's not a bad thing that Daisy has taken to someone outside the family.

Suddenly they hear noises coming up through the floor: shouting, screaming. It's impossible to make out the words, but a slamming door makes everyone jump.

"You crazy bitch!" a man yells.

Eli puts his hands over Daisy's ears.

"Yikes," says Ruth. "Unhappy couple?"

"The neighbors," says Charlotte. "Mother and son. Ariane and Drew."

"Did you say Drew? I used to have a boyfriend named Drew. A total loser, trust me. Definitely one of my worst mistakes."

There's a silence.

"Well, then! Does anyone want seconds?" Charlotte says. "I think we need more Parmesan." Everyone still has pasta on their plates; there's plenty of cheese in the grater. But she needs to escape to the kitchen and take a breath.

When she returns to the table, Eli and Rocco are deep in conversation. Ruth looks at Charlotte. Talk to me. Please.

"How did you and Rocco meet?"

Charlotte can tell she's said the wrong thing. Is she supposed to know or not know? Did they meet on Tinder or some edgy dating/hookup app?

"Rocco didn't tell you?"

Now Charlotte gets it. Ruth is upset that Rocco

didn't rush to tell them the thrilling story of his new romance.

"We've hardly seen him," lies Charlotte. Rocco stays with them every Friday and Saturday night when he sleeps over in the city and isn't staying with a girlfriend. He hadn't mentioned Ruth until he called to say he was bringing her to dinner.

"We met at the Greenmarket. I was buying kale."

"Tell them how *much* kale." Despite himself, Rocco's been drawn into the conversation.

"Ten pounds," Ruth says.

"That's a lot of kale," Charlotte says. "Big party? Restaurant work? What do you do, exactly?"

"I'm a survivalist," Ruth says. "I mean, a survivalist consultant. I help rich people freeze-dry healthy organic foods to stock their panic rooms and bomb shelters."

"Seriously?" So this one is crazy too. It's always something they didn't expect and couldn't have predicted.

"Ruth's messing with you." Rocco smiles. There's something about her he likes. Her joke hints at a sense of humor. Sort of.

She says, "I work for a start-up."

Of course you do, Charlotte thinks.

"Every Friday one of the staff cooks lunch for the

others, and the day I met Rocco was my turn. I thought I'd make them that amazing kale salad they do at Kanji. The kale is fried tempura-style, then mixed with raisins and walnuts. This young chef worked with David Chang, whom I sort of know. Have you guys eaten there? We should all go sometime. Early. For Daisy."

"Sure," says Rocco. "Sometime."

"You should find out about supplying them, Rocco," says Ruth. "That would be a whole new market for the farm, organic Chinese greens and whatever."

"Good idea. I'll look into it." Rocco has no such intention.

"So what does your start-up do?" Eli asks.

"God's work," Ruth says.

Her messing with them is becoming a little much. Unless this time she means it.

"Relief work in Sudan, free schools in Haiti. We finance the saintly stuff by selling rich people junk they don't need. One of our most profitable ventures has been a website called Experience Hunters International. We have contacts in cities all over the world willing to adopt, for up to five days, a business traveler or a tourist. Not for sex, though we don't judge. We do track customer reviews.

"The point is to experience life in a different country. Our carefully vetted contacts' friends are your friends, their hangout spots are your hangout spots. Our algorithms match you with a person who you *would* be friends with, if you lived there. It's been very successful, as you can imagine."

"Charlotte and Eli probably can," says Rocco. "I can't imagine, myself."

"STEP is what the start-up is called," says Ruth. "Solutions to Everyday Problems. We plow the dirty money from Experience Hunters back into our public-minded programs." So that's what Rocco likes about her. She has a social conscience and (unlike Charlotte) is apologetic about working for the rich.

"That's great," Charlotte says. Pieces are falling into place. When they were in high school upstate, Rocco led a student-faculty strike to raise the lunch ladies' salaries and to get them name tags and make the students stop calling them "lunch ladies," which they hated.

"How was the kale salad?" Charlotte says.

"Awesome," says Ruth. "The guys loved it. So . . . Charlotte and Eli, how did *you* two meet?"

Eli says, "I walked into Charlotte's flower shop to buy a Valentine's Day bouquet."

"For someone else," says Charlotte. They've told this story so often they could do it in their sleep.

"And as she was putting it together, I realized I was buying the flowers for the wrong person."

"Eli paid for it. Then he handed me the bouquet and asked me to have dinner with him. And here we are, twelve years later."

Ruth says, "Wow. Can I ask you something else?"

"Of course." Charlotte braces herself.

"Are you Italian? Rocco's an Italian name, but he claims he isn't."

"We're not Italian. Rocco's telling you the truth." It's up to Rocco to tell her that his real name is Rochester. Their mother knew whole paragraphs from *Jane Eyre* and *Wuthering Heights* by heart. Charlotte assumes Mom's forgotten all that. Living in Mexico, she mostly speaks Spanish now.

Ruth says, "Have you done Ancestry.com? I did it for my grandparents and me. We're ninety percent Scandinavian. With a dab of Central Asian. A drop of Genghis Khan. I know this sounds strange, but it felt empowering to be related to one of history's greatest mass murderers."

Another silence follows that.

"Just kidding," Ruth says. "Really."

"How's business, Charlotte? Flowers for the One Percent." Rocco has never hidden his feelings about the fact that most of Charlotte's clients are rich, or trying to raise money from the rich.

"Blooming," Charlotte says, as she always does. It drives Rocco crazy.

Ruth says, "What's your favorite flower, Charlotte?"

Charlotte pretends to think about this as if she hasn't been asked before. "I'd say foxglove. They look like outer space aliens. You have to see them in the wild."

One summer, before Daisy was born, Eli drove Charlotte upstate to an enclave built for Victorian billionaires: massive summer mansions with turrets and verandas. A path led through the forest where huge stands of gorgeous foxglove bloomed. They never returned there. Sometimes Charlotte thinks she dreamed it. Foxglove Brigadoon.

"I *love* foxglove," says Ruth. "How could something that gorgeous be . . . natural? But aren't they . . . poisonous? Loaded with digitalis? Didn't Van Gogh or somebody like that take giant doses of digitalis and that's why he painted like that?"

Rocco bristles. "Lots of people take drugs, and there was only one Van Gogh. There was no 'somebody like that.'"

"Whatever," says Ruth. "Excuse *me*. One more question, Charlotte, and I'm done, I promise. How come you have no flowers in your house?"

"I have enough flowers in my work life."

Eli says, "Daisy has asthma."

"That must be hard," Ruth says.

"You can't imagine," says Charlotte.

It's the truest thing she's said all evening. No one who doesn't have an asthmatic child can know. Not even Eli, though that's not strictly true. The two of them handle it, but not always well. Watching Daisy struggle to breathe, they sometimes snap at each other. It's just fear, they know that, so they forgive each other. But it's not ideal. And Charlotte can't rid herself of the idea that it's her fault—though she knows that's not possible.

A voice says, "Can we eat Ruth's sticky buns yet?" They hadn't noticed Daisy return. How much has she overheard? They try not to talk about her asthma. Daisy has covered her ears and run out of the room when the subject's come up.

"That must be tough," Ruth says to Daisy.

Charlotte is holding her breath.

"It's not so bad," Daisy says. "The hard part is when I lose my inhaler and my mom gets mad at me. Sometimes—"

"Not *mad*," Charlotte says, louder than she means to. "I get scared, is all."

Ruth says, "If that's the hard part . . . there's got to be some practical solution. Let me think about it, okay?"

Why is she asking Daisy?

"The sticky buns?" Daisy says. "Can we have more now?"

"Give us five minutes, honey," says Charlotte. "We're getting to it."

"That's what you said last time," Daisy says.

"I know," says Charlotte, though she's pretty sure she hadn't.

Eli says, "Eye roll alert. Five going on fifteen."

"I'm six," Daisy says.

"Not for a while," Charlotte says.

"Happy birthday in advance, Daisy," says Ruth. "What are you doing for your birthday?"

"It's not for a while," Charlotte repeats.

Daisy looks like she's about to cry, which is *definitely* not what Charlotte wants.

"Okay, come on, Daisy," says Charlotte. "You can help bring in the dessert."

She'd prepared a bowl of clementines and shelled walnuts. But next to the sticky buns, the fruit and nuts seem overly health-conscious, no fun. Daisy arranges the buns on a platter. She gently slides the pastries around to get the arrangement right. Watching her, Charlotte feels happier than she has all evening. Now if only she could keep Daisy from eating more sweets.

When Daisy carries in the platter, Ruth beams as if she's being brought a birthday cake topped with lit candles. She looks around, delighted, slightly embarrassed, as if she's waiting for them to sing.

"This is awesome," she says. "Being able to share my grandma's baking. I can't wait to tell her."

Don't, Charlotte thinks. Don't tell your grandmother yet. Don't tell her anything about us. If she's hoping you'll find someone to love, maybe even marry, you'll only disappoint her.

Ruth says, "The most amazing thing about my grandparents is they're still madly in love after fifty years." Her already flushed face brightens as she describes how her grandparents spend their evenings snuggling on the couch.

Charlotte senses that Ruth has said this before, maybe even to Rocco. But shining through the performance is her love for her grandparents, a good sign. She's able to love, a gift that people don't recognize as a gift, as something you have or don't. Maybe Ruth can love Rocco. Maybe she already does.

Charlotte yawns. "Oops. Excuse me."

"Don't apologize," says Ruth. "We should let you put Daisy to bed. And you guys should get some rest."

Is she saying they look like they *need* some rest? Why is Charlotte so defensive?

"Can we eat the rest of the sticky buns after you leave?" Daisy asks.

"Save them for breakfast," says Ruth. "Heat them at 350 degrees for exactly five minutes. Can you do that?"

"Mom, can we do that?"

"We can." Charlotte thinks: There is no way that's going to happen, even if she has to eat all the rest herself. Which, at the moment, doesn't seem like such a bad idea. The truth is, there's nothing like sugar and butter . . .

Even a neutral goodbye is risky. In the past, Charlotte has said, "See you soon." And she never saw that person again. So now she says, "It was lovely to meet you."

"Thank you, thank you, thank you." Ruth bows and rolls her hand down from her forehead.

"Talk to you soon," says Rocco.

No one has to explain that he's staying with Ruth.

Kiss kiss, and then the sweet silence after the guests have gone home.

Charlotte's thankful that Daisy is so proud of being able to put on her own pajamas that she's eager to hurry off to her room and change for bed. Her pajamas are printed with little ice cream cones and slices of pizza.

Charlotte retrieves Moses from the safe, tucks Daisy in with her giraffe, and turns off the light.

"Wait! Can you read to me?" Daisy's favorite book is about a pig named Pearl who finds a talking bone. Daisy has heard the story so often she knows it has a happy ending, but she still acts scared when Pearl is kidnapped by a fox who wants to cook and eat her. One night Daisy asked Charlotte if they eat pigs. Charlotte didn't want to lie, but neither did she want to create a vegetarian, so she said, We eat potatoes.

"Mom's tired." Only now does Charlotte realize how knocked out she is.

"Okay," says Daisy. "Then we read *two* books tomorrow night."

"Promise," Charlotte says.

"Rocco's friend is nice," Daisy says.

Of course you think she's nice, Charlotte thinks sourly. She gave you sweets.

"She is nice." Charlotte kisses Daisy's forehead. "Good night."

"Good night." Daisy's voice is like a tiny hand squeezing Charlotte's heart.

Eli's already in bed. Charlotte puts on one of his T-shirts and a pair of his pajama bottoms. A signal. Sex is out of the question. They're both exhausted.

They turn to face each other and don't speak for a while. Eli smells of toothpaste. What a blessing, to be able to look so deeply into someone's eyes that he turns into a cyclops.

"She's a little much," Eli says. "Don't you think?" Which makes her love him even more.

"Nice enough. Even Daisy liked her." Charlotte wishes she didn't feel so proud of herself for being big enough to say that. "And we did great. We welcomed her with open arms."

"Your poor brother," Eli says.

"Poor everyone," Charlotte says.

3

Ruth

Everything was fine, or sort of fine, until the Baroness Frieda fired me and left me with thousands of dollars of credit card debt as severance pay. Being the personal assistant to a narcissistic, coke-addled minor celebrity hadn't been the greatest job in the world, but it was a job, and when that ended, I had just enough money to pay for one more month's rent—and then I got evicted.

So I did what I always did when things got really bad: I retreated to my grandparents' house so they could take care of me and feed me and love me until I figured out what to do next.

At night, my grandparents' brownstone is dark. They claim they keep the lights low to save the planet.

It's inspiring to see two elderly people who care about climate change. But I think it's vanity too. Darkness erases the wrinkles, and in the flickering light, they could almost pass for the young couple who fell in love half a century ago.

Every time I visit, I always have a moment of dread, of thinking that one or both of them won't be there. But they're there. The only ones who love me unconditionally. The only ones I love without reservation. I pray that they'll live into their nineties.

Letting myself in with the key I wear on a cord around my neck, I call out, "I'm home; it's Ruth, it's me," so they'll know I'm not a home invader, a murderer, or a thief.

Back before I was born, their neighborhood had gotten pretty sketchy, but by now it's almost totally safe. Emphasis on the *almost*.

Last spring, a woman was killed in her own home, a young mother who had just bought the brownstone with her family and was in the midst of renovating it. The dead woman was found lying at the foot of her stairs. At first they thought she'd fallen down by accident, but later the forensic team found signs indicating that someone else—two people—had been in the house at the time.

I make my grandparents *swear* that they'll keep their

front door locked, which they forget to do. But they're not worried. I'm the one who's scared. Sometimes I'm scared of the dark, though not the dark in *their* house, which feels like hiding under a blanket.

When I lived with them as a child, I'd close my eyes and pretend to be blind, which is useful now as I drift past the shadows trying to spook me, the furniture conspiring to trip me. I navigate by smell (furniture polish, floor wax, dust), by sensations (carpet, rug, wood, linoleum) under my feet, and by the muted explosions of the laugh track on TV.

I've learned to move through the dark house without passing the basement door. I've always been scared of their basement. It's one of those childish fears that won't go away. Granny and Grandpa have shown me countless times: a furnace, old dishes, a shelf of home-canned tomatoes and peaches that no one will ever eat. Nothing to be frightened of! Once, I saw a wolf spider crawl out from under the basement door. Granny Edith says that maybe once, when I was little, I had a nightmare about the basement.

I don't remember a dream like that. I don't want to. I'm just glad to be here.

In the comfy TV room, Grandpa Frank lies on the sofa, his head cradled in Granny Edith's lap. They've already eaten one of her delicious healthy meals—her cooking is probably why they've lived so long. Every evening they watch the news, and later the cable channel I added on for them as an anniversary present. The Time Travel Network shows only old films, black-and-white programs from when Granny Edith was stuck home raising Mom. Even the ads are vintage. Chorus lines of cartoon cigarettes high-kick across the screen; men in shirtsleeves raise beer mugs foaming with brands that no longer exist.

"Ruthie!" my grandparents cry at once.

In a heartbeat they're on tiptoe to hug me. The warmth of their arms makes the world outside disappear. I forget the people who have hurt me, the glances and smirks of the lucky ones who have everything life can offer without having done one thing to deserve it. I forget what the Baroness Frieda did to me. I forget that I'm unemployed. My grandparents rub my shoulders and pat my back until the misery vaporizes like the nightmares I had as a child.

Granny Edith pulls me into the kitchen. Even though I've just eaten. Iceberg lettuce wedges with homemade bleu cheese dressing, crispy roast chicken, buttery mashed potatoes, food so old-fashioned it's trendy again. They have an extra tray table for me so we can fit on the sofa and watch TV.

My grandparents' home is a time machine. Their

Hoboken neighborhood is popular now with young families and trust fund hipsters, but once you get past their front door, nothing's changed. They don't even have a flat-screen. Surrounding the mountainous TV are two enormous stereo speakers on which Grandpa Frank plays opera and Granny Edith plays *Swan Lake* or *The King and I* on *records*, not (hipster speak!) *vinyl*.

Upholstered in an indestructible brownish tweed, the sofa's in perfect shape, except for one leg scratched raw by the Persian cat I had before Grandpa Frank left the door open and Tabibi ran away. That was the only time I ever heard them argue. Granny asked if he did it on purpose. He'd always hated the cat. Grandpa cried until Granny hugged him and said it wasn't his fault. A lover's quarrel, but shocking. I knew my grandpa would never do something like that.

Grandpa Frank still drives the 2009 Cadillac they garage behind their house. It gets eight miles a gallon, which is fortunate. Driving is expensive, and Grandpa Frank is no longer the greatest driver.

For a while, he was always losing their car keys, and we'd search the whole house every time. Now he always keeps them on a little ebony table in the front hall, near the door. He picks up the keys, shakes them three times—*jingle, jingle, jingle*—and off we go.

In case he ever forgets to leave them there, I've bought them a GPS tracker so they can find the keys on their cell phone, which I bought them too.

Granny Edith ties on a scarf with rabbit ears under her chin and tops it off with the ultra-dark glasses she wears because of her macular degeneration. Grandpa Frank wears a fedora in summer, a wool Tyrolean in winter. With a feather! An elderly couple so striking they could get away with anything. Rob banks, swindle pensioners. That's how adorable they are, with their picnic hamper and the road map they never consult.

They turn on the classical station. Loud. And Grandpa Frank floors it through Hoboken and onto the Palisades. There's a landing they like, over the Hudson, with a cute picnic table where they share Granny Edith's fried chicken, coleslaw, homemade lemonade. Willows dip their branches into the water, and at the edge of the clearing are a few apple trees left from an orchard that the highway authority couldn't bear to cut down.

When I ask Grandpa Frank to let me drive, he recites the only poem he knows:

James James
Morrison Morrison
Weatherby George Dupree
Took great

Care of his Mother
Though he was only three.
James James
Said to his Mother,
"Mother," he said, said he:
"You must never go down to the end of the town,
if you don't go down with me."

James James
Morrison's Mother
Put on a golden gown,
James James
Morrison's Mother
Drove to the end of the town.
James James
Morrison's Mother
Said to herself, said she:
"I can get right down to the end of the town and be
back in time for tea."

"Stop it, Grandpa Frank," I say. "You know I hate that poem—"

But he goes right on:

King John
Put up a notice,

"Lost or stolen or strayed!
James James
Morrison's Mother
Seems to have been mislaid.
Last seen
Wandering vaguely:
Quite of her own accord,
She tried to get down to the end of the town—
    forty shillings reward!"

James James
Morrison's Mother
Hasn't been heard of since.
King John
Said he was sorry,
So did the Queen and Prince—

"Okay," I say, "you have to *stop now!*"

Having tortured me enough, Grandpa Frank chuckles and falls silent. A few times he's gone on to the last verse, the scariest of all, because he whispers the letters that begin the words, *J. J. M. M. W. G. Du P.* It's the creepiest thing ever because I know what the letters mean. And because he's whispering.

I guess he thinks it's funny, three-year-old James James bossing his disobedient mom. Did something happen to

Grandpa's mother? Did she leave him, like Mom left me? I never thought it was funny. What is James James supposed to do now that Mother is gone forever?

But I put up with it. Forcing me to listen to every maddening line is the only annoying thing Grandpa Frank does. It's his brilliant way of stopping me from bossing *him* around. Because whenever he recites it, I think: Okay, if he remembers all that, he's probably good to drive.

I sleep in my old bedroom, which has become my grandparents' shrine to me, crammed with relics: my high school spelling trophy, my college degree, school portraits of me grinning as if I'm in pain. Recent photos too: A shot of me on the red carpet with the Baroness Frieda. My certificate from the cooking school. And pictures (I beg Granny to ditch them) of me with various boyfriends.

I sleep like a baby in that room. No insomnia, no Ambien. No nightmares. Every so often I have this recurring dream that I have a pretty little daughter. We love each other more than anything in the world. I promise I will be good to her, treat her better than Mom treated me. Maybe I'm dreaming about myself at that age. I don't care. The dream makes me happy.

I wake up refreshed, basking in the heavenly smells wafting up from the kitchen.

Granny Edith still loves to bake, but she rarely does except when I'm there. Not being all that active, she and Grandpa Frank can't do the daily coffee cake without putting on the pounds. But they roll their eyes when I say I'm watching my weight, and they tempt me with bacon, eggs, pancakes, toast, butter, and more butter.

When I go back to the city, Granny won't let me leave without a container of her freshly baked sticky buns—a taste of childhood to bring with me into the cold, cruel world.

She spends hours decorating them with white icing on the golden brown crust, each pastry topped by a small sun and eight rays of iced sunlight, each ray exploding in a starburst of its own.

"Goodbye, Ruthie," she says, handing me the container. "Stay happy, dear. Stay safe."

I know that's why she gives them to me. For security, not just pleasure. They're like the enchanted cloak, the magic shield that the good witch gives the prince heading into the dark forest. My grandmother means the pastry to work like edible charms to watch over me when I'm alone in the wilderness, lost and too far away for her love to protect me.

Whenever I leave my grandparents' house, I walk several blocks out of my way to avoid walking past the house in which the lovely young wife and mother of two got murdered.

I can't bear to think what it must have been like for the husband who couldn't reach her, and called and called and finally found her among the paint-splattered tarps and paint cans and carpenters' tools. She'd been checking out the renovation of the home they were planning to live in. And now their plans had changed. Because now she lay dead, just inside the front door, at the base of the stairs on which the paint was being scraped away to reveal the oak underneath.

When I heard back from the start-up, it was the first response—the first nibble—I'd gotten since the Baroness Frieda fired me.

I had a good interview. It was a challenge. I don't have much of a résumé, so I had to explain what I'd done for the past two years since the baroness had refused to write me a letter of reference.

Sandy—the boss—liked my energy. I'd helped friends grow their businesses, though I hadn't done it for a living, as he may have assumed from what I said.

Even so, we got off on the wrong foot. I guess you could say that Sandy sexually harassed me, though I have never been sure, since all he did was give me something to read. If he'd made me watch porn with him, that would be clear. But this was a short story by a writer so famous even I'd heard of her.

Sandy suggested that I read the story, which is about a secretary who has an S&M relationship with her boss, who makes her crawl around on all fours and spanks her on his desk. Was Sandy hitting on me? Did he want us to have an intimate two-person book group? Or was he just a guy who likes making reading recommendations? Maybe he thought that being a barely glorified secretary, I might like a story about a secretary and a boss. An office romance. How sweet.

I could have had him busted—maybe I would have if the story weren't so good. Anyhow, if I got Sandy fired, I wouldn't have a job, not even a job at an office where no one speaks to me.

The men (of course they are mostly guys, except for a few women too scared to be friendly to me, or even to one another) work hard to isolate me, to remind me I'm not in their club. They all think I got the job because I had sex with Sandy. But we didn't have sex, though Sandy may have wanted to.

One of our projects—Experience Hunters International—was my idea. Before I went to work for the baroness, I spent six months in Europe. My grandparents paid. I went to Berlin, Madrid, Paris. I watched hot young people having fun, and I wanted to have their lives.

Any desire you have, someone else has it too. *Ka-ching!* Experience Hunters. The guys at STEP take credit for it. I could fight for my intellectual property rights, a he-said, she-said situation. Or I could shut up and keep my job and hope that someday I'll get credit. It'll go on my résumé.

Whenever I read about a gag rule, I think, everyone's under a gag rule. There's so much you can't say. You have to sort out what you want people to know—and what you never want anyone to know. Ever.

Every Friday my coworkers get together at the IT guy's house. I'm not invited. They watch reruns of *The Office* for tricks to play on me, farting near my desk, turning everything I say into a dirty joke. They actually encased my stapler in a mound of Jell-O, like they did on TV. It hurts that these guys go to so much trouble just to make me miserable.

Whatever. As soon as I got the job, I found myself a little one-bedroom walk-up in Greenpoint. I made it homey and cute. My grandparents loaned me enough money for the broker's fee and the rest, since, this being New York, no one will rent you an apartment unless you have enough money to buy it.

I told myself that all that craziness with the baroness was behind me. New house, new life.

Even though it's hopeless, I keep trying to please my coworkers. So I threw myself into the discussion about Friday lunch. Guys? I've been to culinary school. Three Tuscan grandmothers showed me how to make food that will rock your world.

When they said it was my turn, I should have been on my guard. But I wanted to prove myself and maybe change their minds. Granny Edith says, The way to a man's heart is through his stomach.

I asked each guy what food he'd been craving. It was surprising how many said kale. I described the Kanji kale salad, and they said it sounded great, especially when I name-dropped David Chang.

They let me go through all the prep work in the open kitchen, chopping all that kale and frying it and mixing it with the raisins, soy sauce, and sesame oil. Delicious!

I was shocked when they wouldn't eat it.

Sandy said, "If I eat that, I'll grow a vagina."

Tears popped into my eyes.

One of the guys said, "I don't eat this shit." Another said, "I don't eat this shit, either." Then another. I packed the salad into plastic tubs and tossed it into the dumpster behind the building.

But at least I met Rocco. It doesn't always happen that something good comes out of something bad. For once, I was lucky, though it wasn't all luck. Planning played a part.

I'd seen Rocco around the Greenmarket. There was something about him I liked. He was handsome and dark and shy, and really nice to his workers. I began to look for him. Low-tech, old-school stalking. There were other stands that sold kale, but I chose his when my office green-lit my salad.

I asked if I could have a discount since I was buying in bulk. But I didn't care about a discount. I wanted his attention. I never imagined that he would offer to help me carry everything back, or that we'd have a chance to talk, walking up Broadway. Well, maybe I did imagine it, but I didn't believe it would happen. I gave him my phone number, and he called the next day.

On our second date, Rocco drove me up to his home in Claverack, in the Hudson Valley.

Signs of other women were layered in his house like the circles that mark the age of a tree. I wasn't jealous. I didn't care about the past. Rocco's sheets were freshly washed. We laughed. We had fun.

On Monday I took the train from Hudson back to work in the city, and the next Friday morning, early, I met Rocco in the market. The park was lovely at that hour, with a bright mist rising from the wet pavement. I went up to Rocco, he turned, and we kissed. I still had my arms around him when I said, "This could ruin everything, but could I ask you a question?"

"Now I'm scared," said Rocco.

"Don't be scared. It's just stupid. Can I take a picture of us?"

"Deal breaker. I can't be kissing a woman who buys ten pounds of kale and takes selfies."

"It's not for Instagram or anything. It's for me. My grandma says, 'Everyone makes fun of you girls for taking selfies, but I think it's brilliant. Someday you can look back and know that the person in the picture was you.'"

"Your grandmother said that?"

"She's a prophet. A prophet and a saint."

He was warming to my grandma. Everyone does. Especially men.

Rocco introduced me to his workers, Ravi and Tengbo.

I said, "Can I ask them to take a picture of us on my phone? Oops. I guess I mean your phone. I left mine at work."

"Sure," Rocco said. "But I just lost my hard-on."

"You'll get it back. I promise."

"In that case, go ahead," he said. "Tengbo can take it on my phone and I'll send it to you."

Our fake kiss for the camera had turned real by the time we stopped. We were both a little flushed. Tengbo and Ravi looked down. I was sorry that we embarrassed them. But apologizing would only have made it worse.

Rocco saw that I sympathized with his workers. That sort of thing was important to him, and it made me like him even more.

4

Charlotte

Charlotte has gotten so used to passersby stopping to stare at Alma's window displays that she no longer notices. So she's startled when Alma says, "That woman out there is looking at you like she knows you."

It's been a while—three weeks, maybe—since Rocco brought Ruth to dinner and she made them eat those sticky buns. Charlotte assumes her brother is still seeing her. He hasn't been staying with them on his nights in the city. But he hasn't said anything, and Charlotte hasn't asked.

"That's Rocco's new girlfriend," Charlotte says to Alma.

Ruth must see that Charlotte is elbow-deep in a

bucket of delphiniums, but as she walks into the shop, she says, "Is this a bad time?"

"Not at all," lies Charlotte.

"I was wondering. Could we go out for a quick coffee? I know you're busy. You can say no."

"It's a perfect time," says Charlotte. Lying again.

"This place is amazing. Half these flowers, I don't even know what they are. And it smells like . . . heaven . . ."

Charlotte says, "Alma, this is my brother's friend Ruth."

Ruth holds out her hand to shake Alma's, smiling so engagingly that Alma—who's not in the best mood— can't help smiling back.

Ruth says, "I'm playing hooky from work. Just for a little while."

"Is that all right with them?" Charlotte can't help turning into the anxious big sister, making sure that no one's getting in trouble.

"They probably won't notice."

"Half an hour," Charlotte says. "We can go some-where close." She looks at Alma, as if for permission.

"I'll be fine," says Alma.

The tattooed barista at Big Cool Bean hardly hears Charlotte's order, he's so enchanted by the wide-eyed vivacity with which Ruth asks for a skim milk latte.

Ruth waltzes her coffee to a table. Charlotte sticks a dollar in the tip jar and follows Ruth.

Ruth says, "I used to work at a place like this. What matters is who you're working with. Believe me, what matters is not 'Should I leave room for milk and sugar, sir?'"

Charlotte recalls the intensity with which Ruth talked to Daisy. Something childish and odd about her spoke to Daisy's shyness. Charlotte would have been wary if a man glommed on to Daisy that way. But people like it when childless women are comfortable with kids. Teachers, librarians, aunts.

"Daisy's a great girl," says Ruth, as if she's read Charlotte's mind.

"She is. I know I worry about her too much. My therapist—"

"You're in therapy!" Ruth says. "I would never have thought that!"

"Thanks," Charlotte says uncertainly. "Ted helps me keep everything in balance."

"Ted?" Ruth says. "This is weird. I once dated a therapist named Ted."

"Ted Lewin," Charlotte says. "It couldn't have been the same guy. Ted's an older man—"

"It wasn't Ted Lewin," Ruth says. "It was Ted . . . Franklin."

"Not the same guy," says Charlotte.

"What a coincidence *that* would have been! Sometimes I think that *I* should be in therapy. Seriously. I'm dealing with some unresolved bad-mom issues that surface when I least expect them."

"Everybody is," says Charlotte. "Everybody has some bad-mom issues. Daisy probably will too." Charlotte regrets this the minute she says it. Why is she telling Ruth about the problems that her daughter may or may not have?

"I doubt it," Ruth says. "You guys are so cool with her. I know Rocco had some problems with your mom. But he's pretty closemouthed about it."

It's Rocco's business to tell Ruth what he wants her to know. There's a silence. Then Charlotte says, "Whom *did* you work with? At the coffee shop."

Ruth laughs. "This guy Russ. We had this long vibey thing, and then this short hot something else. He had more tattoos than *that* guy, piercings everywhere. I thought, I've never made it with a guy like that, and I may never have another chance, so why not? Am I right?"

Charlotte nods uncertainly.

"The sex was . . . unusual. But good. Better than good. Maybe rougher than I would have liked. But consensual. So . . . one Saturday morning he picks me up in his Honda Civic. We drive to an empty lot under the George Washington Bridge and meet these other guys, all driving shitty cars. Someone shoots off a gun, and we're racing down the West Side Highway, scaring the shit out of people. Whoever reaches Battery Park first without killing someone wins. The loser buys everybody drinks. Then they do the same thing uptown, only drunk."

"What happened then?" Charlotte is a little shocked by how rapidly this conversation has progressed from a polite, friendly chat into something much more . . . intimate. She reminds herself of how quickly Rocco's girlfriends have appeared on the scene and then vanished. Reminds herself: Watch out. This woman is *not* your friend.

"After that? I stopped taking his phone calls and texts. Do I look crazy to you?"

"No." What else can Charlotte say? A little crazy, maybe. But not nearly as nutty as Rocco's previous girlfriends. And there's something appealing about Ruth, something innocent and open, a brave refusal to be defeated by whatever life has in store for her.

"So tell me something." Ruth fiddles with her necklace, then smiles. "What was the strangest sex *you* ever had? Weirdest place. Kinkiest. Whatever. Come on. I won't tell your brother."

Charlotte squints into the mist. She still can't believe how quickly this conversation has progressed. "Once, I went home with a guy who started howling like a coyote when we were having sex."

Ruth burst out laughing. "No! And?"

"I laughed. The guy asked me to leave."

Charlotte hasn't told that story in a while. All her friends have heard it. And Eli, of course, early on. She likes it that Ruth laughs. Maybe Ruth and Rocco will work out. Maybe they can be happy.

"Poor guy," Ruth says. "Trying to find a woman who won't mind his . . . special thing. Seeing them all freak out. The disappointment!" No one has ever said that before. Not one person—including Charlotte— wondered what it was like for him.

"My boyfriend before Rocco was so kinky, I kind of forgot what halfway-normal sex was like. He was the all-time worst, really . . . He worked at a place like this. So, okay . . . can I talk to you about something?"

Here it comes. This won't be the first time that one of Rocco's girlfriends has cried on Charlotte's shoulder. She's heard all sorts of theories about why he's such a frustrating boyfriend.

Ruth says, "I care about your brother. Maybe he's a tough nut on the outside, but he's thoughtful and decent and nice. But what I want to know is . . . what did your mom do that got her sent away? Rocco's hinted at something, but when I press him, he goes radio silent."

Charlotte's half smile freezes on her face. "I think that's Rocco's call . . . what he wants to tell you . . . It's something . . . he doesn't like to talk about . . . Neither of us do . . ."

"Not even a hint?" says Ruth. "I want to be there for Rocco."

Charlotte thinks, Don't tell him we've had this conversation. She hesitates to say anything that Ruth might interpret as an offer of friendship. Who is Ruth . . . really? Charlotte has the strangest sensation of seeing a forest creature streak by, just past the edge of her vision. She thinks: I've already said too much. Ruth's surprisingly easy to talk to. Under other circumstances, they might have become friends . . . or, anyway, *friendly*. But these aren't "other circumstances." Ruth is Rocco's girlfriend. Charlotte knows better than to became even slightly attached.

She says, "I'm so happy to hear you feel that way. I love my brother. I want him to be happy."

"I do too," Ruth says. "And . . . just to clarify: I want him to be happy with *me*."

5

April 19

Charlotte

Now Ruth has taken Daisy. Ruth has stolen Daisy from her school.

Charlotte is on her way to meet Rocco and then Eli at Ruth's apartment. Maybe Ruth will be back already. Maybe she'll be there with Daisy.

Charlotte doesn't feel like she has the stamina to go up and down the subway steps, especially if there's a crowd. She taps an app on her phone. The car will arrive in two minutes. She checks the app that finds Daisy's inhaler. Once again she gets nothing—and panics all over again.

Erzilie, the Uber driver, is a middle-aged Haitian who handles her RAV4 confidently and well. She has a soothing presence, and it takes all of Charlotte's will-power not to tell her that she is in terror.

Her daughter has been taken (she'll avoid the word *kidnapped*, for now) by her brother's girlfriend. It could turn out to be nothing. It could be a tragedy. At the moment she can't tell. She's in mortal fear. She can't help it.

The driver will sympathize. She'll shake her head and make soft, kind noises at Charlotte and maybe aim an angry growl at the brother's rogue girlfriend. But will that mean she'll drive faster?

Charlotte wants and doesn't want that. She doesn't know what she wants. She wants this not to be happening.

Waze's bright, soothing electronic voice warns Erzilie (and Charlotte) in advance of what they are supposed to do, then reassures them that they haven't made a mistake. The voice tries to make the long torturous drive seem like fun. Let's take Nassau Avenue!

For a few seconds, Charlotte's terror subsides. She wonders how often people remark on how the neighborhood's changed. Then Charlotte remembers the pleasure of being in a car with Eli and Daisy, and a dentist drill of fear grinds at the back of her throat.

In their woolen caps pulled low and their big dark overcoats, the hipsters look like the old Polish people whose neighborhood they've overtaken. Camouflage, thinks Charlotte.

Charlotte calls Eli, but he doesn't pick up. Maybe he's talking to the police. More likely he's waiting on hold, yet another thing he is better at than she is.

The weathered vinyl-sided houses are so identically grimy and dull that the driver passes the address and continues for an entire block before they realize she's overshot their destination. She tells Charlotte she has a pinched nerve and doesn't like to twist around and back up, but she can drive around the block and get it right on the next try.

Charlotte says no thanks, that's fine, it's only a block. She can use the walk.

She gets out of the car and runs.

6

November, Five Months Earlier

Ruth

I'm not sure if Charlotte likes me, and when I'm uncertain, I babble. Later I can't remember one word I said. She seemed friendly enough over coffee. If she hadn't wanted to leave work, she could have said no. Her assistant seemed annoyed. Obviously, they were busy, and I tried not to keep Charlotte away too long.

She hugged me goodbye, an impersonal hug but better than a handshake. I decided to stop by my office; then I went back home to wait for Rocco.

Sometimes Rocco seems totally present, sometimes not so much. Sometimes he seems to like me; sometimes I drive him crazy. Already I worry that Rocco is bored and planning to leave me. I honestly don't know what I'll do when he tells me it's over.

I don't trust myself not to let things get out of hand.

I decide to ask Granny Edith. It's surprising how well she understands modern guys. She always gives me good advice—usually: Dump him, Ruthie!

Watching her roll out the dough for a chicken potpie comforts me as I describe dinner at Charlotte's house. I leave out the awkward moments. Why make Granny feel embarrassed on my behalf?

Granny says it might be helpful to understand Rocco's history. I say *he* doesn't understand it, so how can I? She says women can understand things men can't.

I tell Granny Edith that Daisy is the only one who likes me. Her mom keeps insisting that she's shy, but she isn't shy with me. I keep having this weird feeling that I know Daisy better than her mom does. And Daisy looks so little like either of them—I sometimes wonder if she was adopted and they're keeping it a secret.

Whenever I think about Charlotte and Daisy, I think about the poor young mother who got murdered in her own home, not far from Granny Edith's.

"Is the door locked?" I ask.

"I think so," she says. "Ruthie . . . leave the little girl alone, or you'll make the mother hate you."

"I *like* the little girl. I like her best of all."

"Fine. But don't let on. The mom will *never* trust you. Do you really want to know the way to these people's hearts? Through their stomachs. They care about food."

"Which is why I brought them your sticky buns."

"That's my girl," she says.

7

Charlotte

Rocco calls Charlotte at work and says Ruth wants to take them all to dinner. There's a spot in Flushing. The cuisine's from a distant corner of China. Super funky, super cheap, super excellent. Ruth says it's really special.

Charlotte's so shocked to hear her brother use the words *cuisine, really,* and *special* that she says yes. He would never agree to go somewhere trendy or over-priced. But this place seems to say to him: Immigrants flinging themselves into the melting pot. Democracy in action. Ruth must have figured out Rocco.

Rocco says, "We should go before the food bloggers ruin it."

Daisy's thrilled by this break in her weeknight

routine of the nutritious dinner with both parents at home. Pajamas, a story, bed. The happy domestic evening every kid is supposed to want. That's why she's so happy to escape.

Eli likes to drive. They garage their car, a 2017 Saab, on Avenue A, though they rarely use it.

It's an unseasonably warm evening. Charlotte likes being in their little world on wheels heading for the Brooklyn-Queens Expressway. She opens her window, but when they pass a cemetery where someone has made a bonfire of lopped-off branches, Daisy coughs. Maybe she's just clearing her throat, but Charlotte rolls up the window.

The GPS coaxes them around cloverleafs and down quiet residential streets. On a block of one-family houses, the GPS voice insists they have arrived. They drive back and forth, annoyed. Getting lost isn't something that Charlotte and Eli handle well. Each blames the other and blows up way too soon.

It's Daisy who says, "Maybe it's there." She points down an alley lined with snarling stone lions. "Are they real, Mom?"

"No," says Charlotte. "They're made of rock."

"Cement," says Eli.

"I meant cement," says Charlotte.

Eli says, "You knew they're not real lions, Daisy. You're just messing with Mom."

Daisy giggles. "I know, Dad. I'm not a baby."

Delicious smells—soy sauce, roasting meat, garlic, onions—drift in through Eli's window.

"Are you hungry?" Charlotte asks.

"I am now," says Eli. "Starving."

They park a block from the restaurant. Daisy skips between them, holding their hands, asking them to fly her. Anyone passing would think: Happy, happy family. Charlotte feels a rush of gratitude, and then a jolt of dread. She knocks on a tree they pass.

"What was that for?" asks Daisy.

"Mom believes in the spirits in the trees. She thinks they're waiting to harm us. So every time she has a positive thought, she knocks on a tree."

"Why does knocking help?" Daisy asks.

"I don't know," Charlotte says.

"So why do you do it?" asks Daisy.

Charlotte says, "To let the spirits know I know they're there."

"Mom's crazy," Daisy tells Eli.

"Just careful," Eli says.

Charlotte says, "I have a good feeling about the food."

Eli says, "I'm not looking forward to this."

Charlotte says, "Try. Let's make it fun."

Outside the restaurant, Rocco and Ruth sit on a bench, tapping their phones. A small crowd mills around, waiting to be seated, scanning the walkway for someone they're meeting. Most of them are also looking at their phones.

"They won't seat us till our whole party's here," Rocco says.

"Kiss your Uncle Rocco hello," Charlotte says. Daisy creeps over to Rocco, who scoops her up and lifts her in the air and then onto his lap.

"Hi there, Daisy," says Ruth.

Daisy dislodges her head from the crook of Rocco's neck. "Hi."

"Remember me?"

"Yes."

"I have a present for you!" Ruth says.

"What is it?"

"Let's wait till later. It'll be a surprise."

"We're all here," Charlotte says. "They can seat us now."

"Finally," Rocco says.

"I'm on it." Ruth jumps to her feet. Through the window they watch her talking to a Chinese couple. Everyone's smiling.

Ruth's still smiling when she comes back. "They're friends of a friend of a chef I know. That's how I heard about this place. Follow me."

As they trail Ruth into the restaurant like a family of ducklings, people step aside.

Special, Charlotte thinks. Ruth makes Rocco feel *special*. That must be so nice for him.

The brightly lit room is crowded with bare Formica-covered tables. Still more enticing smells are coming from the kitchen.

"No frills," Rocco says. "I like that."

Ruth beams.

They sit at the round table: Eli on Charlotte's right, then Rocco, Daisy, Ruth, then Charlotte, who longs to ask Ruth to move so she can sit next to her daughter. Charlotte wants Ruth to *offer* to move. It irks her that she doesn't.

Ruth introduces the owners, Mr. and Mrs. Moy. The woman puts her hand on Ruth's shoulder and murmurs something that Ruth leans in to hear.

"Can I let Mrs. Moy order for us? She'll bring us the best dishes on the menu."

"Dream come true," says Rocco.

Eli and Charlotte order beers, Rocco and Ruth drink tea, and Daisy begs for—and gets—a Coke only after Uncle Rocco intercedes on her behalf.

A waiter announces each dish as he sets it on the revolving platter. Thick white rice noodles with peanuts and scallions, a crab-meat-and-cucumber salad. The waiter points at Daisy and shakes his head—hot!—when he brings out the chicken with chilies.

The grown-ups are fine with chopsticks; Daisy uses a fork. Mrs. Moy produces a pair of chopsticks tied together with a rubber band and explains that this is how Chinese children learn. She hands the child-friendly chopsticks to Daisy, but Daisy recoils, as if the wooden sticks are knives. No one knows what to do, and they sit there until Ruth says thank you and puts the chopsticks in her tote.

"We'll work on it," she says, which pleases the owners. Daisy gives her a grateful look.

Rocco's lips glisten; he looks happy. After their mother retreated to the attic, Charlotte sometimes called out for Chinese food—a special treat. China Clipper was ten miles away, and the food was soggy and cold by the time it arrived. But those dinners provided some of Rocco and Charlotte's warmest moments, living together in the big house without adult supervision.

Charlotte raises her glass. "To great food."

"To pleasure," says Ruth.

Rocco's gaze is fixed on Ruth, and Charlotte thinks,

unkindly, that he's doing a good impersonation of a man in love.

"I know a lot of chefs," Ruth says, "from my time in cooking school. Having those guys in my database was helpful when I worked for the Baroness Frieda."

Charlotte knows who she means, but Eli and Daisy look puzzled.

"The baroness with the TV cooking show. *Skinny Baroness Frieda*? You've probably never watched it, right, Daisy?"

"My parents only let me watch TV an hour a day," Daisy says primly.

"Good for them," says Ruth at the same moment Rocco says, "Poor thing."

Ruth says, "I don't think you'd like this show. It's not for kids. The Baroness Frieda is Norwegian. She was married to a cousin of the king of Norway. Before that she was a supermodel. And when her career tanked because of some bad . . . habits and then that huge scandal, she had to rebrand herself. She got herself together— with *my* help, not that she admits it—and now she's become the spokesperson for a lifestyle mega-brand."

"What's a scandal?" asks Daisy.

"It's a problem," Eli says. "A problem that becomes a bigger problem when everybody knows about it."

Ruth pulls out her phone and flips through some pictures until she turns the screen around to show them a photo of herself and a tall blond woman on a red carpet in front of a sign that reads, "Healthy Women Eat. Gala Benefit, 2015." Both wear little black dresses and the deer-in-the-headlights look of a borderline-famous person swarmed by shouting paparazzi.

Ruth says, "My best friend from high school worked for her. She left to get married. She warned me not to take the job. I thought, How bad can it be? Well, I found out. A serious coke addiction does not make for the greatest boss."

Daisy looks at her father quizzically, then at her glass.

"Not that kind of Coke," he says.

The snapshot of the Baroness Frieda has jogged a distant memory. Charlotte read about her, several haircuts ago. For a while the baroness was in the news, but why? A scandal.

The phone comes around to Daisy, who says, "Is that your sister?"

"God no," says Ruth.

Ruth and the Baroness Frieda do look alike, and it's more than their blond hair, blown out and streaked by the same stylist. They have the same dazed expressions.

"Everyone asked us that," says Ruth. "I think that's

why she hired me. I could be her body double when they were shooting the show and she refused to get out of bed. You can't imagine how much kale I ate for *Skinny Baroness Frieda*, which makes it so ironic, since kale was how I met Rocco. A few times she made me pretend to *be* her at some event she was too messed up to attend. Want to hear my Norwegian accent?"

"I've heard Ruth's Norwegian accent," says Rocco. "It's pretty persuasive."

"Also I understood her. She wanted to be free. To be loved. She always has to smash down her true self so no one will judge her."

Charlotte wonders if Ruth is describing herself, or the person she believes she is. Maybe Ruth began to feel like the baroness's fun house mirror.

Ruth says, "All she wanted was to escape the Norwegian royal family. There were so many things they expected her to do. Though that didn't explain why she was always losing her shit—excuse me, Daisy—going off on waiters and salespeople and leaving me to sneak back into restaurants and overtip or pick up the clothes she'd flung around dressing rooms. At the end of the day, I'm grateful for the wild ride. I got to experience this totally decadent lifestyle that I don't personally want."

Rocco is looking approvingly at Ruth again, as if

she's expressing a political view, when in fact it's pure memoir. In any case, he seems contented. Ruth has introduced him and his family to this super cool, cheap, excellent spot in Flushing. He could do worse. He's done worse.

"Most people think they'd be good rich people," says Eli.

"It's worked out for you, Eli," says Rocco.

Ruth says, "Luck is luck, am I right?"

"You're right," Charlotte hears herself say.

"How's the play?" Rocco asks Eli. "Lady Macbeth still trying to wash the blood from her hands?"

"Not great," says Eli. "It's taking everyone's energy trying to talk the director out of doing the crazy shit in his head."

"Language," Daisy says.

Eli says, "Sorry. Now he's decided that Lady Macbeth should wear a blue Marge Simpson wig."

Ruth says, "Eek! In high school, we played it in street clothes. It made it even more scary—"

"And they've cut the budget," Eli says.

Ruth says, "That play is the most frightening thing ever. This murderous psycho couple egging each other on. She's up to her elbows in blood. It was hard to imagine someone ordering the murders of those two princes in the tower."

There's a silence. Rocco and Charlotte look at Eli, the nicest of them, to break the bad news about Ruth's mistake.

"I think that's *Richard III*," he says. "The princes in the tower."

Ruth's face turns red. "Oops," she says. "My bad."

Eli signals the waiter: more beer for Eli and Charlotte, then a platter of orange slices, and when nothing's left but peels, dinner's over. Even Ruth has run out of steam. She has just enough energy left to make eye contact with the owners and check-sign the air.

"We can't let her pay," Charlotte mouths at Eli, who reaches for his wallet.

You would have thought he'd reached for a gun, that's how fast Ruth jumps up.

She nearly bumps into a crowded table as she goes back to the owners. As they run her credit card through the machine, they stand there in the half-relaxed, half-attentive poses of people waiting for something to appear on a screen.

The owner swipes the card again. He calls Ruth around to look, and Ruth shakes her head. She brings the owners over to the table. Ruth's face is working strangely.

Ruth says, "I have no idea . . . except . . . wait. I've been using my grandparents' address for my credit card statements because some creep keeps breaking into my mailbox in Greenpoint. I've been identity-thefted twice. My grandparents are pretty organized, but sometimes they file something in the wrong cubbyhole. Maybe they forgot to pay the bill. It's happened, but not often . . ."

Charlotte has seen so many cards denied, by now she thinks she can figure out who's surprised and who expected it to happen. But she can't tell about Ruth.

"Identity theft is awful," she says.

"Awful but fixable," Ruth says. "In return for a big chunk of your time and your life."

The owners thank Eli for his card.

"I feel terrible," Ruth says. "Mortified. This was my idea and my treat and my—"

"Don't worry," says Eli. "We wanted to pay. The credit card god has ruled in our favor."

"How charming," Rocco says darkly.

"Next time's on me," says Ruth. "I'll straighten this out."

"Don't worry about it," Charlotte says.

"I'll pay you back. I promise. I am *so* embarrassed."

They're getting up to leave when Daisy says, "Where's my present? Ruth?"

"Daisy, honey, don't whine," Charlotte says.

"My God," Ruth says. "I almost forgot. The most

important thing." She reaches into her tote and pulls out a small package covered with cellophane: a glittering metallic bunny on a chain. She finds a piece of paper, the size of a playing card. She gives Daisy the bunny and card with a ceremonial flourish.

"The bunny is cool," Daisy says.

"Cool indeed," says Ruth. "You chain this bunny to your inhaler. And you give this card to your mom. It will tell her how to open a special app on her phone that will find your inhaler no matter where you left it. It's a GPS tracker. Everybody has it. I gave one to my grandpa so he could find his car keys."

Daisy stares at the bunny, then at the card, then at Charlotte.

"Give it to Mom," says Ruth.

Daisy hands Charlotte the card.

"Good girl," says Ruth.

Daisy's face shines. "Thank you."

Charlotte has no choice but to find Daisy's inhaler in the special zippered pocket where she puts it when they leave the house. The inhaler is supposed to look like a pink snail, like a toy instead of a life preserver. Question: What child would want to suck on a snail? Answer: A child who can't breathe. She attaches it on another link on the chain with the bunny. A bunny, a snail. How brilliant.

"This works," Charlotte says.

"It does work," Ruth says. "Now you always know where it is."

Charlotte should be grateful. A problem has been solved. Instead it annoys her that Ruth (not Charlotte or Eli) found the solution. One of them should have thought of it, not her brother's goofy girlfriend. It's just because she's younger, more savvy about the tech that can put them in constant touch with the thing that might save Daisy's life.

"Say thank you, Daisy," Charlotte says.

"She already did," says Ruth.

"I already did," says Daisy.

"See you soon," says Rocco, with quick hugs for Eli and Charlotte and a big hug for Daisy.

"Can I hug you too?" Ruth asks.

"Not yet," Daisy says.

You go, girl, Charlotte thinks.

"Gotcha," says Ruth. "Later."

Charlotte's relieved to say good night and walk back to the car.

"Can you drive?" she asks Eli.

"I'll be the soberest guy on the BQE."

"That was fun," Charlotte says. "The food was great, wasn't it, Daisy?"

Still holding their hands, Daisy nods her head so hard that Charlotte feels it up her arm.

As soon as they get back to the loft, Daisy says, "Let's try out the magic bunny."

Charlotte wasn't sure that she'd understood, but obviously she has. Five-year-olds know more about technology than grown-ups. And though it's late, and they're tired, and Daisy has school tomorrow, they say okay—how long can it take? It takes less than a minute to download the app onto Charlotte's phone. They wait. And there it is, the tracking icon is a bunny, bouncing on her phone.

Eli tries to download it, but error messages keep coming up, even when Daisy helps him. Eli says he'll figure it out, but he won't. It's yet another responsibility he's going to leave to Charlotte. Eli does that a lot. There's just so much to do even with only one child. No wonder her mother went crazy taking care of two.

"Okay," Daisy tells her. "Turn off your phone, I'm going to hide my inhaler."

Charlotte turns off her phone, and Daisy tells her parents to close their eyes. They hear her running around the loft. She stops, turns, laughs. Tricking Mom and Dad is fun.

"Okay," she says. "Now turn your phone back on and find it."

It's not the same as when she's struggling for breath. It's a fun game. They've got all the time in the world.

Charlotte opens the app, and a series of little blue runway lights and a beeping sound guide her to the bottom of Daisy's laundry basket.

"Mom!" cries Daisy. "Mom found it."

The chip found it. Ruth found the chip. But Charlotte will take credit. And now she will always know where Daisy is.

The next morning, Rocco calls to say that he's moving in with Ruth. He'll stay with her in Greenpoint, then drive up to the country Thursday nights to load up the van Friday mornings and bring the vegetables back to the city.

"That's quite a commute," Charlotte says.

"I've been doing it anyway. You and Eli and Daisy can have your Friday and Saturday nights back. Family time."

"We *liked* seeing you," Charlotte says.

"You still will," he says.

Charlotte says, "I have to ask. What was that credit card thing?"

"What credit card thing?"

"With Ruth. Come on," Charlotte says. "Please."

Rocco says, "You've never had a card denied? Bullshit. You never had a customer whose credit card was denied? Double bullshit."

"No and yes," Charlotte says.

Rocco says, "Ruth called her grandparents this morning, then the credit card company. She's got it straightened out. It was nothing. I'm sorry, Charlotte. I'm sorry if you don't like her. I'm interested in her. I'm not bored. I want to see how this turns out."

"We *do* like her." It's mostly true. Charlotte even—sort of—likes being around her.

But she doesn't trust her.

Charlotte gazes over her therapist's head at the African masks on his wall. By now, she's looked at them so often, it's as if they're people—faces—she knows.

"Something's off about her," says Charlotte.

Ted says, "Do you realize this is the third session you've started off by talking about your brother's girlfriend?"

Charlotte knows and she doesn't know. She thinks: I don't have time for Ted to tell me what I already know. She doesn't have time for therapy.

But she needs this as much as she needs anything. More. Ted helps her make sense of the world. He helps her deal with her anxieties about Daisy's health, with her worries about not being a good-enough mother. He helps her deal with her guilt about what happened in the past—and what she can't change. He helps her cope with her feeling that Eli isn't doing as much as she is, with her suspicion that just because he pays most of the bills, he can leave the heavy lifting to her. Or maybe it's a man thing, a half-Latino-man thing. The woman is the one who has to take on the burden of caring for their home and their child.

She loves how old-school Ted is. His office looks like a therapist's office from Freud's time, with its tribal weavings and statues, its Persian rugs—really, it could have been interior-decorated by Freud! She likes the fact that he keeps his records and patient files in a separate room, out of sight, so that she doesn't have to think about all the unhappy people who have passed through this space.

"I worry about Rocco," she says. "You know that. Better than anyone. He's had so many crazy women. I worry he's found another one."

Ted says, "Do you expect that at some point you'll realize he's an adult, so you no longer have to be his big sister? Protecting him? Taking care of him like you did when your mother left you in charge?"

"I'll always be his big sister. But okay. Sure. Yes.

Whatever. Look . . . this girlfriend scares me a little. More than a little. I have this feeling she's not telling us things. That she's got some awful secret . . ."

Ted's silent for a long time.

"What are you thinking?" asks Charlotte.

"I'm a little hesitant—"

"Say it," Charlotte tells him. "Go ahead."

"What I want to say is . . . Do you think you might suspect her of having secrets because of the secrets *you* have? The things *you* haven't told anyone, that you've kept from Eli—"

"Me?" says Charlotte. "Secrets? What secrets?"

She's joking.

"You know, Charlotte," says Ted. "You know."

8
Ruth

Every day I spend at the start-up feels like being hazed by frat boys at the world's most horrendous fraternity initiation. When my coworkers crazy-glued my mouse to my desk, I had to pry it loose with a crowbar I borrowed from the janitor. It left a hole in the laminate, and I had to install a new mouse with everyone watching. I felt like punching someone. Okay, think: What was the very worst day of my job with the baroness? There were so many bad days. Whatever happens at the start-up is better.

For about a half minute, working for the baroness was fun. Her idea of entertainment was to rent high-end sports cars and floor them on the Palisades after she'd had a few drinks. No one but me would go with her. No one had told me that risking my life was part of my job description. It was a good thing I'd had practice, riding with Grandpa Frank.

I'm not scared of much. Spiders. The basement at my grandparents' house. And being abandoned by men.

It was cool when the baroness and I went to clubs and they chased hot young A-list types away from prime tables for us. They wanted their club to appear on the Baroness Frieda's show. Once, I made a move to refill our glasses and she slapped my hand. Let the waiter do it. She'd had a lot to drink.

Sometimes she would ask me to *be* her on the phone and say the first thing that came into my head, even to a reporter, as long as I did my Norwegian accent. She was all right with whatever craziness appeared in the press. She knew a lot of famous people. Every time a famous person died, she'd make me post an archival photo of her with that person. She has over a million Twitter followers. Her photo archive had its own closet in the rambling Upper East Side apartment she'd inherited from her Dutch grandfather who sold scrap metal to the Nazis.

Her TV show was all about her eating what she wanted—*half* of what she wanted—and staying skinny. Wicked self-denial. She'd cook (or pretend to cook) small portions of exquisite food while the audience watched, and then she'd eat half of it. Very, very slowly. High-end portion control.

Off camera she drank like crazy, so she had to go on these awful fasts and cleanses. Sometimes drugs killed her appetite, which helped. When she did eat, her routine (or so she told the magazines) was to fast all day, then eat half of whatever she cooked. Then a glass of lemon water at bedtime. She left out the marshmallow peanuts in bed, then the puke. She left out the eat, puke, repeat.

So what was the low point? The night she sent me, in a cab, to deepest Brownsville because someone told her a dealer there had the best coke in the city. Why couldn't she pay him to make a house call? Maybe part of the fun was having me step over passed-out crackheads. Or maybe it was when she made me call Jimmy Choo and ask them to deliver their entire fall line in sizes 9, 9½, and 10. When they asked where to send the invoice, Frieda—listening in on the landline—started screaming. Didn't they know who she was?

I knew who she was. I knew how much of her story was true.

I found a letter from Princeton saying they couldn't find the baroness in their alumni records, but being a Princeton graduate stayed part of her story. She could hardly spell! What did she learn at Princeton?

One afternoon she made me come with her and her kids, Angus and Marlene, to a celebrity's kid's super-crunchy birthday party in Tribeca. All around the loft were trestle tables groaning with nutritious nut-free snacks, raw vegetables, candy for those lucky kids whose moms allowed it.

A bouncy castle had been blown up in the great room, and the Baroness Frieda's kids were flopping around, unaware that Mom had gone out for a smoke and not returned. It was my job to smile and stay chill as the other moms jumped ship, my job to reassure the hostess until Frieda finally answered my texts and left the young man she'd been chatting with at the bar on the corner.

On the sidewalk outside the birthday boy's high-rise, she screamed at me. She made me go back upstairs to get the swag bags that her children had left behind. Angus and Marlene were sobbing! Those poor kids were right to fear and distrust her—she had cameras and monitors and nanny cams all over the apartment.

She fired me when scandal finally drove the stake through the vampire corpse of her name-only marriage to the gay Norwegian baron. You couldn't go to the supermarket without seeing fuzzy shots of her in St. Barts, belly to belly with the hunky personal trainer. As the phone calls flew between New York and Oslo, the baroness—while talking to the Norwegian queen mother—mouthed the words "Handle this, Ruth! Make it go the fuck away!"

My mistake was asking her what I should say. She shouted, "That's what I pay *you* to know!"

After that, she was pure meanness. She accused me of being a fraud, of lying about my past. In fact I'm the most truthful person ever. She was talking about herself.

I don't know why I kept quiet. Maybe I hoped for a reference, which she refused to write. She swore that if I ever disclosed any personal information about her or tried to sell an unauthorized photo, she would personally make sure I never worked in this town—this universe—again. It wasn't until I met Rocco that I could begin to hold up my head and quit apologizing to everyone I bumped into on the sidewalk.

If I still have credit issues, I can thank the baroness, who was always forgetting her purse and borrowing my card. At first she was careful to pay me back. But she started forgetting that I'd paid the terrifying bill at the restaurant or at the clothing store that refused to comp her, no matter what level tantrum she threw.

By the time I canceled my card, she'd run up $6,000 of debt. She accused me of piling up the charges myself. She said, "Call my lawyer if you're confused."

Rocco and I had been dating for a while before I told him. I must have trusted him. You are always taking a risk with a story about bad luck. Some people will feel sorry for you. Other people will blame you for what happened, though they might not know it.

And there's nothing you can do to change their minds.

9
Charlotte

When Charlotte was pregnant with Daisy, the doctors made her spend the last two months in bed. The anxiety and boredom were torments. The only way she could cope was by imagining the summer day when she would bring her daughter (by then they knew it would be a girl) to Love in a Mist, the farm that provides most of the flowers for Charlotte's business.

In Charlotte's fantasy, Daisy was around five or six, the age she is now. She imagined her little girl running through the flower farm, her bare feet hardly touching the earth as she raced past the rows of zinnias and snapdragons. She imagined her stopping in front of a gorgeous pink dahlia.

Often, at that moment, Daisy kicked hard, as if she couldn't wait to be born and see for herself.

She arrived three weeks early, underweight and frail.

Maybe those kicks meant something else: Not yet. Please. Not yet.

The birth was more painful than Charlotte expected, but painless compared to the agonizing intensity of her love for Daisy. And even that pales beside Charlotte's burning need to protect her.

Daisy was three the first time Charlotte took her to the farm. It was mid-August, Charlotte's favorite time, when the garden goes crazy after its midsummer nap.

Charlotte had been so excited, she didn't sleep for days. Eli warned her not to expect too much. Charlotte hates it when he warns her about something she's worried about already. Anyway, what could go wrong? Daisy could walk long distances. She enjoyed walking. And when she got tired, she was still light enough to carry. She would like Matt and Holly, who ran the farm—and whom Charlotte adored. She could play with the cake-baking app on Charlotte's phone while the grown-ups had lunch.

Each time they passed the blazing red poppies and blue cornflowers massed on the median strips along the Palisades, Daisy asked if they were there yet.

The first time Charlotte heard Daisy cough was on the highway. The air was thick with pollen. A light green film coated the windshield during the few minutes it took to buy water at the rest stop. Charlotte rolled up the windows. Daisy looked content, spaced out, napping in her car seat.

Unless Charlotte drives miles out of her way, it's impossible to reach the flower farm without passing the farm where she and Rocco grew up. Long after Andrew John knocked down the charred ruin that used to be their house and built his extraordinary modern home farther up the hill, Charlotte would still avert her eyes when she passed.

Too many memories. Too much grief.

It hurt her that she couldn't tell Daisy: Look, there's the place where Mommy and Uncle Rocco lived when they were your age!

And yet . . . and yet . . . if you didn't know, you'd be amazed by the extraordinary beauty of Andrew John's land, by the way in which he'd consolidated and transformed a few barely sustainable farms into a valley that was protected, magnificently landscaped, fertile—and completely organic.

Walking from the road to Matt and Holly's house, they passed banks of hydrangeas and butterfly bushes, rows of lipstick-colored dahlias with deep burgundy leaves, velvety spires of the snapdragons for which the farm was known.

Matt and Holly squatted to greet Daisy.

Holly said, "Great to meet you, Daisy. Your mom says such wonderful things about you."

Already extremely—worryingly—polite, Daisy said, "Nice to meet you too."

Matt said, "Got a little cold?"

Daisy shook her head.

Already the trip seemed like a big success. Charlotte chose to ignore Matt's question about Daisy having a cold.

Matt got a phone call he had to take. Holly was almost done preparing lunch. Maybe Daisy and Charlotte would like to take a walk in the garden.

Holly said, "Check out the cleomes. Kids either love them, or they're terrified, I guess because the plants are bigger than they are."

Charlotte decided to say nothing and just let Daisy experience the garden, to wander where she wanted and see what she wanted to see.

Charlotte heard her cough. One cough, then another. Charlotte told Daisy to drink from her water bottle, but the dry little cough continued.

Daisy looked up at the cleome plants. Some *were* twice her size. She and Charlotte had watched *Alice in Wonderland*. Did Daisy think she'd fallen down the rabbit hole—and shrunk?

Daisy began to wheeze. The soft crackle in her breathing got louder and harsher until it shrilled like a police whistle. That was how it sounded to Charlotte. Daisy stared at her mother. Gagging, frightened, she began to cry. Her little face turned pink, then red, then a horrifying purple.

Charlotte thought she was going to faint. She was useless, totally useless. Then some instinct kicked in. She scooped up Daisy and ran to get Holly. They piled into Holly's car and drove to the hospital in Albany. Holly felt responsible because her garden display included ragweed, to which many people are allergic but which looked lovely with the dahlias. She'd been thinking of pulling out the ragweed, and now she definitely would. She told Charlotte she was sorry.

"It's not your fault," said Charlotte. Charlotte couldn't help thinking that it was *her* fault. Her punishment.

The ER doctor gave Daisy some sort of steroid, and she recovered quickly.

But it's taken Charlotte longer to recoup, if she ever has. Well, it's hardly the worst that could happen. Asthma can be managed. Inhalers, doctors' visits, nebulizers, better vacuum cleaners. Caution. It was good to be cautious. Charlotte hates the idea of her daughter suffering. But if she can draw a lesson from this, it's a warning about watchfulness, about not letting down your guard.

There's a shower in the back of the shop, and Charlotte changes clothes before she picks Daisy up after school. At home, purifiers ensure that the air they breathe is as clean as the water they buy in gigantic bottles. It's another expensive option of privilege. But how would they feel if they cut corners and something happened? It's why Charlotte is often happy to get out into the dirty city air. She's like a dog sniffing everything, even the car exhaust and whatever rots under the sidewalk in the summer.

Once, Eli asked Charlotte if she thought Daisy might be exaggerating her symptoms to get attention. It started the ugliest argument they ever had. He accused her of having lost her sense of humor, and Charlotte said hurtful, possibly unforgivable things about his work in the theater.

Charlotte would like to have a rescue inhaler in every room. But Daisy's pulmonologist, the ironically named Dr. Ash, is a Puritan about prescribing them. He says it's wasteful. They expire. Also, he says, having just one, or even two, helps the child grow up into an adult who will take responsibility for her own health. Five seems early to start training a future adult to be in charge of her breathing. But Charlotte and Eli still hope that Daisy will grow out of it.

Early one morning, Eli calls Charlotte at work. "Don't push the panic button. But Daisy's starting to wheeze, and I cannot find the fucking inhaler."

Charlotte says, "Look for it. You have to find it."

"I know what I *have* to do, Charlotte. And I already looked. Do you think I would be calling you otherwise? You've got the app on your phone."

How could Charlotte forget? She finds her phone and opens the app and presses LOCATE.

"Wait a second," Eli says. "Listen. Hang on."

Charlotte hears footsteps. Then a noise. As Eli walks through the loft, the beeping gets louder. Charlotte's phone shows a cartoon man approaching a cartoon bunny under a sign that says: 30 seconds!!

Thirty seconds later, Eli says, "Gotcha!"

Charlotte's phone says: Device located. The bunny icon is bouncing.

"Where was it?"

"Under the plastic hippo in that pail she plays with in the tub. Let me get Daisy off to school. Then I'll call you back."

"Promise?"

"Promise," says Eli. "I love you. Isn't it weird that crazy Ruth is saving our asses?"

"I don't know," Charlotte says. "The last girlfriend stole things, and this one finds lost things. I'd say things are looking up. Or, anyway, leveling out."

Charlotte hasn't seen Rocco for weeks when he walks into her shop. He looks happy, relaxed.

Rocco says, "I come in peace, with flowers." He's holding two large pails packed with long-stemmed sunflowers in a range of colors. "Hydroponically grown. Andrew John's latest science experiment. Say what you will, the guy's amazing."

Charlotte flinches every time she hears Andrew John's name. She tries not to think about him. Rocco is okay with working for the guy who bought their farm; she should be fine with the fact of his existence. She herself doesn't want all that land, all that responsibility. But still . . . why does he have all that money? Why not them?

Rocco says, "Alma, can you give me a hand with these? I'm double-parked."

Charlotte keeps watch at the door while Alma and Rocco carry in four more pails of sunflowers. Charlotte's already imagining what she can do with them.

"The MacCrae wedding," says Charlotte. "How hard will it be to talk the bride out of pink roses and blue delphiniums into something brighter and bolder and . . . yellow?"

"That's what I was thinking," says Alma.

Rocco says, "I have a favor to ask."

Charlotte should have known.

"Ruth's birthday is coming up."

"Let's do something fun." Charlotte instantly reverts to the welcoming-older-sister mode.

Rocco says, "The weird thing is, her birthday is right around Daisy's."

"That never came up," Charlotte says coldly. But why would it? She can't remember telling Ruth when Daisy's birthday was.

"Ruth wants the three of us to celebrate together. She wants me to get tickets to the Moon Circus for her and me and my little niece."

It takes Charlotte a beat to figure out that *little niece* means Daisy. Then her heart starts to pound. A series of disasters plays out in front of her, a shuddering loop of horror. They will lose Daisy in the crowd. A stranger will take her. Car crashes, mass shootings. Children screaming, blood everywhere. They won't know what to watch out for.

Charlotte falls into a chair. She can hardly breathe. Come on! The city is full of lucky kids being taken to the circus by their uncles. It's called family. That's how the childless play at parenthood. The survival of the species depends on couples practicing on their relatives' kids.

Charlotte trusts Rocco. Daisy loves Rocco; she seems to like Ruth. They're capable of taking Daisy to the circus and having fun and bringing her safely home. Still, Charlotte wishes that everyone would just forget about it and the whole thing would go away.

"Is the circus in town?" She's stalling. "Where?"

"Where it always is. Under a tent at Battery Park City."

"Daisy's got parties coming up. And school and . . . she has a lot on her plate."

"Charlotte. Seriously? How much can a five-year-old have on her plate? I'm asking you. As a favor. Daisy's my niece, Ruth is my girlfriend. We won't keep her out late. We could pick her up at school and bring her home afterwards."

It's the most that Rocco has said to Charlotte at one time in a long while. "I'll ask Daisy."

"Good," says Rocco. "Do that. Ask a five-year-old whether or not she wants to go to the circus."

Charlotte says, "Let me ask Eli too."

Rocco says, "Is this a complex decision?"

"You should try making one of those sometime."

Oh, why did she say that?

"A pleasure to see you as always, Alma," says Rocco, and he stalks out of the store.

A few minutes later Charlotte gets a text.

Yes or no on the circus. Don't contact me to discuss.

She knows that Eli will urge her to say yes. He's sure to think that a tiny bit of independence will be good for Daisy. And, though he's too tactful to say it, that it will be good for Charlotte as well. A baby step toward . . . the future.

She texts back to Rocco, OK. GIVE ME TIMES AND DATES.

It feels right, like a gesture of surrender, of trust and faith. At the same time Charlotte is praying that the circus will be sold out, or that Daisy won't want to go.

10
Ruth

I was Daisy's age when Mom left Dad and loaded me and Tweets the parakeet into the family car. I've seen films in which a movie star does something like that. But real life was less of a madcap adventure than it looks like on-screen. Tweets died outside Taos. We stealth-buried him in a church known for its sacred dirt. We drove around a lot. Mom waitressed and met the kind of guys who pick up waitresses.

I was ten by the time Mom landed in Tucson with my stepdad, who was not interested in having me around.

One day Mom took me to visit my grandparents in New Jersey and went out to get something from the car and didn't come back. I loved my grandparents so much, I didn't even miss her. Or maybe I did, for a while. Granny Edith says I cried myself to sleep at first, but I don't remember that. I just remember how sweet my grandparents were. How safe they made me feel.

Maybe Mom did me a favor. The best times I ever had were with Granny Edith and Grandpa Frank. At Christmas, we'd go into the city to see the department store windows. Wonderlands, Victorian holiday parties, scenes from "The Night Before Christmas." That pure wonder was what I wanted Daisy to experience when Rocco and I took her to the circus.

I couldn't wait to see Daisy's reaction to the opening act, which borrows from Chinese acrobatic ballet, with pyramids of silver-clad gymnasts and rippling silver streamers. Everything is silver because the circus is supposed to be taking place on the moon. There used to be a silver tiger, but I was glad that the animal rights people stopped that. I wouldn't want to bring Daisy somewhere where there was a wild beast, even in a cage.

I couldn't remember looking forward to anything as much as I looked forward to the circus. From the minute Rocco told me Charlotte agreed, nothing they did to me at the office bothered me.

When one guy accidentally-on-purpose spilled hot

coffee on my desk, I said, "That's okay. Accidents happen."

Maybe it wasn't even all about Daisy. Maybe it was that Rocco cared about me enough to ask his sister, which couldn't have been easy. She struck me as the type who didn't trust anyone with her kid, not that I would, with *my* kid, if I'd had a child like Daisy.

Rocco kept reassuring me that his sister and brother-in-law liked me, that they thought I was good for him. That we were good together. But I wasn't convinced. I'd had a bad feeling about Charlotte ever since that first dinner at her loft. What a disaster! I'd thought it would be such a nice, friendly gesture to bring them some of Granny's sticky buns. But as soon as I met them and saw their amazing loft and looked at how Charlotte was eyeing the greasy bag of pastry I was holding, I knew I'd made a terrible mistake. Of course I realized immediately that she's one of those super-health-conscious moms who's extremely careful about what her child eats—and who thinks sugar is the devil. After that, nothing seemed to go right. I was so uncomfortable, and everything I said sounded so stupid and trite. I couldn't wait for the evening to end.

My getting the tracker for Daisy's inhaler helped

some. In fact it had been a big plus. Score one for Ruth. But anyone could have figured that out. Anyone younger than Charlotte and Eli. Or more tech-savvy than Rocco. Anyway, Charlotte said yes.

I wanted things to go right. At first we planned to pick Daisy up at school. Charlotte put us on the pickup list. But when I couldn't get us tickets for the five o'clock show and we had to go to the seven, we decided we'd get her at Charlotte and Eli's loft and take a car service to Battery Park.

Charlotte looked haunted, bereft. I wanted to say, Chill! We're just taking her to the circus.

Charlotte said, "Daisy dressed herself."

When Daisy emerged from her bedroom, Rocco and I burst into applause. She was dressed like an Egyptian princess in a golden crown with a snake curling up from her forehead, a triangular black wig, a purple skirt, a white T-shirt, and lots of costume jewelry. A pair of silver boots completed the look.

I was impressed that Charlotte would let Daisy dress any way she wanted, and even more impressed by Daisy's choices. If I ever had a daughter, I'd want her to be just like Daisy.

Daisy looked proud, then miserable—as if she wanted to run back to her room and change.

"Fashion gold!" I said.

Rocco looked at his phone. "We should go. The car's downstairs."

"How are you getting there?" asked Charlotte.

Rocco turned his phone around. "Suleiman in a red Toyota Camry."

"That's a tiny car," said Charlotte. "Make sure she wears her seat belt. Daisy, wear your seat belt."

"I will, Mom, don't worry," Daisy said with a clarity that shamed us into action.

"We'll be back by ten," I said.

"It's a school night," Charlotte said.

"We talked about that," said Rocco.

"Have you got your inhaler?"

Daisy got it out of her backpack, which she'd tossed on the floor by the door. She hesitated, deliberating over who should keep it. I opened my purse for her to put it in. I shifted house keys and old tissues so the inhaler could have its own compartment.

"I've got this," I said. But I could tell that Charlotte didn't believe me. Or trust me.

Daisy grabbed her uncle's hand and hardly looked back at her mother.

"Jail break!" Rocco said.

I asked, "Daisy, do you want to tell the driver where we're going?"

Daisy shook her head.

"The circus of the moon," I said, squeezing Daisy's hand.

I was glad to see that the driver checked his mirrors before pulling out. He found Daisy in his rearview mirror.

He said, "Going to the circus with Mommy and Daddy?"

Daisy didn't correct him.

Mommy and Daddy. Sure. Why not? It was none of the driver's business.

He drove carefully, for which I was grateful. As Rocco and Daisy got out, I gave the driver a 25 percent tip.

Milling among the crowd at the entrance were ticket takers and ushers dressed like astronauts and space aliens. Daisy grabbed my hand.

I whispered, "Don't be afraid, they're not real."

Daisy said, "They *are* real. Real people in space suit costumes."

Did Charlotte know how smart her daughter was?

Daisy said, "You can die like that. Painted all over silver."

The inside of the tent was like a cross between an ice palace and a Mylar balloon. Daisy beamed like those glowing kids in ads about taking the grandchildren to Disneyland. My grandparents would never have taken me to Disneyland. They wouldn't have known what to do there.

As far as I knew, they never went farther from home than that picnic spot overlooking the Hudson—their happy place.

When I asked Granny Edith for advice on what to do with a child at the circus, she said, "Popcorn and cotton candy. That's how to keep everyone happy."

Daisy smiled when I asked if she liked popcorn. What a ridiculous question!

It was a good thing I'd seen the circus before, because I kept looking at Daisy and forgetting about the tightrope and the trapeze, the pyramids of acrobats and unicycles. She was transfixed, bewitched. I felt like I *was* Daisy, starting over, redoing my childhood with a better family. She'd have a happier life than I had. I wanted to be her favorite aunt. She could learn from my mistakes.

More than anything, I wanted to have a family of my own. I wanted Rocco and me to have a child—a little girl just like Daisy.

When the circus ended, and all the performers strutwalked a victory lap around the ring, and the bareback rider made the silver horse's bottom twitch goodbye, the lights came on, the magic spell wore off, the carriage turned back into a pumpkin.

I'd hired a driver for the ride home. I didn't want to depend on an app. The driver was waiting just where he said he would be.

Despite everything, I was grateful to the Baroness Frieda for certain survival skills: the know-how to make a car be where you want it to be, exactly when you need it.

11

Charlotte

Daisy doesn't want to wear her Egyptian princess costume from last Halloween. She wants to wear a party dress to the circus.

But Charlotte persuades her that it will be fun. Also it's very cute, but mostly Charlotte thinks it might be harder to kidnap a child dressed as Cleopatra. She'd wanted to beg Eli not to go to rehearsal but to stay home and babysit her while she waits for Daisy to return. Last night she mentioned her anxiety, and Eli said, Wait until Daisy's in high school, staying out all night and dating unsuitable boys.

But Daisy will be older then, better able to watch out for herself. Right now she's so little, so helpless. It's only the circus! Daisy will love it.

Charlotte gives Daisy an extra hug goodbye, pet-rified that she will never see her again. Be safe, wear your seat belt, hold your uncle's hand. She thinks how people always warn you about the wrong things, about missed sleep and changing diapers and the terrible twos, when the real problem is the fear that never goes away.

Please let Daisy be all right and once a month I'll do flowers pro bono for a charity fund-raiser. I'll never be impatient with Eli again. I will never fall apart in a crisis. I will never—ever!—wish that Rocco were easier to get along with. I will never wish that Daisy would fall asleep and let me get some rest. I will stop looking for signs that prove that Ruth is just another one of Rocco's crazy girlfriends.

Charlotte falls into the couch and tries to remem-ber what she learned in the yoga classes she took a few years ago. Inhale, let the air out, count backwards from ten.

Maybe food will help. Charlotte eats standing up at the refrigerator. Spoonful of peanut butter, spoonful of jelly. Daisy's favorite snack. Oh, Daisy!

It's only then (why has it taken so long?) that Char-lotte remembers the app. She practically sprints to get her phone and clicks on the icon. After a brief heart-stopping pause, she sees a little bunny stalled in traffic. A great sense of peace comes over her. Charlotte watches it, transfixed. The bunny bounces in place, then inches toward the circus, then stops. Red light. Gridlock. It's hard to tell.

The image shatters into pixels, and Charlotte feels a stab of panic, but now the bunny is back again, bouncing. Daisy's in the circus tent; they must have found their seats. So far, so good. How long can Charlotte watch the bunny? All night, if she has to. But after a while she puts it aside and turns on the TV. Normally, she likes mindless Westerns and Scandinavian noir, but tonight nothing holds her attention, and she watches half of a French procedural before she realizes she's seen it. The murdered woman is a drug mule for a Moroccan gang.

She checks her phone. They're still at the circus. Probably safe, but then the trip back home . . . She pours herself a tall whiskey and takes a Xanax.

Charlotte's asleep on the couch when Rocco and Ruth and Daisy come in. Is she dreaming? She can't believe it's real. Daisy's fine. She's fine! She buries her face in Daisy's hair, which smells like popcorn and some sweet chemical.

Daisy says, "I got cotton candy in my hair."

Charlotte says, "We can fix that." Anything is fixable as long as Daisy is here.

Just then Eli walks in, and Daisy flings herself against her father. Eli registers the whiskey bottle on the coffee table. He knows why she'd needed to pass out. How she loves her husband and their daughter and Rocco and even (if only at this moment) Ruth!

Daisy's saying, "The only thing I didn't like was the people painted silver. Did you know you can die from that?"

"Where did you hear that?" asks Eli.

"This boy in my class said so, and Miss Amy said he was right."

"What *did* you like?" says Charlotte.

Trying to describe some high-wire artist doing flips at the top of the tent, Daisy's talking so fast she's sputtering.

Just then Rocco's ringtone sounds: the opening bars of Beethoven's Fifth Symphony. *Dum dum dum DUM.* Who's calling at this hour? He looks at the screen, considers not picking up, then takes the phone into the kitchen, where he remains for a long time. Mostly he seems to be listening. Charlotte senses trouble, but she no longer trusts that instinct, given her pointless panic about Daisy's trip to the circus.

When Rocco returns, it's clear something's wrong.

"Jesus," he says. "That was Mom. She's insisting we all come to Oaxaca for her sixtieth birthday."

"I'm not going," Charlotte says.

"I want to see Grandma," says Daisy.

"We have to go," says Eli. "She's your mother. Daisy's grandmother. It's her sixtieth birthday."

Charlotte sighs. Eli's sense of family is so much stronger than hers, perhaps because he actually has a family. Then they all fall silent.

Charlotte says, "It's high season. I shouldn't leave work."

"Alma can handle it," says Eli. "There's email. Texts. Phones. We're not going to Mars."

"Great!" says Ruth. "Then it's decided. Let me know when so I can tell the office. But wait . . . sorry . . . Is this family only? Would it be okay if I tagged along?"

Charlotte looks at her brother. It's Rocco's call.

"Sure."

She can tell that Rocco wants Ruth to go. He'll feel braver if she's with him, better able to handle their mother. Doesn't that count in Ruth's favor? Even if it's just that Rocco doesn't want to hurt Ruth, that thoughtfulness is new for him, and reason for celebration.

Charlotte says, "The more the merrier."

All that matters is that Daisy is safe. Everything else will work out.

12

April 19

Charlotte

When she gets out of the Uber and runs toward Ruth's apartment, where she's supposed to meet Rocco—and where she prays that Ruth is back with Daisy—she can only run half a block before she's hyperventilating so hard that she has to sit down on someone's front steps.

If she doesn't stop, she'll pass out. Then she'll never find Daisy.

She was right to distrust Ruth. She just had the wrong time, the wrong event. The circus!

That had worked out fine. She'd been lulled into a false sense of security. Well, maybe not security . . . She'd learned to manage her anxiety. To tell herself that those fears were in her mind.

Well, they weren't in her mind!

She forgot the one thing—the one thing!—she needed to remember to do: take Ruth off the pickup list.

Charlotte can't breathe.

This is how Daisy must feel when . . .

The inhaler!

She takes out her phone and presses the app again.

A spinning blue wheel.

Nothing.

Inhale. Exhale. She stands. Spots jitter in front of her eyes. She sits down again. She has no time!

She could crawl down the street if she has to.

She starts to rise and feels dizzy again, and sinks back onto the steps.

She texts Rocco: ???? That's all she can manage.

Rocco doesn't text back. How can he do this to her? How did he do this to *them*—bring this madwoman into their lives? It's all Rocco's fault. Oh, her poor brother! How ashamed he must be!

But . . . didn't Rocco see this coming? How could he *not* have seen the signs and warned them?

The recent past drifts back in fragments. Mexico . . . home . . . the meeting . . . the shop . . . Daisy's school.

Now this.

Charlotte tries to stand and collapses again. She needs to call 9-1-1!

Instead she does something she's only done once before in nine years of therapy.

She calls Ted.

She's called to make and break appointments, but never—except for once, from Mexico—to say that she's in hell. Please. Can Ted help her get through this without exploding into a million pieces?

The last time—the only other time—was not that long ago.

She'd called Ted from Mexico. She'd felt desperate then too. But not as desperate—not as terrified—as she does now.

Both of those calls had to do with Ruth. That's what Ruth has done to Charlotte. She's turned Charlotte into a person who calls her therapist—in tears. Hysterics.

Maybe he's between patients; maybe someone canceled. Maybe he knows it's important. Even more important than the last time, when she called from Mexico.

Miracle: He picks up.

"I hate to bother you." Even when her child's been kidnapped, Charlotte's apologizing. Maybe they should talk about *that*! As if there will be a future in which she and Ted will discuss her little problems! What if she never gets Daisy back? They won't ever talk about anything else.

Better not to think about it.

"Daisy's been stolen. Ruth took her."

"Are you sure?" he says.

"I'm sure," Charlotte says.

"Oh, dear God," says Ted.

There's a long silence, like sometimes in therapy sessions. Charlotte doesn't have time!

Ted says, "I was going to call you."

"Call *me*?"

Another silence.

"A woman called this morning. Weeping. Terribly disturbed. She asked if I was taking any new patients. That is, any new couples for couples therapy. Her fiancé has broken up with her. They'd only recently gotten engaged. She wanted to know if she could see me. Right away."

What does this have to do with Charlotte? Why would Ted call her about it?

"And . . ."

"She kept referring to the fiancé as Rocco. Your brother? What a coincidence, huh?"

"Rocco's not engaged," says Charlotte.

Daisy's aunt. Charlotte's sister-in-law. What has

Ruth been saying? She never worked for the baroness. Her car was never swarmed by children.

"Then she said something about kale. I couldn't understand. Maybe she did mean your brother. So I asked his last name. It's him."

"Rocco isn't engaged," Charlotte repeats.

"I'm only telling you what she said."

"Did she say what her name was?"

"Naomi," says Ted. "Naomi . . . I couldn't catch her last name. She was crying too hard. But I'm sure she said Naomi."

"Rocco's girlfriend's name is Ruth," Charlotte says. Could he have been cheating on Ruth with a woman named Naomi? Had he gotten engaged to this other person, and Ruth found out and kidnapped Daisy as some kind of crazy revenge?

Rocco has done stuff like that in the past. It wouldn't be totally out of character.

But it isn't Charlotte's fault! And it certainly isn't Daisy's.

Who the hell is Naomi?

"I tried to keep her on the phone because I had a bad feeling that she was going to do something—"

"She did. She did do something."

"I thought she was going to do it to *herself.*"

"Wrong on that one, Ted." Poor Ted. It certainly

isn't *his* fault.

Charlotte's phone beeps.

Eli is trying to call.

"I need to get this," she tells Ted.

Ted says, "Try to stay calm. I don't know what else to say."

Ted has never *not* known what to say before. It scares Charlotte as much as anything.

"I'll keep you posted." She switches over to Eli's call.

"Where are you?" he asks.

"Right near Rocco's. I mean Ruth's. Catching my breath. Did you call the cops?"

"They're on their way over." Eli's voice breaks. Not a good sign.

"What's taking them so long?"

"It's not like on TV," he says. "They said they were going to have to write this up as a family abduction. No Amber Alert. It wasn't clear."

"Ruth isn't family!" Why is Charlotte yelling at Eli?

"I know that. But . . . she was on the list."

There's nothing Charlotte can say.

"But wait," Eli says. "Something really strange happened."

"Something *else* strange? What could be stranger than this nightmare we're—?"

"Listen. Okay, Charlotte? Just listen for once."

Charlotte forces herself to stand and start walking toward Ruth's apartment as she talks to Eli. Everyone's on their phones, and in her panicky state, it makes her feel more invisible.

Maybe she looks like a normal person and not like a woman who wants to beg every passing stranger to please help her.

"'For once'?" she says. "Listen '*for once*'?"

"Sorry. So . . . I was walking upstairs to the loft. And Drew heard me pass by his mother's door. He came out of Ariane's loft and stopped me on the landing.

"He said that this afternoon, around two, when he went out for cigarettes, a woman stopped him outside the door and asked if he lived in the building. She said she was Daisy's nanny."

"Daisy doesn't have a fucking nanny!"

"I know that, *amor*. You need to calm down."

"Okay. Then what?"

"I asked him what the woman looked like. He described Ruth. It couldn't have been anyone but Ruth. And Ruth asked if he would do her a favor."

"Please," says Charlotte. "Drew? What does Drew have to do with this? Is Drew mixed up in this? Jesus, not Drew. Please not Drew. Do you think Ruth and Drew are in this together? Do you think they're planning to kidnap Daisy and hold her for ransom? Do you think Drew and Ariane could be in on it too, that they've been planning to kidnap Daisy for money or revenge or—"

"No," says Eli. "I don't. I don't think any of that. What I think is that you're letting your imagination run away with you. Anyway, this person . . . probably Ruth . . . she told Drew she was Daisy's nanny and—"

Oh, why hadn't they been friendlier to their downstairs neighbors? Drew would have known that Daisy didn't have a nanny. Not that he would have cared—

She'd made Eli look Drew up on the sex offender registry, just because he gave off a weird vibe. Instead they should have asked Drew to dinner. Maybe he would have helped them today. Maybe he would have saved Daisy.

"Ruth told Drew that you asked her to pick up Daisy after school. But Ruth said she wasn't feeling well, and would Drew go with her? In the event of an emergency, like if she had to find a toilet fast or get herself to the ER, maybe Drew could watch Daisy for a while or even bring her home. Obviously, he knew where she lived. And Ruth could get to the ER before . . . well, she didn't want to say."

Now of course she remembers the after-school teachers' description of the man with Ruth. No wonder it sounded familiar! Drew. Charlotte's downstairs neighbor.

The light turns green. Look both ways. This is when people get run over.

Charlotte reaches the other side of the street. Inhale. Exhale.

"Did you ask Drew what happened then?"

"Obviously," says Eli. "They left the school. They went outside. She said goodbye. By the time he'd turned around, she and Daisy had disappeared."

Charlotte is trying not to cry. For Eli's sake, she's trying.

She says, "Has Rocco ever talked about someone named Naomi?"

"Not that I remember," says Eli.

Charlotte starts to run again. She doesn't care who sees.

13
Three Months Earlier
Rocco

As Rocco puts on speed, gathering momentum to get his truck up the long, steep climb that's Andrew John's driveway, he thinks he can smell smoke.

That's crazy. He knows that. It's been almost twenty years since the family house burned down. There's not even a charred place where the house used to be. Just weeds and saplings, like every spot that's been cleared from the rocks and forest.

Rocco knows where the spot is. His house used to be visible from the road. That's how Charlotte saw the fire. Saw it burning, that day. That's how Charlotte saved him.

He can't let himself forget that. He can't let himself

remember. When he tries to remember, his memory doesn't match Charlotte's.

He always looks as he drives past the spot where the house used to be. He always sees nothing, feels nothing.

Andrew John's house is an all-glass rectangular box perched on the peak of the mountain, a multimillion-dollar see-through Noah's ark. Rocco likes being there. It would be just as easy—easier—to meet with Andrew John in his city office, near Union Square, where Andrew John works one or two days a week. But Rocco likes coming to his house. It's more casual, friendlier, less like a business meeting, though of course it is a business meeting.

From the outside, the house looks icy cold—but it's pleasant inside. Warm but not too warm. Like its owner.

Andrew John gives Rocco a light hug, which Rocco returns, first because Andrew John is his boss, and it would be awkward to just stand there, and second because he likes to feel the rich fabrics of Andrew John's shirts and jackets. Even his country clothes are expensive. If he has the money, and that's what he wants, so what? He's giving back enough. He's repairing the planet.

Ordinarily, Rocco might hate a guy like Andrew John—a privileged rich guy who doesn't have to work.

But Rocco has respect for him, partly because Andrew John is so cool about this weird situation: Rocco, the farm's former owner, working for him. It might be really uncomfortable if Rocco's boss were anyone else.

Rocco's grateful for the job. He likes the work. Andrew John hired Rocco right after he got out of rehab. It might have been tough to find work. And Rocco wants Andrew John to be glad that he took a chance on him.

Delicacy, tact, respect—something about Andrew John's humility and simple good manners smooths over the awkwardness of the fact that a billionaire Argentine, with vast *estancias* in his homeland, now owns the land that used to belong to the dispossessed American guy, who transports the vegetables from his farm. Rocco couldn't have taken on the responsibility; he doesn't have the vision or the resources. He wouldn't know how to hire the people Andrew John has hired to advise him on how to turn the valley into an organic, productive, profit-making—and beautiful—farm.

Andrew John shows Rocco to what he calls his "napping couch." It's been almost seven years since Rocco began working for Andrew John, and he's gotten used to the little jokes that Andrew John makes, the catchphrases he uses over and over. He's so rich he can repeat himself without worrying that anyone will judge him. But there's a purpose to it. Everything Andrew John does has a purpose. The little repetitions—"my napping couch"—create a kind of ceremony, a sense of continuity. They remind Rocco of how many times he's been here, of how well he and Andrew John know each other without knowing each other at all.

Rocco always thinks the same thing. Who could nap on this couch? It isn't as comfortable as it looks. Rocco sits on the couch, and Andrew John accordions his tall frame into an armchair beside it.

"Coffee? Tea?"

"Coffee would be great."

Andrew John transmits a message—telepathically, it must be—and Margarita, his "house manager," appears with two cups, a coffeepot, and a pitcher.

"Hope you don't mind that it's heavy cream. My weakness. None of us live forever."

The coffee is delicious, and the gas fire in the free-standing fireplace is surprisingly warm.

"How is your mother?" asks Andrew John.

This too is a delicate subject, best handled with care.

"Mom's fine. She loves being in Mexico."

"And your sister and brother-in-law?"

"Charlotte's business is booming, Eli's working on a play."

"And your niece?"

"She's great. I took her to the circus for her birthday."

Rocco notices that he's said *I*. First person singular. And the circus was for Ruth's birthday, not Daisy's. It's a good thing that Ruth's not here.

"Was it fun?" says Andrew John.

"Was what fun?"

"The circus."

"Lots."

Andrew John's wife and son and daughter elected to stay in Buenos Aires until their kids finish school. They agreed it would be too much of a change, not just from Argentina to America, but from the city to the country.

Rocco knows this from the internet, where he's seen pictures of his boss's wife—a beautiful woman with beach-streaked hair and two fashion-model-grade children. Andrew John visits them every few weeks. Otherwise, he never talks about them, and Rocco never asks.

Andrew John walks over to the window. He has a habit of standing up in the middle of a sentence, drifting over to the glass, and talking with his back to Rocco. Rocco can't blame him. If he had that much money and land, he wouldn't be able to look people in the eye, either.

Andrew John returns, sits down, and grabs a sheaf of printouts from the table. They go over the figures, discuss the shelf life and the popularity of each hybrid or heirloom vegetable and fruit. How are Tengbo and Ravi doing? What can be done to help them? Both are citizens now, but their families have immigration issues. Andrew John has contacted lawyers who will help them, if need be.

Rocco likes these conversations: calm and highly focused. He often feels as if Andrew John is looking slightly past him, into the future. That must be what a visionary is.

Rocco certainly isn't one. He can't see into the future. In fact, some days—some more than others—he feels as if it's an accomplishment to get up and put one foot in front of the other. That's another reason he doesn't mind working for someone who pays him well enough to be paying off the mortgage on his own little house, and who makes him feel as if his work is important and valued.

After their business conversation ends, Andrew John invites Rocco to tour his greenhouse, where he is working on multiple projects: easily grown lichen that is nutritious and delicious, organic aphid-resistant cabbage, hydroponically grown sunflowers.

Today he shows Rocco pots in which he is raising a

beautiful species of daffodil with delicate petals, frosted silver.

"What do you call it?" Rocco asks.

Andrew John loves naming brands and breeds. It's my poetry, he often says.

"Lunar narcissus," Andrew John says.

Rocco thinks of the circus.

He'd been amazed that Charlotte let them take Daisy. Mostly he disapproves of how Charlotte is raising his niece. He loves his sister, but he wishes she were different, and he suspects that she feels the same way about him. It's not just envy of her easy life, her money. Charlotte and Eli have no real respect for labor, for hard work. Eli hasn't had to work in years, and though Charlotte spends lots of time at her job, it's not like loading turnips and carrots on and off a truck.

Charlotte shelters Daisy, teaching her to be frightened of her own shadow and then obsessing about why she seems so timid. Maybe Rocco wouldn't be so concerned if their mother had been different. Sane. Maybe he wouldn't find himself worrying that Charlotte's wound so tight she might snap. If Eli weren't a sensible guy, Daisy would have been in therapy when she was in her baby carrier, her little limbs flopping helplessly against the adult chest propelling her through the world. If Rocco has children, he will do a better job. He thinks Ruth wants children, though—thank God—the subject never comes up. When they pass a child on the street, her gaze catches and lingers.

He has no idea how long this whatever-it-is with Ruth will last, but already it's set a record for how long he can stay interested. He doesn't know what it is, maybe some brightness of spirit. She's a fighter. She's not going to drown, and she means to keep Rocco dog-paddling right alongside her.

She's never tried to psychoanalyze him, in that irritating way so many of his other girlfriends did, even though *they* were the crazy ones. Maybe it's because her childhood was as bad as his. They both had mothers who were, to say the least, unreliable. Both of their mothers are far away now: Rocco's mom in Oaxaca and Ruth's in Scottsdale.

Rocco likes having sex with Ruth; she likes to try new things, and when it doesn't work, when their bodies won't fit together a certain way, she laughs. He's never met a woman who thought sex was funny. It was always so deadly serious, you had to check your sense of humor at the bedroom door. In bed and out, Ruth is energetic and generous, but never freaky or weird. Well, maybe a little weird, just enough to make things interesting. And she has never asked—never seemed to care—about the other women he's been with. Another first, in his experience.

Lately he's been feeling as if a page has been turned. Ruth has her quirks, but she's not insane. He must have been a different person to have gotten involved with those others. Who *was* that guy who dated cutters, suicidal shoplifters, gambling addicts, closet alcoholics, each time choosing to ignore the signs or to be the last person to figure it out?

He even likes staying over at Ruth's apartment: also a first, for him. She's decorated her place with stuff she's gotten from her grandparents and rescued from the street, and it has a breezy charm, like her—neutral, not too girly. There's a big TV, a comfortable couch, which—she learned from her grandparents—is the secret of domestic bliss. Her grandparents are regular gold mines of good advice. She cooks well, mostly Italian food she learned to make at a cooking school run by Tuscan grandmas.

On the way to the circus, in the car that Ruth organized, Rocco felt doors swing open before he and Ruth and Daisy bothered to knock. By the time the performers finished their opening parade, strutting around the ring, Ruth was beaming. All through the show, she was in another world, high in the stratosphere. She'd looked more sparkly than he'd ever seen her. He couldn't stop looking at her.

He wants Ruth to be happy. He's never cared about someone else's happiness before. It's a new experience that he's not entirely sure he likes.

Ruth's birthday falls on a Wednesday, so Rocco can stay in the city if he drives upstate the next day.

He asks Ruth how she wants to celebrate. He likes it that she doesn't expect him to guess her secret birthday desire. He's seen women get furious because he wasn't a mind reader. Ruth will be twenty-four, eight years younger than he is. He's glad that she doesn't seem to care about the difference. She pretends they're the same age.

Ruth wants to go out to dinner. And she's found a restaurant, a collective in East New York that grows vegetables on the roof and trains neighborhood kids for careers in food service. It's community-based, affordable, delicious, serving the neighborhood. Rocco's dream restaurant.

The place is called There Is Such a Thing as a Free Lunch. Ruth says, "Let's not judge it by its name," just as Rocco is getting ready to judge it by its trendy name.

They agree to meet there at six. Rocco offers to pick Ruth up in Union Square, near her office, but she says the rush hour traffic will be terrible. It will be much faster if she takes the train. Rocco admires the fact that she's got the energy to trek out to East New York by subway.

When Rocco wakes up, sunlight is streaming into Ruth's apartment. She's left for work. He decides to buy her flowers and surprise her at her office. He knows that she's working with a bunch of frat-boy sadists. Twice she's burst into tears describing how they treat her, and though he's offered to punch them out, they both knew he was joking.

Now he thinks it might be helpful to show the frat boys that Ruth has someone in her corner, a boyfriend who brings her flowers.

Charlotte would be happy to put a great bouquet together. For free. But he decides not to ask her. It's not that he doesn't want his sister to be happy for him, or that he wants to waste money. It's about privacy. He doesn't want Charlotte charting the progress of his emotional life, especially if his relationship with Ruth doesn't last.

Rocco drives out to the Park Slope Greenmarket and buys an armload of flowers. Then he layers the flowers in a cooler and drives to Union Square. He parks in a garage—he's living large, it's Ruth's birthday!—and walks to the office building where he'd left her with all that kale the day they met.

In the small foyer, a middle-aged black guy in a short-sleeved shirt stands behind a counter. The doorman watches Rocco look for STEP on the letter board on the wall. The businesses are listed alphabetically, and he looks from Sayers Inc. to Title Research International. No STEP, nothing like it. Rocco knows that start-ups sometimes operate out of other offices. He asks the doorman, who says there's no business like that in the building. All the firms listed have been there forever, and the management company doesn't permit subletting office space.

Rocco takes out his phone and shows the doorman the picture of himself kissing Ruth—the photo Tengbo took in the market.

"No, sir, I never saw her before."

"Can you take another look?"

"Sir, please. I would tell you if I had seen that girl, but I'm sorry, I haven't."

Rocco says, "Okay, sorry, I must have the wrong building."

"I don't work here every day." The doorman's trying to make Rocco feel better. He sees the damn bouquet! This poor slob is bringing flowers to a girl, and he doesn't even know where she works.

"That must be it," Rocco says. "I've got the wrong building."

"No problem." The guy thinks a moment, as if deciding whether to say more.

"I heard from the janitor that something happened here last week. Ambulances and cop cars."

"Jesus," says Rocco. "What was it? Some kind of workplace shooting?"

Why did his mind go directly to that? Because of the times they live in.

"Nah," says the man. "More like some kind of workplace food poisoning. I clean my hands"—he produced a bottle of hand sanitizer from under the desk—"every half hour."

"Thanks," Rocco says. "I'll keep that in mind." He tries the next building and the next. Nothing like STEP. No one has seen Ruth; no one recognizes her photo; no one knows what he's talking about. Yet he knows he left her here with those bags of kale.

A couple of times, he'd tried to look her office up on the internet. He'd been unable to find it, and Ruth said that they'd taken down their website. They'd been hacked, and they were undergoing a redesign. He hadn't bothered to follow up.

Now he thinks, This will be easily straightened out, the mystery cleared up. He's gotten things wrong before. He's gotten people wrong. Especially women.

He would ask her tonight. Except that . . . it's her

birthday! Just in case things got awkward, it might be better to wait . . .

Lit by an enormous skylight, the restaurant occupies a cavernous repurposed garage. Straw mats and picnic tables cover the oil stains. Strings of lights are wound around posts and looped around scraggly trees in planters.

Rocco arrives early and waits at the bar. He watches Ruth cross the atrium. She's dressed up in a black-and-red flowered dress and high heels. He sees how envious the other guys look when she kisses the lucky guy. That lucky guy being . . . him.

A waitress in a tight orange T-shirt and blue jeans shows them to their seats on benches, across from each other at a picnic table. There are people on either side of them. It's hard to hear.

"Happy birthday." Rocco hands Ruth the flowers, and she begins to cry. He's always been squeamish about women's tears, but tonight he's so focused on the mystery of Ruth's job that it hardly registers. The flowers look only a little worse for having been dragged around the city all day.

Ruth's eyes are glistening as she gives the waiter a disarming smile and asks if he could please "do something" with the flowers until she can take them home. He agrees, whether he knows what to do with them or not.

Rocco wonders why his good mood has been so rapidly spoiled. Or maybe his mood wasn't nearly so good as he imagined.

He can't help asking, "How was work?"

Something in Ruth's expression turns wary. Has she heard something in his tone? "Pretty quiet. Not horrible—for a change. What about you?"

"I was off today," Rocco says.

"I know. I mean this weekend. How was your visit with Andrew John? What are you trucking into the city?"

"The first pumpkins," he says. "The last summer squash. Apples and gourds."

"Ooh," says Ruth. "Let's make a pie."

The prospect of a pie sounds wonderful, until he remembers his . . . doubts. No point spoiling her birthday. He'll ask about her job when they get back to her place. Or he can wait.

The meal is delicious, but the dishes have too many edible flowers for Rocco's taste—nasturtiums in the ramen, a daisy peeking out from under the arctic char, violets atop the crème brûlée. He's trying to think of a joke about being served the bouquet he's brought Ruth. But nothing seems funny. He concentrates on not cross-examining Ruth. Let her talk about the circus, about Daisy. How wonderful it was! How much fun!

At the end of the meal, the waiter brings individual little chocolate cakes with sparklers shooting off splinters of light. Ruth's face is as luminous as it was when she watched the trapeze artists sailing through the air.

But Rocco can't forget his conversation with the doorman. Maybe she got Rocco to leave her and the kale at a place that wasn't really her office. Maybe she was ashamed of her workplace. Maybe she'd been afraid that one of her coworkers would say something that would make Rocco think less of her. Probably it's something like that. Still, he can't help wanting an explanation.

Driving back to Ruth's, he decides he might regret having sex with Ruth if he's thinking that she might have lied about her job. It's unfair to her and . . . distracting.

Strangely, it makes the sex hotter. Ruth has taken off most of her clothes, and then most of his clothes, within moments of their walking in the door. All he can think of is how good it feels, and how mysterious—how inexplicable—these feelings are. Lying beside Ruth, steeped in the pleasurable after-chemicals, Rocco is willing to believe that he's made a mistake about where she works. But he can't bring himself to ask her outright. First you have sex with a woman . . . and then you suggest that she might not know where her own office is.

He wants a cigarette; he wants a drink. Two things he hasn't wanted in . . . he can't remember how long. Rehab saved him, he knows that . . . If it hadn't been . . . That's not what he wants to think about.

The only light leaks in from a streetlamp outside, but still Rocco shuts his eyes—he doesn't want to see Ruth's face—when he asks, "I was trying to remember today . . . I know you told me a million times. But . . . what's the name of your company?"

"STEP," Ruth says guardedly. Or is he imagining guardedness? "Actually, I told you a *zillion* times. Don't you listen to me at all, ever?"

Once Rocco's started, he can't stop, perhaps because he can't figure out how he can return to the subject later without making it seem more important than it is. "I know you told me. But the thing is, I went there today, and there's no such company."

There. He's said it. He wishes they weren't both naked. He wants to pull the blankets over her, to protect and shield her.

Ruth doesn't flinch. "Why would you go to my workplace?"

"To give you the flowers. Ruth, there is no such company."

"Not anymore," she says.

"And you don't work there." He touches her shoulder, as if to soften what he's saying, but she brushes his hand away.

"I did. The company dissolved overnight. My boss went MIA. I think the frat boys were involved in something darker than glorified Airbnb. Maybe they pissed off the wrong guy in Moscow or Juárez. I think they were into some heavy dark stuff."

"How long ago was this? How long ago did your company *dissolve overnight?*"

Rocco's afraid that he sounds as if he's imitating her when he's just repeating what she said. He can't bring himself to say that none of the neighborhood doormen recalled ever having seen her. Ruth might reply that's no surprise, that it's a terrible picture of them kissing, her face is practically squashed into his, and besides, doormen have come and gone, the management companies are nightmares, they hire and then fire the workers before they have to start paying benefits. Why is he interrogating her?

She'd have every reason to get defensive. Or would she? If she doesn't have a job, where does she get her money? She dresses well, wears expensive perfume. Do her grandparents support her?

"Hello-o!" Ruth snaps her fingers, close enough to

his face to be annoying but not close enough to be infuriating. "Are you still with me? The start-up vanished into thin air . . . let's see, three days ago. No, wait. Four. You were up in the country. My God, Rocco, we must be in really close touch, I mean psychically, if you sensed there was a problem there—and you went to find me."

"The doormen had never heard of you and your company." Rocco is sorry the minute he says it.

Ruth coughs so long and hard that Rocco hands her his water glass and makes her take a sip.

After a while, Ruth croaks, "Everybody got threatened. The consensus was: What happened never happened. There never was a STEP start-up. I wasn't supposed to know, but I heard that two guys showed up in the lobby with guns. I wouldn't be surprised if the doorman quit on the spot."

"And it took you all this time to tell me?"

"Listen, Rocco, please. I know this might seem strange, but will you watch a movie with me? I want to show you something."

They get up and get half dressed and go into the living room and nestle on the big couch in front of the flat-screen. Ruth clicks through the streaming channels until she finds a French film about a guy who gets fired and can't tell his family and leaves for work at the same time every day and goes and sits in his car and comes home when his workday is supposed to be over.

Rocco's tired. The subtitles flash across the screen too fast for him to read. Twice he nearly falls asleep. By the end, the French guy seems to be back with his wife, and they seem happy about it.

Over the credits Ruth says, "I couldn't bring myself to admit I didn't work there anymore. Not even to myself. I couldn't process it until I'd figured out some answers. How could I not have known? How could I not have picked up a signal that things weren't what they seemed? I would have told you eventually, I swear. I would have admitted defeat.

"Except . . . you know what? I don't feel defeated. Right now I have this idea for an indie feature film: A woman gets fired from a shady start-up and sits in Union Square and feeds the pigeons and becomes friends with all the unemployed people, male and female, old and young, black and brown and white, also hanging out and feeding the pigeons."

It's the kind of movie Rocco would like someone to make, if not the kind that he wants to see. It's interesting that Ruth would try to explain her being newly unemployed by making him watch a film with one pathetic star on Netflix. How did she even find it? Did the movie give her the idea? Or did she have the idea first and find the film and wait to show it to him until he figured out the truth?

Ruth says, "People do stupid things, and then they admit them. That's what it means to be human. And then we try to do better."

That's what Rocco believes, what he wants to believe. He wants forgiveness for everything he's done: Forgiveness from the crazy girlfriends he's mistreated in ways in which he is determined not to treat Ruth. Forgiveness for what he did when he was drinking. Forgiveness for nearly attacking his mother . . .

Why not let Ruth make this one mistake and pick up where they left off? Or start over? She would be more careful. More trusting, poor thing.

That's what he decides to do. And they go back to bed.

In the morning, he wakes up, and the first thing he thinks is how sorry he is that he agreed to let Ruth come to Oaxaca. What if she lies about something . . . and Mom catches her in a lie?

Lately, Rocco sees his mother two or three times a year. Mostly she flies up north to visit Daisy. She stays with Charlotte and Eli, and she drives them crazy. But she prefers her family to come visit her. She has also, it's turned out, made some wise investments, wise enough so that if she adds the interest to the income she cobbles together from her various jobs, she can live simply and even hire a maid, the sweet-tempered, endlessly patient Luz.

Her house is big enough for them to stay. When he goes down there (Mom pays for his ticket), she seems happy to see him, though she soon grows bored with him. It annoys her that Rocco has quit drinking, and though she knows that for him sobriety is a matter of life and death, some part of her thinks it's self-righteous of her son to spoil everyone else's fun.

Ruth has offered to pay for her own ticket to Mom's birthday celebration. They're flying separately. Because of a difference in fares, Ruth will be arriving a few days after Rocco and Charlotte and her family, and they'll all fly home together.

At least, Rocco hopes, Mom might be interested in Ruth even after she's lost interest in him.

PART TWO

Our Mexican Adventure

14
Charlotte

This will be the first time that Charlotte and Eli have brought Daisy to Mexico. Charlotte's not sure why they've hesitated before, especially since Mom always assumes they'll bring her, and it always takes her days to get over her rage at them for having left her granddaughter at home. Charlotte and Eli aren't worried about drug crime and kidnappings, which are uncommon in Oaxaca. But kids get sick . . . Maybe they just fear that they'll feel more . . . vulnerable with a child.

Besides, there's Daisy's asthma. Charlotte has asked their doctor, who says she'll be as safe in Mexico as she would in New York, or almost as safe. But he warns Charlotte to keep Daisy's inhaler readily accessible in the Mexico City airport.

Seven thousand five hundred feet in the air with some of the world's worst air pollution are not words guaranteed to reassure the anxious parent. Is Daisy an actual person to her doctor or just another wheezy little chest? Charlotte decides to change doctors, if need be, when they get home.

Charlotte's never anxious or restless in Oaxaca. She always feels happy there, especially when she manages to get away from Mom and her expat friends. A few times Eli has stayed in New York with Daisy, and Charlotte has gone alone, or with Rocco; a few times Eli's parents came up from Florida to watch Daisy so Eli and Charlotte could go together.

Charlotte loves the soft clear mountain light, the brightly colored walls, the hilly cobblestone streets, the gorgeous vegetation, and the smells of someone cooking something delicious behind the kitchen windows. Turning a corner to find herself in the middle of a parade with brass bands and people throwing baskets of candy at the happy children—that's when Charlotte would miss Daisy most and wish they'd brought her along.

It's Mom's—Daisy's grandmother's—sixtieth birthday. Daisy has a right to be there. She belongs there. They can always fly home if something goes wrong. Mom will understand. Eventually. She'll be frosty and then defrost after a couple of months. Anyway, nothing is going to go wrong.

There was only once—just once—when the trip was a nightmare.

That was before Daisy was born. Rocco and Charlotte had gone down there to help Mom get settled, only to find that she was already settled. She'd hired the endlessly kind, resourceful Luz to help around the house.

Rocco had been drinking heavily. He was unemployed. Probably homeless, though he never admitted that to Charlotte, who would have insisted that he come stay with her and Eli.

He'd gotten the money for the fare from Mom.

And one night, after who knows how many tequila shots, he'd pulled a knife—a kitchen knife, but still—on Mom and demanded to know why she'd burned down their house.

With Rocco inside it.

It's one of those family . . . what? Not secrets, exactly. They all know about it. Charlotte and Eli. Mom and Rocco, obviously. But no one ever mentions it.

It's one of those family . . . *things* that no one talks about. Ever. One of those things they all pretend to have forgotten, though no one will ever forget.

Charlotte was a senior in high school then, getting ready to leave for college.

One afternoon, walking home from the school bus stop, she had to jump out of the way of the town fire engine speeding toward . . . It took her a while to realize where the fire truck was going, but on this stretch of the road, it could only have been heading for her house.

She began to run. She could hardly breathe. She was already weeping. The wind—the same wind whipping up the fire—blew her scream back in her face.

Rocco would have been walking home from the bus stop with her . . . except that he'd stayed home, sick with a bad cold that day.

He'd stayed home with Mom.

Oh, Rocco!

A passing motorist had called in the fire. Flames were already shooting out of the roof of the house. The fire had started in the attic. Where Mom lived. Where Mom had been hiding out.

The sheriff was the first to arrive, and he and his deputy had gotten Mom out of the attic, and she had directed them to the bed where Rocco lay asleep.

Later Mom would stress that point. Didn't that prove that she meant to save him? That she hadn't been trying to kill him? That it was an accident . . . she'd fallen asleep smoking . . .

The police believed her. But Rocco and Charlotte

never did. Without ever discussing it, they both believed that Mom had been living out the end of her *Jane Eyre* fantasy. The madwoman in the attic sets fire to the house.

None of the authorities seemed to notice—and no one pointed out—that Mom didn't smoke. That is, she didn't smoke then. Later she would start. As if to prove that her story could have been true.

The problem was that it wasn't true.

By the time Charlotte got there, Mom and Rocco were standing on the front lawn, wrapped in blankets, shivering. Watching everything burn.

Mom had gone to the hospital. Charlotte and Rocco had gone to live with their father's sister in New York City. Charlotte left for college. Rocco started drinking.

And no one talked about any of it until Rocco held the knife to Mom's throat, in her kitchen in Oaxaca, and asked her why she'd done it. How could she?

Mom was crying. It was an accident. An accident, she swore.

Screams, Mom's and Luz's, had woken Charlotte, who'd run into the kitchen and gently, gently—it had been shockingly easy—taken the knife from Rocco.

She'd flown home with him on the next plane, and within a few days she and Eli got Rocco into rehab.

No one talks about that, either.

Rocco has been sober ever since. But Charlotte has never forgotten how it felt to take the knife from her brother's hand, the knife poised just a few inches from their mother's throat.

If she closes her eyes and imagines it—which she tries not to do—she can see, with perfect clarity, the scene in her mother's kitchen. She can still feel the terror. And she dreams about it sometimes—not directly, but nightmares that, when she wakes up crying out in her sleep, she knows had something to do with that day.

She never believed that Rocco would have gone ahead with it. He wouldn't really have hurt Mom. He just wanted to scare her the way she'd scared him all those years ago. He was a sweet guy, basically. But he'd been a crazy drunk. It meant that everyone, Rocco included, was doubly committed to his staying sober. And it meant that Charlotte would never be able to think of her little brother in the same way again.

She'd never trusted him as completely as she had before. Maybe that was part of the reason why she'd been so hesitant when he and Ruth wanted to take Daisy to the circus. She was sending her child off with a guy who'd threatened their mother—*his* mother—with a knife.

Ever since that day, there had been an undercurrent of tension—of things unexpressed, unexamined, unforgiving—between Rocco and Mom. Well, it was hardly surprising.

Anyway, they didn't mention the cause. They acted as if nothing had happened.

And when they all met in Mexico this time, for Mom's birthday, no one would mention it. Or think about it.

Charlotte wonders how much of this Ruth knows. Or if she knows any of it at all.

Charlotte prepares in real ways—passports, extra socks, OTC medicines—and in magical-thinking ways. When Charlotte tells Daisy's teacher that she wants to keep Daisy from feeling overwhelmed by all the new sights and sensations, Miss Amy tells Charlotte to buy a notebook in which Daisy can record her experiences and impressions. It doesn't matter that she can hardly write yet; she can draw. If Charlotte buys scissors and a glue stick, Daisy can cut and paste pictures of what she's seen. It will help her feel more in control if she can keep the explosion of sight and sound contained between two covers.

The cover of Daisy's notebook is silver cardboard studded with tiny rhinestones. On the first page Charlotte prints, *Our Mexican Adventure*, and Daisy signs her name. Charlotte prints out images from the internet and gives Daisy a head start: marigolds and celosia in the market, a woman with a jug on her head, a massive pre-Columbian stone figure—it all goes into Daisy's book. The thought of what Daisy might learn has a calming effect on Charlotte's anxiety.

It will all be worth it. Besides which, Mom will insist. It's her sixtieth birthday. Not bringing her only grandchild is not an option. She loves Daisy, and she wants to show her off to her large community of locals and expats.

Charlotte and Eli should have realized that going to Mexico would be *better* with Daisy. People have always been nice there, but now they're even nicer. It's as if Daisy's existence proves that her parents are members of the human race. Who would have imagined that Daisy would *like* being smiled at by strangers, and that she would begin to smile back, which never happens in New York?

Mom lives half a mile from the market, and every day she walks there and back, which may be partly why she still has a stringy marathon-runner's body even with the tacos and mezcal-tamarind cocktails. She dresses in comfortable, loose-fitting clothes. The ponytail she's worn for decades bounces and gives her walk a youthful spring; pulled tightly back, her hair tugs at her skin and makes her tanned face look taut and attentive.

She's different from how she was when Rocco and Charlotte were kids. She's lost interest in playing the tragic mad heroine in the attic. She's a modern woman now, living on her own. She's proud of how she's built a life here. Her Spanish isn't perfect, but good enough for her to have friendships with people whose English is no better than her Spanish. And she understands enough to watch the telenovelas on TV. She knows a lot of older gay men, divorced women, retired Mexican teachers of English, and retired American teachers of Spanish.

Everyone in the neighborhood knows Mom. Señora Sally. Daisy tells Charlotte that Grandma must have shown everyone pictures of her, on her phone. The women selling chilies and mangoes call out her name. Señorita Daisy!

Daisy's delighted to be with her grandma. Charlotte feels as if Daisy is the world's most inspired hostess gift, a present so well chosen for her mother that Mom even seems happy to see Charlotte and Eli.

Mom has never been affectionate. When Charlotte hugs her, she grudgingly allows herself to be embraced. Charlotte has worried that Mom would treat Daisy that way. But she's been surprised by the heartfelt affection that Mom lavishes on Daisy when she visits them in New York.

For Mom, love seems to have skipped a generation. It doesn't bother Charlotte. Not really. She's glad that Daisy has a loving grandmother.

Freed from the duties of childcare, liberated from their worries about whether Daisy is bored or entertained, hungry or thirsty, Eli and Charlotte can enjoy the city. Eli likes speaking Spanish. They take long walks and sit in cafés and eat churros and chocolate and talk. It seems like a good sign to Charlotte that, after being married for years and having a child, they can still have fun.

They explore antiques shops, go to the art museum, and cool off in the incense-laden chill of the cathedral. They ask Luz what she needs in the market, and they do the shopping. They buy artisanal mezcal and woven place mats that Charlotte can't resist, even though they don't need them. They purchase a painted wooden donkey that Daisy names Sig. After little white worms begin crawling out of the wood, Charlotte has to spirit Sig into the garbage when Daisy is sleeping.

Charlotte and Eli buy Mom an air conditioner, not because the weather is so hot, but because Mom is developing a worrisome wheeze, a little like Daisy's. And it will be better for Daisy to have the air filtered. They ask Luz to find a man to install it.

They've been in Oaxaca for a day when Rocco arrives. He and Mom seem wary around each other. It's hardly a surprise. After all, they don't share a great mother-son history.

Rocco has learned Spanish from two of the guys he works with. Unlike Eli, who is fluent but reluctant to talk to strangers, Rocco will talk to anyone. One night the three of them leave Daisy with Mom and go to see the masked wrestlers. They drink beer and eat potato chips drenched in hot sauce, and cheer and boo along with the rest of the crowd.

Rocco has always liked Oaxaca. But this time he's not quite his usual Rocco-in-Mexico self. He seems preoccupied. Distant.

One night, after a couple of Mom's cocktails, Charlotte gets up the nerve to ask if everything is all right with Ruth.

"What's it to you?" he says. "You and Eli don't like her."

"We do," Charlotte says. "We both do."

Is that true? They *do* like her . . . with reservations. But it wouldn't be helpful to say that.

"*Daisy* likes her." There's something challenging, even hostile, in Rocco's tone.

Ruth is coming down for Mom's party. But when Charlotte asks Rocco when Ruth is arriving, he shrugs. She's been through enough of his breakups to read the signs, but she can't decipher these. She can't tell if he's getting ready to leave Ruth or if he's nervous about her safe arrival. Or both.

"She's coming Wednesday," Rocco tells Eli, ignoring Charlotte, though she's the one who asked. "Flying in from Mexico City."

Charlotte and Eli spend Wednesday exploring the ruins at Mitla, and by the time they get back, it's evening. Rocco keeps checking his phone and trying to call or text Ruth, but she's not picking up. Mom says that the last plane from the capital landed around six, so if Ruth isn't there by eight, she probably isn't coming and they should go ahead and eat without her and assume she'll arrive tomorrow.

Rocco says, "You're okay with that, Mom? That's how we're going to leave it? Jesus Christ. She texted me this morning that she was arriving tonight."

"What am I supposed to do?" says Mom. "Call out the Federales? Believe me, dear, we don't want the police mixed up in this. That is the last thing we want."

"That's reassuring," says Rocco.

"It is what it is," says Mom. "This place isn't for everyone."

"No place is," says Rocco.

"Amen, son," says Mom.

Charlotte puts Daisy to bed, then returns to the kitchen to find Rocco still trying to reach Ruth. Mom keeps mixing margaritas, and she and Charlotte and Eli keep drinking.

In the morning, Charlotte awakens with no memory of how she got to bed. She assumes Eli tucked her in. A star of pain blazes between her eyes.

Daisy runs into the room and jumps into bed between her parents. Charlotte's throat hurts. She needs water. Now. She rolls Daisy over toward Eli and goes into the kitchen.

Rocco and Mom are sitting at the table, and there, standing by the sink, is Ruth, doing all the talking. Rocco has his back to Charlotte, who sees that Mom is openmouthed. Dumbstruck. That Mom is listening to someone else for this long is shocking in itself.

Charlotte's surprised by how happy she is to see Ruth, or maybe she's just relieved. When she hugs Ruth hello, she can sense Ruth making sure that Mom is watching. Ruth wants Mom to see that she belongs, she's already part of their tribe, so Mom might as well get on board. It's not exactly the truth, and besides, Ruth is misjudging Mom if she thinks that Mom cares what the rest of them think.

"When did you get here?" asks Charlotte.

Rocco answers for her, "Three in the morning. Tell Charlotte what you told us."

"The short version," Ruth says, "since I already told you."

"Definitely," Mom says. "The highlights." It seems possible—no, clear—that Mom doesn't like her, and that Ruth doesn't notice or doesn't care. This evening, Mom will not appreciate her turning down a margarita to show that she's supporting Rocco.

Ruth says, "I missed my connection. This nice woman at the airline desk helped me find a driver who would get me here, so I wouldn't have to stay in Mexico City."

"That's a seven-hour drive," Charlotte says.

Ruth says, "Six and a half. And the driver wasn't speeding. He seemed like a nice guy. He drove very smoothly. His English wasn't one hundred percent. But we could communicate. *No problemo.* He made it clear that he wasn't going to rape and murder me—or charge the stupid gringa a fortune.

"But here's the crazy part. Outside Oaxaca he stopped the car for no reason, and all these . . . all these . . . skinny dirty children ran out from the bushes. They swarmed the car, they just . . . *swarmed* it. They had their hands out, begging. The driver yelled at me to roll up the windows, but I had the feeling that he was part of it, that he'd brought me there because he wanted me to give them money. I asked him if he could drive on without hurting the children. He edged through the crowd, and finally the kids scattered and ran back into the shrubs. Wasn't that a crazy thing to happen in the middle of the night?"

"That *is* the crazy part all right." Rocco sounds impatient. And tired. Especially tired.

Mom says, "In all my years here I've never heard anything remotely like it."

Charlotte doesn't know if any of them believe Ruth's story about the kids. But why would Ruth make that up? Charlotte can hardly interrogate her brother's girlfriend, who has come all the way to Mexico to celebrate Mom's birthday. It would only make the situation more awkward than it already is.

Charlotte says, "Strange. Really strange."

Rocco and Mom are disappointed. They'd expected something more from Charlotte, more inquisitorial, more conclusive. A swarm of children? *Really?* But Ruth seems satisfied with her introduction to the household, and Charlotte's glad to leave it at that. For now. Still she wonders how this has happened so fast. Mom is a powerful personality, yet somehow even Mom seems to have rolled over for Ruth—at least enough to let her absurd story go unchallenged.

Mom says, "Are you sure you weren't dreaming? Once I took a sleeping pill for a flight, and I had no idea how I got to the place where I wound up."

Ruth says, "I never take pills. Not even to go to sleep."

"Lucky you," says Mom.

"Trust me," says Ruth, "I can tell the difference between a dream and reality."

"You take Ambien," Rocco says. "I've seen you."

Ruth glares at him, then says, "TMI, dear. Too much information," she explains to Mom.

"I know what 'TMI' means," says Mom.

"I'll take a pill maybe once in a million years," says Ruth. "Everyone has those nights."

"You must be very tired." Doesn't Ruth hear how unfriendly Mom sounds?

Ruth goes straight to sleep and spends most of the next day working on her laptop in Mom's courtyard. She doesn't eat anything, and she makes a glass of orange juice last all day. At home she's always had such a thing about food. Surely whatever Luz is offering is no more unfamiliar than that Chinese meal in Queens. Is Ruth afraid of getting sick?

"Is she all right?" Charlotte asks Rocco.

Rocco says, "Leave her alone. She's fine."

But Rocco doesn't seem fine.

Mom is making a genuine effort to be hospitable. A superhuman effort. Unheard of, for Mom. The first evening Ruth's there, just before dinner and just after Mom's gotten Eli and Charlotte (and herself) trashed on margaritas, Mom asks what Ruth would like to do in Oaxaca. Is there anyone she wants to meet?

Ruth says, "My favorite thing, wherever I go, is to meet a cool local chef. It was useful when I traveled with the baroness, to scope out the best cooks, even though she made such a production of eating half of whatever she was served, a tiny portion. It was my job to explain that it wasn't an insult or a sign that the Baroness Frieda didn't like the food. Half portions were her brand."

Waiting for Mom to ask who the Baroness Frieda is, Ruth pauses. But Mom doesn't care, or already knows. Charlotte waits for Mom to say that leaving half of what you're served is the most decadent thing she's ever heard of, unless you're planning to give the other half to someone who's hungry. But Mom doesn't say that, either.

What Mom *does* care about is showing her family the fabulous life she's made for herself, without their help, in Oaxaca. That includes having a chef on her contacts list. A young Mexican rising star would have been better, but at least Mom knows an expat cook. Chef Basil, who ran a fine-dining restaurant in Atlanta, has retired with his partner to Oaxaca, where they run a cooking school.

"Have you heard of Chef Basil, Ruth?" asks Mom. "I believe he appeared on *Martha Stewart*."

"Yes, I think so," says Ruth.

"He's one of those guys who puts the *fun* in cooking *fun*damentals." Mom giggles, and Charlotte wonders how many cocktails she had before she started mixing them for her and Eli.

Chef Basil owes Mom a favor. She watered his plants when he and Ernesto went back to Atlanta to collect an inheritance. Maybe he'll agree to give Ruth a quick *free* lesson. Their classes are usually sold out for weeks, but Mom will give it a try.

Mom likes creating the impression that all of expat Oaxaca is at her beck and call. She leaves the room, and they can hear her purring into the phone. Then she tells them that it's all set up for two people tomorrow morning at Chef Basil's house. Two people? She must have assumed that Rocco and Ruth—the happy couple—would go, but Rocco says, "I wouldn't go to a shit show like that if someone held a gun to my head."

Well! Charlotte's puzzled. Rocco loves food. Normally, he'd go along just to see what it was like. It reinforces Charlotte's sense that some strain is making him watchful around Ruth. Maybe her implausible story about the car swarmed by children has put him on guard. It did seem preposterous, yet Charlotte is still puzzled by why she would invent it.

Mom says, "Obviously *I* can't go. My party's the next day, in case you've forgotten."

They haven't forgotten. Thirty friends will be assembling in her courtyard for champagne and street food made by everyone's favorite vendors. Mom looks at Charlotte, imploringly. That is, imploringly *for Mom*. Would Charlotte go to Chef Basil's with Ruth?

"Sure," Charlotte says, "I could use a few tips on how to cook great Mexican food."

"Not just great," says Mom. "Fabulous. I can take care of Daisy. She's always helpful. Right, honey?"

Daisy nods without looking up from her *Our Mexican Adventure* notebook. She's pasting in pictures she's cut out of the airplane magazine, images of cathedrals nowhere near Oaxaca, of snorkelers diving in turquoise water, of tourists doing yoga on expanses of bleached sand. It's never occurred to Charlotte to say: That isn't *our* Mexican adventure. Daisy's pasting the pictures in her book makes them part of their adventure too.

The next morning, Ruth and Charlotte set off for Chef Basil's house. Ruth prattles about how she adores Charlotte's mother, what an inspiring example she is, what a great life she's made for herself here. Ruth hopes she'll be like Mom someday. No wonder Mom raised two such wonderful children.

Charlotte decides that Rocco hasn't told Ruth about their childhood, about Mom's illness, the house fire, her hospital stay. Maybe if she knew the truth, she'd realize: The wonder is that Mom's children still talk to her. The *true* wonder is that they are walking and talking at all.

Oh, and Ruth admires Charlotte's mother for being such a terrific grandmother. Daisy loves her to pieces! That's how Ruth puts it: *loves her to pieces.* If there's one thing Ruth knows about, it's the importance of the love between grandparents and children. If it weren't for Ruth's grandparents, she'd be a total basket case.

Something inside Charlotte curdles and shrinks. She hates it when Ruth talks about Daisy, that sugary note of fawning admiration and . . . *fandom* that creeps into Ruth's voice.

Ruth says, "I was nervous about meeting your mom. I'm so relieved that she seems to like me."

"I'm glad too." None of this could be further from the truth. Does Ruth not see Mom rolling her eyes every time she opens her mouth? Charlotte hopes Ruth doesn't notice, and that she's oblivious to how much—and how guiltily—Charlotte enjoys her mother's response.

Ruth also doesn't notice that Mom has been going out of her way not to be left alone with her, or talk to her for too long. Ruth prefers to think that she's won Mom's heart with her . . . *what?* With her energy, friendliness, pluckiness, with her having worked for the Baroness Frieda, with any of the qualities that Ruth thinks are her strong points.

Ruth says, "Your mom is *practically the queen of Oaxaca*. She can make one phone call and hook us up with the coolest chef."

Charlotte stifles the impulse to say that the city has lots of cool Oaxacan chefs, and Mom is sending them to a gringo expat who gives lessons to tourists. What stops her is knowing how self-righteous she'd sound, how snobby and aggressive. Probably Mom is introducing them to the kind of guy she thinks Ruth deserves.

A few blocks from the zocalo, behind an unassuming facade, a Mexican woman in a bright folkloric costume admits them to a colonial palace, an urban hacienda, its walls banded with murals of white ladies in long gowns parading around the zocalo trailed by indigenous people keeping the trains of the ladies' dresses out of the dust.

"Wow. Do you think those are hand-painted?" Ruth asks Charlotte.

Charlotte can't trust herself to answer, and the Mexican servant either doesn't understand or pretends not to. Charlotte can see the staff through a set of French doors. A woman, a man, and a girl around Daisy's age sit at a table, concentrating on some sort of food prep.

Chef Basil vaults into the room and lands on both feet with a thump. His pudgy face is so shiny and pink it looks scraped. He sweeps off his chef's toque, revealing a mesh of reddish hair pasted over his blotchy scalp. He's wearing a white coat, navy-and-white-striped chef pants. He wipes his hands on a towel before shaking their hands—first Ruth's, then Charlotte's.

"My God," he tells Ruth, "you look just like your beautiful mother."

"I'm Ruth. Rocco's fiancée." Ruth looks nothing like Mom.

Rocco's *what?*

"Ah, yes," says Chef Basil. "Ruth. The cook. So *you're* the beautiful daughter."

"Charlotte. I'm Charlotte."

"Of course. Will you ever forgive me?"

Charlotte can feel her face contorting in a frozen grin that she hopes signals forgiveness. Chef Basil ushers them out onto the patio planted with flowering vegetation. He says, "Ruth and Carla—"

"Charlotte."

"What's wrong with me this morning? Ruth and Charlotte, this is Lydia, Ricardo, and Marisol, who is out of school on holiday. I wouldn't want you to think we're using child labor here."

The child giggles.

But this *is* child labor, thinks Charlotte, even if it's a school holiday. Thank God Rocco isn't here.

Lydia touches her daughter's arm. The child smiles to show that spending her day off working in the gringo's kitchen is fine with her. It's fun! The child and her mother are shredding turkey. The man is peeling charred green chilies.

"Wow, this is so beautiful!" Ruth's face is shining, enchanted. Charlotte can see Chef Basil deciding that she is the audience he should play to. By now Rocco would have stalked out and left Ruth to patch things up with the chef, who, Mom warned them, will be at her party tomorrow.

"Have a seat," says Chef Basil, and they sit— awkwardly—at the table with the Mexican family.

"Lydia will show you how to prepare the marvelous handmade tortillas we make in this magical region."

What do you mean *we*, white man? Charlotte's determined to get through this without unpleasant thoughts. No judgment.

Lydia pinches off a lump of dough, slaps it between her palms, and motions for them to do the same. Lydia's tortillas are as thin and soft as handkerchiefs. Ruth's and Charlotte's have tiny cracks around their thick, lumpy edges.

"Good try!" crows Chef Basil, returning from the kitchen. The Mexican family's smiles are kindly. Good try, señoras.

"Onwards," says Chef Basil. "I warned your adorable mother that I only have a little time. I'd love to give you my whole day. But I have students coming, clients who signed up months ago."

"We understand," says Ruth. "We're grateful."

The kitchen is a paradise of copper cookware and gleaming tile, the heartbeat of a hacienda in another century, updated with a Thermador range, a Sub-Zero fridge, an electric pizza oven. A pizza oven in Mexico?

"In a regular class, we'd grind the mole, but in a pinch, ha-ha, I'll give you each a packet of the *most* extraordinary mole you can find in the market. I love taking students to our *mercado*, teaching them how to shop—and bargain. So many gringos can't even tell when an avocado is ripe! But that's another treat we'll have to put off till next time."

Ruth looks as if she expects Chef Basil to set a date. Her face darkens slightly when he rattles on.

"I've made a fabulous turkey mole for my afternoon class. Obviously no Oaxacan in his right mind would eat this for breakfast. But since we're together such a short time, and since a big part of the expat lifestyle is escaping those no-fun rules we left behind . . . what would you ladies say if we tried some mole with Lydia's fabulous tortillas?"

"That would be excellent," Ruth says. Charlotte tries to look excited, though Luz made them filling fruit smoothies just before they left.

Chef Basil fills three small bowls and sets them on the counter, where three elaborate place settings make the occasion seem not quite so spontaneous, so spur-of-the-moment. He sits at the counter and invites them to join him.

The mole is so good that it's easy to eat even on top of a fruit smoothie. Its deliciousness does a lot to dispel Charlotte's reservations about Chef Basil, and she says yes when he asks if she'd like more.

"We should have had beer," Chef Basil says. "Or tequila. What the heck? It's cocktail hour somewhere."

In Mongolia, Charlotte thinks.

"I don't know . . . ," says Ruth. "I don't drink . . . I gave it up for my fiancé, who's in recovery . . ."

"Good girl," says Chef Basil. "Not many ladies would do that. And *no* men would. Anyhow, I was kidding. Do you ladies know how you can tell the real alcoholics? They wait for cocktail hour. Not a drop before. The amateurs hit the bottle first thing in the morning. Would you like a cup of Mexican chocolate?" There's chocolate in the mole, and Luz's smoothies were sweet, but again Chef Basil makes it impossible to refuse.

"So what do you do, Charlene?" he asks, more relaxed now that he can see the light at the end of the tunnel of their visit.

"Charlotte. I run a flower shop in Manhattan."

"We love flowers down here. As you can see—"

"It's not just a *flower shop*," says Ruth. "Charlotte is one of the most successful florists in New York City."

"Well, then," says Chef Basil competitively. "I wish I'd known! I would have asked our gardener to stop by. The man is a genius. We owe all this to him. Ernesto and I would have killed every green thing long ago . . . And you?"

"I work for a start-up," Ruth says. Chef Basil nods. *Start-up* could mean anything, but he doesn't care what.

"Ruth used to work as the personal assistant to the Baroness Frieda of Norway. Who, as you probably know, has a cooking show." Charlotte wants to think she's inspired by the same generous desire to praise—to shine light—that has made Ruth rave about Buddenbrooks and Gladiola.

Chef Basil puts down his cup. "Is this the world's most amazing coincidence, or is this the world's most amazing coincidence?"

Chef Basil was on the Baroness Frieda's show just a few months before.

"That would have been ages after I quit working for her," says Ruth. Some new tension in her face makes Charlotte wonder if the circumstances under which she'd left the baroness were even worse than she described.

"Wise move," Chef Basil says. "I mean, your quitting. The lady is a piece of work, am I right?"

"That . . . you . . . are," says Ruth, whose lips are so tight she seems to be squeezing the words out, one by one. "She *is* one of the world's *biggest* pieces of work."

Chef Basil says, "She was here for two weeks. The longest two weeks of my life. She expected me to wait on her, to be her slave, to be in constant touch with her assistant, that guy with the satellite-dish ears." He waits for some sign of recognition from Ruth.

Ruth says, "Poor guy. That was me. I mean, that was my job."

"Poor you. What's your last name, Ruth?"

"Seagram. Why?"

"I was curious. Your boss—"

"Former boss."

"Your former boss, Queen Frieda, would call me at three A.M. with some teensy request or complaint. Ernesto threatened to divorce me if I didn't set some limits. And for what? So she could haul her entourage down here, the makeup and hair people, the tech crew—"

"Tell me about it," says Ruth. "No, *don't* tell me. I've been there."

"All crowding into this kitchen. I could hardly breathe, let alone work. Yet somehow I managed to cook her *spectacular* food. And Princess Frieda doesn't even thank me. She barely tasted it. She divided it in half and ate half."

"That's her MO," says Ruth. "Her brand. She wanted to call the show *The Baroness Frieda Goes Halfsies* until the network talked her out of it."

"*The Baroness Frieda Goes Halfsies?*" says Chef Basil. "I wish I'd known. I would have been less insulted. Anyhow, I shouldn't complain. That show got us tons of new students."

"That's great," Charlotte says weakly.

"My oldest friend is her accountant. I suppose that's how we got the gig, and I am endlessly—*endlessly*—grateful."

"It aired already?" Ruth says.

"Three months ago," says Chef Basil. "You would not believe the spike in traffic to our site. Who would have thought that an anorexic Norwegian could have such an enormous following?"

"Modern life," Ruth says.

"Speaking of," Charlotte says. "We should get back. Mom has a lot for us to do. The party is tomorrow."

"I'll see you there," says Chef Basil.

Ruth says, "*¡Muchas gracias!* Your house is so beautiful, the food was scrumptious, I love what you're doing here. This is going to be the highlight of my stay in Oaxaca."

"Thank you," says Chef Basil. Something in his expression softens, and his pinkish skin turns a shade redder. "That means a lot."

"No, thank *you*," says Ruth.

What does Rocco see in her? Except maybe that she's pretty, and so ferociously *nice*?

"Wait! One more thing," says Chef Basil. "Can Lydia take a photo of the three of us together? I like to have a record of my students and new friends."

"Sure," Charlotte says, though she hates the idea of having her picture taken with Ruth and Chef Basil. Relax. A few more minutes and they'll be gone.

"Sure . . . but . . . I have conditions," Ruth says.

The way she says *conditions* makes everyone, including the Mexicans, pay attention.

"This *cannot* go online. I'm very protective about my privacy. I always say no if someone plans to post it—"

"No worries!" says Chef Basil. "This is for personal use only." And he giggles, almost lewdly.

"All right then," agrees Ruth.

Chef Basil stands on tiptoe to drape his arms around their shoulders while Lydia photographs them against a grouping of potted palms.

"Would you ladies like a copy?" he asks.

"No thanks," says Ruth.

Charlotte shakes her head, though she instantly wishes she'd said yes. She could show it to Eli when she tries to describe this.

"See you tomorrow," Ruth says.

"I love endings like this," says Chef Basil. "Not having to say goodbye."

15

Ruth

Obviously I planned to tell Rocco that I no longer worked at STEP. But first I had to process the shock. I told myself to be grateful I hadn't known what was *really* going on, grateful that the frat boys excluded me from their inner circle. I didn't have to disappear or go to the dark side or underground—or wherever they went.

One day my boss and coworkers were there; the next day they weren't. One day STEP was up and running; the next day it wasn't.

I didn't care if I ever saw them again, except that I wanted to ask, What the hell? Also I missed the paycheck, tiny as it was.

There was a new doorman on duty that day. That

last day. Gus, the regular doorman, had been there for-ever. I knew people left jobs, quit, and got fired. But Gus would have said goodbye. We'd been friends.

The new doorman asked me to sign into the visitors' log. He was new. I wasn't a visitor.

I explained that I worked in the building, on the sixth floor. He said there was nothing on the sixth floor but empty office space. I explained: That wasn't possible. Friday I'd gone to work there, and it was only Monday morning. He said he didn't know about that. He'd started on Sunday. The previous doorman had a health emergency. Something crazy happened in the building. Some cops and an ambulance came.

A chill ran down my spine. What kind of a bullet had I dodged?

"What happened?" He *had* to tell me. "I mean, what happened to Gus? What *kind* of health emergency?"

"Gus? I'm sorry. I don't even know the dude's name."

He'd started work on Sunday. We'd never had a Sunday doorman before.

I said, "Can I go take a look?"

"Go ahead. Be my guest. But do me one favor. *Two* favors. One: Don't tell anybody I let you up there. And two: Don't steal anything. Anyhow, there's nothing to steal, which is the only reason why I'm letting you do this."

The glass door to the office was locked. I saw cubicles and a few desks, overturned chairs.

A ghost office.

Where was the African violet I'd kept on my desk? It looked as if no one had been there in ages, as if no one had *ever* been there. My head was starting to ache in a way that felt like the start of a red-alert, heavy-duty migraine.

I thanked the doorman as I left. He didn't even look at me.

I sat on a bench in the park. I put my head (seriously hurting now) in my hands.

I should have called Rocco. I should have begged the doorman to let us back in and taken Rocco up to the sixth floor and asked him to help me figure it out.

I don't know what stopped me. Maybe I didn't want to admit how out of the loop I'd been.

The guys didn't trust me. They didn't like me. No *maybe* about that. Would this be an unsolved mystery? It made me look so flaky, so naive. So stupid!

I needed to think of the least embarrassing way to tell Rocco.

Maybe I *was* stupid. Rocco found out on his own. All the time I'd worked there, he never once came to see me at work, though it would have been helpful to let those frat boys know I had a cool boyfriend who had my back.

And now he decided to drop by and . . . surprise! No more frat boys. No more office.

I gave myself a few days to rest and recuperate with Granny Edith and Grandpa Frank. I stayed in my old room and cried. Every so often Granny Edith would knock on my door and ask if I wanted something to eat. I could smell the delicious food she'd brought to tempt me; I could hear Grandpa Frank telling her to leave me alone.

They'd seen me melt down before. They weren't worried.

When I finally ventured out to the TV room, Grandpa Frank turned off the TV, maybe to spare me the news about the ongoing investigation—no suspects so far!—into the murder of that young mother who'd been renovating the brownstone near my grandparents' house.

She smiled into the camera. Her hair was blond and shiny, her face open and trusting. She had a little mole on her cheek. She must have really loved whoever took that picture.

"Is the door locked?" I said.

"I don't know," said Granny Edith.

"Check," I said. "Please check. You know that poor young woman was murdered in her own house—"

"I'll check later," she said.

Grandpa Frank said I needed to get back on the horse that threw me. I should look for another job. It was good advice, except that the horse had run away, leaving no trace in the stable.

Granny Edith's voice was unusually sharp when she said, "What you need, Ruthie, is to get away for a bit. Travel. We'll be fine without you. I promise to keep the door locked. Isn't there *anywhere* you want to go?"

It was the perfect moment to ask if they could pay for a ticket to Mexico for Rocco's mom's sixtieth birthday party. They liked the sound of Rocco, though they hadn't met him yet.

Grandpa Frank asked, "When are we going to meet him?"

"Soon," I said. "I promise."

"Let's celebrate," said Granny Edith. "Drive out to our picnic spot and have a bite to eat."

It wasn't clear what we were celebrating, and it was a cold day. But I never refused to go.

"Can you drive?" I asked Grandpa Frank. "I mean, do you feel like driving?"

My grandfather began his stupid poem: James James Morrison Morrison Weatherby George Dupree took great care of his mother, though he was only three.

Grandpa recited it like a threat. Or did I just imagine that because I was paranoid?

Grandpa Frank drove to the picnic spot. We ate my grandma's fried chicken and drank her homemade lemonade and watched the light sparkle on the river.

It always cheered me up. I felt ready to go back out and face the world.

Meanwhile I was going to Mexico. *¡Adios, abuelitos!*

16

Charlotte

As soon as they leave Chef Basil's and step out into the burnished Oaxacan sunlight, Charlotte says, "Thank God Rocco wasn't there."

Ruth gives her a puzzled look, then hesitates at the corner. Charlotte knows how to get back to Mom's, so that makes her the leader. She crosses to the shady side of the street, and they fall into step.

Ruth says, "Rocco likes good food. Your brother's got political principles. But give him a good meal, and he's yours. It runs in the family, Charlotte. You and Eli like to eat. And Daisy eats a wider range than most kids her age. You probably have to watch out for her in Mexico. Stuff can make kids sick. Is the water at your mom's okay to drink? I've been embarrassed to ask."

Daisy! That Charlotte has forgotten her for an hour is alarming. Irrational, really. Daisy's with Mom, who loves her and will take good care of her. It's Mom's city. She's better qualified than Charlotte to navigate these streets with a child.

Mom set fire to their childhood home. Mom tried to murder Rocco. That Charlotte's not supposed to remember makes it harder to forget. Mom is a different person now. Responsible. Together. Well . . . reasonably together.

Charlotte says, "The city water's fine. Plus Mom's got a filtration system."

"Glad to hear it," says Ruth. "Hey, let's go check out this fabulous antiques shop." She points at a cluttered, grimy window. "Do we have time?"

Charlotte trails Ruth into the tiny store. Why has she never noticed this shop, crammed with marvelous paintings, textiles and furniture, treasure and junk? A dusty skylight lets in just enough sun for customers to see what everything is. Toward the front of the shop is a case of antique wristwatches.

Ruth says, "Wouldn't one of these make a great gift for Rocco?"

Maybe, maybe not.

The store is a cabinet of wonders, crammed with old religious paintings, picture frames made from tiny seashells, bits of embroidery, tinted portrait photographs. Charlotte drifts toward the back of the shop, hoping to find a dollhouse or an antique doll that Daisy might like, though she knows that modern kids sometimes think old dolls are scary.

On one wall are several rows of wooden masks: conquistadors, mermaids, snakes, eagles with giant beaks. The most amazing mask is in the dead center of the wall. Obviously very old, it's divided into two halves. On one side is an angel, on the other a grinning scarlet devil. A thin chain dangles down between the two sections.

Charlotte's startled when one of the masks says, "Pull the chain."

The talking mask, which has the face of an old man with two wings of slicked-down gray hair, yawns and lifts its chin. Charlotte utters a little yelp of fear.

It's not a mask that has spoken to her, but the shop's elderly proprietor. Judging from his sly chuckle, she assumes he often plays this trick on new customers.

Again he motions at the angel-devil mask and gestures for Charlotte to pull the chain. She gives it a tentative yank, and the two halves of the mask divide. The angel and devil come apart, revealing a third mask beneath them: a pretty young woman with black hair, pink cheeks, blue eyes.

Why does the mask seem evil? Then it stops seeming evil and seems beautiful. She wants it.

"How much?"

"Six thousand pesos." About three hundred dollars.

Ruth is standing beside her. Charlotte hadn't noticed.

"Birthday gift for your mom?" says Ruth.

Charlotte's mother doesn't want gifts. She's threatened: If they give her anything, she'll "regift" it to the first beggar she sees. Charlotte's mother would love the mask, but Charlotte's not about to spend all that money on something that Mom might give to one of the women who sit on the sidewalk in the *centro*.

"Just looking," Charlotte says. "At that mask with the angel and the devil."

Ruth says, "Ugh. I hate masks. I must have been scared by one as a child. I've always hated Halloween. Everybody swanning around in pirate and kitty-cat costumes, and I'm at Granny Edith's with my head under the blankets. But that's another story. Let's go. Your mom probably needs help."

"*Gracias, señor*," Charlotte tells the old man, who says, "*Hasta luego, señora.*"

Ruth and Charlotte walk another block, then turn onto a crowded pedestrian street that leads to the zocalo. People stream toward them, locals and tourists moving at different speeds, in different rhythms, looking at different things.

Suddenly Ruth grabs Charlotte's forearm and pulls her through the nearest doorway, into a cavernous café. Small groups of Mexican men are drinking coffee at long bare tables. There's no music, hardly any light, almost no conversation.

"Stay," Ruth says. "Don't move. Don't speak. That's him. I saw him. I'm sure." Ruth has gone rigid. Her voice is shaking. "He passed right by me. He saw me."

"Who?"

"Rafael," she says. "The guy who drove me from Mexico City. The one who took me to the place where we were swarmed by children and pretended he didn't know what was happening. Pretended he didn't set it up."

"Why didn't you say hello? I thought everything got sorted out by the time he dropped you off."

Did Ruth say that? Or did Charlotte just think she did?

"Because he's looking for me."

"Why?"

"Why does anyone look for someone else unless it's about money?"

Charlotte's surprised. Ruth has always struck her as having a hippy-dippy nonchalance about finances.

"I assume you paid him." Charlotte regrets the sharp impatience in her voice, but it's too late to blunt the edge.

"Of course I paid him. In cash. Pesos. I changed money at the airport ATM. But I think he thought I didn't give him a big enough tip. Maybe he was right. I hadn't got the exchange rate thingy down. Maybe I undertipped him."

"Then why didn't you stop him just now and say so? Apologize—give him some pesos? I could have loaned you the money, it probably wasn't much."

"I was embarrassed. I didn't know what to do. Is he looking for me? Can you see him? You go check. I'm scared."

Ruth waits inside the café while Charlotte goes out to look. No one is stopped on the street; no one is looking for them. Rafael, if that was him, has gone on his way.

In the café, Ruth is sitting at a table. She looks shaken.

Charlotte says, "You can relax."

"It's not that big a deal," Ruth says. "I wouldn't have thought about it if we didn't pass him. I don't think he was thinking about it, either."

But Ruth just said he was looking for her, looking straight at her. And now she says he wasn't.

"I guess I'm just being paranoid," Ruth says. "I get

that way. I haven't been here long enough to figure out how things work, south of the border."

"It takes time," says Charlotte.

"I ordered coffees," Ruth says. "I hope you don't mind. All that great food at Chef Basil's made me sleepy."

Charlotte minds a lot. She wants to get back to her mother's, to see if her mother needs her help and to check up on Daisy.

"Sure" is all she trusts herself to say.

A girl, not much older than Daisy, brings two small black coffees.

Ruth says, "Chef Basil's was amazing."

"Amazing," Charlotte says.

"I need to talk to you about something."

Rocco, thinks Charlotte. She knew there was a problem. She's seen it in Rocco's face ever since he got to Oaxaca. She just wishes she was hearing about it from him.

Ruth says, "I have a crazy question. Totally loco."

"Go ahead."

"Is Daisy adopted?"

Charlotte puts down her coffee cup.

"Why would you ask that?"

"She doesn't look like you. She doesn't look like either of you."

Charlotte tries to laugh. "Unless I'm getting this wrong, I gave birth to her. I was pregnant. I stayed in bed two months. And I don't think they switched babies in the hospital."

"She's not anything like you."

"She looks like Eli," says Charlotte. "Everyone says so."

"Actually, she doesn't," says Ruth. "Can I ask: Is Eli Daisy's biological dad?"

"Of course he is. And no, you can't ask. Why would you ask a question like that?"

"I don't know. I'm sorry. Sometimes I just get this feeling about things."

"A wrong one."

"It's like I have a sixth sense," says Ruth.

It's important not to react, not to do anything to show that Charlotte's blood pressure has spiked. Where is Ruth getting this from? How could she possibly know?

No one knows about Daisy. Not even Eli.

No one.

Charlotte should have been an actress. It's quite a performance, walking the rest of the way to her mother's with Ruth and not seeming completely crazed.

How tasteful and unpretentious and *real* Mom's house looks compared to Chef Basil's.

"Is Mom back?" Charlotte asks Luz. "Is Daisy still gone?"

"Your mother and Daisy are still at the market."

Eli and Rocco have also gone out. Luz's husband, Paco, has driven them to check out a rug-weaving village near Monte Albán.

Charlotte's anxious because Daisy isn't back yet. Fear doubles the dose of the fight-or-flight chemical that's been running through her since Ruth asked if Eli is Daisy's real father.

She's glad that Eli's not here.

She goes into her bedroom and dials her therapist. Ted.

In all her years in therapy, she's never called him except to make or break an appointment. But she needs to call him now, or she'll never stop shaking. She doesn't have to fake the emotions she leaves on Ted's answering machine.

She's arranging flowers in the courtyard when Ted returns her call.

Back in her bedroom, she locks the door and goes into the bathroom and runs the water. But now Ted can't hear her, so she returns to the bedroom and tries to keep her voice steady.

"She knows. Ruth knows the truth about Daisy. No one knows but you and me. And I didn't tell her."

Ted is silent for a long time.

"Are you still there?"

"I'm here," Ted says. "I'm thinking."

Charlotte has the weirdest thought: Ted told her. But she's just being paranoid. Ted would never betray a professional confidence. And he doesn't know Ruth. She trusts Ted more than anyone in the world except Eli and Daisy.

After another silence, Ted says, "Your brother's girlfriend may have some very serious problems."

Charlotte's heart sinks even lower, as if that was possible. "What do you mean?"

"I worked with schizophrenics early in my career. And I still remember the ones—there were several of them, I recall—whose intuition was so strong, they actually seemed to have ESP. Or to be mind readers. Or something."

"This can't be that," says Charlotte. "She can't be that good. Or that crazy."

"Maybe she's not," says Ted. "Maybe she's taking a guess."

Charlotte has learned to recognize those moments when Ted is about to say something she doesn't want to hear.

"Look . . . I was going to tell you this when you got

back . . . I didn't want to alarm you or spoil your vacation. But . . . a young woman left a long message on my answering machine. She said she was writing a profile on Andrew John for the local paper. She wondered if I knew anything about the family that owned the land before he did. It seemed that the papers had run a story about a fire. She'd found it in the archives—"

Charlotte says, "The local paper up there folded. A couple of years ago. There *is* no local paper. I'm scared. Really scared."

"Of what?"

"Of everything."

"You can't be scared of everything. So don't be. Maybe this means nothing. The woman who called me—let's assume it was Ruth—was fishing. Or stalking you. Or both. My sense is that she knows nothing. Just stay calm. Keep busy. I'll see you when you get back."

"Okay," Charlotte says unsteadily.

"One more thing," says Ted. "Just on the off chance that this . . . Well! We might want to begin to discuss your finally having that talk with Eli."

Charlotte can't move for several minutes after her conversation with Ted. Then she goes back to the courtyard. She doesn't want to think about the implications of what Ruth said, of what Ted said. She doesn't want to imagine how badly—how *really* badly—things could go from here on. Her whole life could be upended because Ruth had some weird intuition . . .

Daisy still isn't back. Time refuses to pass. Charlotte takes a Xanax and lies down on her bed.

She wakes up when Daisy runs into her room and pulls her out onto the patio.

In one hand Daisy holds *Our Mexican Adventure*. And in the other she clutches her glue stick and a stack of elaborate package wrappings—soap, honey, chocolate—that Grandma got her in the market and removed from the products they'd adorned.

Daisy sits down at the table and begins to paste the papers into her composition book.

Later Mom and Luz string the courtyard with paper flags, lacy cutouts of skeletons, and Christmas lights in case people stay late. Mom and Daisy have bought a Bart Simpson piñata, which they hang from a clothesline. Who is the piñata for? Only one of Mom's friends has kids, though perhaps some have visiting grandchildren.

Charlotte and Ruth don't look at each other, which is fine with Charlotte. How much does Ruth really know—and how does she know it? The question is spoiling everything. No matter what Charlotte does, she can't get it out of her mind.

The street vendors wheel in carts of steaming tamales and tacos, tortillas to wrap around the meats that begin to sizzle on the grill. If Charlotte were passing by, she'd envy the people inside.

The mariachis are arriving at eight. That's four hours into the party. What if the guests (some are older than Mom) leave before the musicians come? But Reyna, Mom's closest Mexican friend, a young woman who works with her in the American Library, has told her: It's a common mistake gringos make. They bring in the mariachis too early, before everyone has had enough to drink. Sober, the guests think the mariachis are corny. After a few margaritas, they love it.

By five, no guests have arrived. Maybe the expats are trying to operate on "Mexican time," to rid themselves of the tight schedules that, in their former lives, made them show up on the dot.

Surely Mom expected this. But she looks forlorn, like a child afraid that no one will come to her party. It reminds Charlotte of how Mom looked just before she abandoned Rocco and Charlotte and retreated upstairs to play the madwoman in the attic. She was always a difficult person, and even though Charlotte knows that her mother had been ill when they needed her most . . . she was never a great mother. Not even close. Plus she set the house on fire with Rocco inside it.

Charlotte is glad that she has grown up enough to be happy that Mom has found a community that cares about her and probably doesn't know much about her past.

Daisy senses her grandmother's sadness and goes and sits in her lap. She's more relaxed and chattier than she is with Charlotte or even Eli.

Charlotte doesn't like feeling competitive about her daughter, especially when she's competing against her own mother. Daisy's grandma. It's much worse when she feels that way about Ruth.

Ruth and Daisy like each other. So Charlotte does everything she can to make sure that they are never alone together. Something feels creepy—almost dangerous— about the way Ruth acts around Daisy. And though Charlotte tries to tell herself that she's imagining things, she can't shake her growing sense of dread.

Daisy gets *Our Mexican Adventure* and shows Mom, which leads to more laughs and grandmotherly kisses.

Yesterday Daisy asked if she can wait to show Charlotte the notebook until they're on the plane to New York. Daisy wants the book to be perfect. She doesn't want Charlotte to see it until it's done. Charlotte is pleased that Daisy takes her project so seriously, and she'd said yes, of course. But why is Daisy showing it to Mom and not her? Because Mom won't be on the plane, and good-hearted Daisy knows that it will be a nice distraction for her grandma as she waits for her friends.

Finally the guests trickle in. Fred and Arnie, Charisse, Martine. Charlotte has met some of them before. Quite a few look like Mom. Their yoga pants and cotton shirts are like a uniform. Underneath that baggy homespun, their bodies are nobody's business. Some have put on shifts embroidered with bright flowers. A few men wear guayaberas and straw hats.

Mom introduces Charlotte to everyone, even the people she already knows. Gypsy and Melody have moved down from Marin County to make Melody's trust fund go further. Seraphine is a translator who puts English subtitles on Spanish telenovelas. Maria Luisa, an Argentine doctor, is a single mom with a six-year-old son, Rodrigo. Charlotte is glad that her mother is friendly with a doctor. Maria Luisa has been summoned every time Charlotte visited, because Rodrigo is Daisy's age, and Mom wants to show Charlotte that if Oaxaca is safe for Rodrigo, *who lives here, for God's sake*, it will be fine for Daisy.

Now Rodrigo and Daisy have finally been introduced. They regard each other with terror from opposite ends of the courtyard.

Just as Daisy said, all of Mom's friends greet Daisy like old pals. They've heard so much about her! They recognize her from her pictures—except she's grown so tall! But they seem less clear about which of the adults—Charlotte, Rocco, or Eli—are related to Mom.

Obviously not Eli.

Charlotte is so distracted, she doesn't notice that Ruth is missing until a real estate agent named Harding (he claims to have met Charlotte before) asks Rocco if he's married yet. Rocco says no. Does he have a girlfriend? Or a boyfriend? Rocco looks as if the information is being extracted under torture. His girlfriend has come to Oaxaca with him. And where is the lucky girl? Oh, Rocco says, Ruth's around. She went out for a walk to clear her head. She'll be back any minute.

Charlotte thinks: He's worried. Well, fine. Charlotte's worried too. She can't stop thinking about that conversation with Ruth about Daisy. How much does Ruth know?

Maybe Ruth is gone for good. And for a moment Charlotte thinks that she would be just as glad if Ruth never came back. It would solve lots of problems. Problems that haven't really happened yet, but still . . .

"Where's Ruth?" Charlotte asks Rocco when Harding wanders off for another tamarind margarita.

"She went out about an hour ago. To get something. She wouldn't tell me what. It's strange that she's not back yet. I hope she's not lost."

"Oaxaca's hard to get lost in. Ruth can find her way. She's a smart girl, as you know."

Is he really afraid that she's lost? Did Ruth tell him about the driver stalking her, demanding his tip? Was that even true? The story seems improbable, just like the story about the swarming children. If she lied about that . . .

Charlotte should have mentioned the driver to Rocco, but she doesn't want to scare him. She'll wait and see what happens. Ruth will be back. Unless . . . Ruth was telling the truth about being stalked by the driver.

Charlotte has three choices. One: She can assume that Ruth will return any moment. Two: She can forget about Ruth and deal with her absence after the party. Or three: She can ruin everything by leaving to find Ruth or insisting that someone go search for her.

It does seem strange. Ruth had put so much effort into charming Mom. She'd hardly want to destroy what little headway she's made with Mom by showing up late, or not at all.

"Look!" Charlotte tells Rocco. "There's Reyna! Go talk to her."

Reyna, Mom's friend from the library, is very pretty. Unlike most of Mom's friends, in their shapeless embroidered sacks, she's stylishly dressed in a short lemon yellow dress that makes her skin glow with youth and health.

Reyna has a two-year-old daughter. Adorable, Mom says. They've lived with Reyna's mother ever since the girl's father hit Reyna. A few days later he'd come to her mother's house with two friends, and they'd stood outside until Reyna's mother called some tough male relatives to persuade them to leave.

No one here calls the police. Ever. No matter what.

What mischievous impulse made Charlotte send Rocco over to Reyna? Is she hoping that he'll find her more attractive than Ruth? At least Reyna's sane. But she lives in another country and has problems of her own. Maybe Charlotte just thinks that a conversation with a smart, beautiful woman will keep her brother occupied until Ruth returns.

Charlotte crosses the patio, chatting with the people she knows, introducing herself to strangers. They are all easy to talk to, even if they all have only one topic of conversation: how happy they are in Mexico, what a great decision they've made.

Mom's Mexican friends are harder to figure out. Most are artists or writers or retired teachers. Maybe they think it's important to meet different kinds of people; maybe they hope for art careers in the US. Mom and her friends must seem different from *their* families and most people they know.

After a while Charlotte sees a man waving to her from across the courtyard. Without his chef's jacket, in a salmon-colored T-shirt and jeans, Chef Basil is barely recognizable. Holding his elbow, as if he's afraid of losing him, is a taller man with a black mustache in a sharply pressed navy guayabera.

"Ernesto," Basil says, "this is . . . this is Sally's daughter. Sally's daughter . . . Carla."

"Charlotte."

"Poor dear Basil," says Ernesto, who is quite a bit younger. "Don't take it personally, Charlotte. My husband does this all the time. Our cooking school would be more successful if there weren't so many one-star reviews on TripAdvisor about him not bothering to learn students' names."

"That may be more information than . . . our new friend needs." Now Charlotte can see the sadness beneath Basil's maddening qualities. It's also Ernesto's sadness. He loves Basil and is struggling to cope with his memory deficits. His forgetting Charlotte's name really *isn't* personal.

"I was so hoping to run into you here. And where is your darling sister-in-law?" He looks past Charlotte into the party.

"Ruth's not my sister-in-law," Charlotte says. "She's my brother's girlfriend. She stepped out for a minute. She'll be right back."

"Good," he says. "Because I have a very—*very*— strange thing to tell you. I don't know what to make of it. I'm sure it's a mistake. But last night . . . I happened to talk to my old friend, the Baroness Frieda's accountant. I told him I'd run into a former employee of the baroness. I told him her name, I described her. I assumed he'd know her. He's been with the baroness forever. He basically lives at her house, that's how often she demands his physical presence.

"Well, here's the strange part: He'd never heard of your sister-in-law. He didn't recognize her description. He never had her name on a payroll, never cut a check with her name on it. So I sent him the picture that Lydia took of us. And he swore he'd never seen her before. Isn't that *peculiar*?"

Why is Chef Basil telling Charlotte this? Does he want her to doubt Ruth's credentials as a former abused employee of the Baroness Frieda? Does he relish the possibility that his accountant friend's memory is as bad as his? There's a chance that he's trying to sow suspicion and discord in the family. But that seems like the least likely possibility.

"I'm sure there's a simple explanation," Charlotte says.

"I'm sure there's a *very* simple explanation," says Ernesto. "Which is that poor dear Basil has no *idea* what that girl's name is."

"Ruth," protests Basil. "Her name's Ruth. Carla just said *Ruth*. And what about the photo? I sent him her picture."

By now the patio is crowded, and with the party swirling around her, Charlotte doesn't have time to consider the fact that a man with a memory problem has just told her that his friend can't remember meeting her so-called sister-in-law.

Still, it is unsettling. The black mark beside Ruth's name is getting darker.

Across the courtyard, Charlotte's mother is sitting on top of a picnic table, surrounded by fascinated listeners. How can this be the same woman who made Charlotte take care of Rocco while she played the tragic abandoned wife? How can this be the person who burned down their house and almost killed Rocco?

Charlotte says, "Try the cheese-and-green-chili tamales. They're the best."

"Oh, yes," says Basil. "I know the woman who makes them—Estella. They are *the* most delicious in Oaxaca. And believe me, Carol, the bar is set pretty high for that.

"Ta-ta," says Basil, and as he walks away, it occurs to Charlotte that he remembers the name of the woman who makes the tamales—and not hers. But of course he and Estella live here. Charlotte is the outsider who will be gone by tomorrow night.

Rocco and Reyna are chatting in a corner of the courtyard. Daisy has sidled over to them and is leaning against him. Rocco and Reyna are smiling and nodding. Rocco looks relaxed and—

Of course it's just at that moment that Ruth arrives.

The air around her crackles. Ruth looks semi-demonic, like one of those Satan-haunted girls in horror films whose heads spin on their necks. She's holding a large package in front of her as she struts through the crowd and places herself squarely between Rocco and Reyna.

"I'm Ruth," she announces, loud enough for everyone to hear. "Rocco's fiancée."

Charlotte reaches them in time to hear Reyna say, "Rocco's told me so much about you. He's been telling me what a wonderful time you both are having in Oaxaca."

By now the party guests notice: Something's going on. Like Moses parting the Red Sea, Mom charges through the space that opens up around her.

Ruth wheels around to face Mom. "Happy birthday!" She thrusts the package at Mom.

"Thank you," says Mom. "I'll just put it on the table with the other presents, even though I insisted there be no presents. I remember saying that any gift would be given to the poor. I'm still considering that, though I would be lying if I pretended my decision didn't depend partly on how much I like the presents—"

Mom laughs at her little joke, and the guests chuckle, relieved that the tension generated by Ruth's arrival seems to be dissipating.

"Open it," Ruth says. "Now."

Charlotte remembers how Ruth insisted they eat her grandma's sticky buns.

Astonishingly, Mom obeys. As she rips apart the package, Luz gathers up the shredded wrapping paper. Mom holds her gift up for the others to see.

It's what Charlotte knew it would be.

The angel-devil mask.

"Wow," says Mom.

"Pull it," says Ruth. "The chain."

Mom pulls the chain and the mask splits, the angel and the devil separate, and the woman's face appears beneath them.

Mom says, "This is me. This is a mask of me *on the inside*."

"It's a mask of everyone," says Ruth.

Ruth said that masks scare her, and then went back and bought the one that Charlotte loved. Where did she get $300? She's taken a risk, assuming that Charlotte's mother would like it. But it's worked, and she's won. Charlotte tells herself to be glad that at least someone in the family has the mask.

"Thank you." Mom puts her hand over her heart, a gesture totally unlike her. "I love it."

"Don't thank me," Ruth says. "I mean, don't thank *just* me. It's from me and Rocco."

17

Rocco

Ever since the vanishing start-up, Rocco has been weighing Ruth's good points versus her bad. It's something he used to do with women, and he's come to think that it's wrong. Anyone weighing *his* good and bad points might come to some disturbing conclusions. He is, after all, a guy who threatened his own mother with a knife. That was when he was drinking. He's not drinking anymore.

On the night before Mom's party, Rocco and Ruth lie beneath the ceiling fan evaporating the light film of sweat from their bodies.

Ruth asks, "What did you get your mom for her birthday?"

It seems like a sign of intelligence, or at least sensitivity, that she waits until after they've had sex to ask the difficult questions.

"Nothing. She said no presents. My mom is capable of giving the gifts away, just like she threatened."

Ruth says, "People say they don't want presents, but everyone wants presents. You *need* to get her something. I saw the perfect gift. Trust me on this, Rocco. I know what people want. I inherited it from Granny Edith, the world's best present giver. She gave me clothes and heels and makeup when my mom was still giving me Barbies."

Rocco says, "The party's tomorrow."

"No worries. I'll go. I'll buy it for us both. I'll be back long before the party starts. But listen . . . This thing I have in mind is a bit expensive. Worth every peso, but news flash, beauty isn't cheap, not even here. We could split the cost, so it could *really* be from us both . . ."

That's how Ruth gets Rocco to give her his credit card. She says she'll ask the store to divide the charges between his card and hers. He knows she's had credit card trouble, but he can't bring himself to mention it.

When Ruth isn't back when the party begins, Rocco knows she's probably buying the gift. But still he worries that she's lost, or that something has happened. He's also afraid that he's set her loose on the town with his credit card—and that she's *never* coming back.

But they're flying back to New York together. That's reassuring. Sort of.

It's hard to enjoy the party when he's constantly looking for Ruth. The only thing that's any fun is talking to Reyna, who is charming and funny and, despite her domestic problems, which he's heard about, lighthearted. She cares about his mother, and better yet, she respects her. Señora Sally. Soon they're laughing—affectionately—about what an impossible person Mom is.

Reyna says she wants to send him a picture of Mom surrounded by the kids she reads to at the library. Rocco types his number into her phone, and she texts him so that he has her number too, just in case he ever needs her to help get in touch with Mom.

He senses Ruth's presence before he sees her, the way—when he lived in the country as a kid—he always thought *snake* a few seconds before he saw one.

It's Rocco's luck that Ruth walks in just when he and Reyna are exchanging phone numbers.

Ruth sees him; she sees Reyna. Ruth looks . . . fierce. For the first time, he's actually scared of her. Then the feeling passes.

Ruth had warned him that jealousy is one of her "fatal flaws." He'd never heard it as a warning, exactly.

Now he thinks maybe he should have paid attention to the implicit threat. Be faithful . . . or else.

Ruth pushes her way through the guests, holding a package like a shield or a weapon.

Mom and Charlotte sense the tension and come over to them. Ruth hands Mom the package, and—against all odds—Mom obeys Ruth and opens it.

The mask casts a spell on the party. For a moment no one breathes.

Reyna says, "That's a very beautiful mask."

"I know." Ruth's voice is so cold that Reyna flinches.

Mom seems to like it. "Thank you," she says.

Everyone starts breathing again.

Around them, everyone's eating and drinking. Several feuds are patched up. No one wants the evening to end. Rocco looks at his watch. When do the mariachis arrive?

Everyone except Rocco and Ruth and Daisy drinks margaritas. It's a miracle that Rocco has stopped thinking of sobriety as a torture. He appreciates Ruth abstaining for his sake. Solidarity is a good thing for a couple, if that's what he and Ruth are.

Yet even without alcohol, he feels a little high. He finds himself talking to his brother-in-law in the way you can only talk to someone in the middle of a crowded party.

Eli is complaining about the theater director whose ideas are becoming more impractical. Not only does he want the witches to fly in harnesses, but when the knocking portends the discovery of Duncan's murder, he wants it to be a blast of electronic noise.

Rocco has heard most of this, but now Eli complains that no one takes him seriously. Because he made his money in business, no one believes he knows anything about the theater. Rocco's about to say something encouraging when they hear, from the kitchen, a loud male voice.

Then Luz shouts, in Spanish, "You can't go in there!"

Rocco thinks: Reyna's boyfriend.

Reyna seems to think that too. She moves behind a pillar.

A man in a neat white shirt and black pants rushes onto the patio. Rocco takes a few warning steps toward him, stands between the intruder and Reyna. But the man isn't looking for Reyna.

It's Ruth. The stranger confronts her, glowering and shouting.

Rocco could take the guy out if he had to. He had to do that once, in a bar, to protect a waitress from a drunken customer. He hadn't liked it, but he'd done it, and he could do it again.

The guy's saying that Ruth never paid him for driving her from Mexico City. He makes a check-writing motion. *Rechazado.* Bounced. Ruth's check has bounced. Is this guy an idiot, accepting a *check* from a gringa tourist?

Ruth is very persuasive. Maybe she convinced him that it was the only way she could pay him. Maybe she knew that no one here goes to the police.

Either Ruth's Spanish is better than she's let on, or she recognizes the guy. She understands what he's saying.

"I paid you," she says in English. "I asked for a receipt, but you said it wasn't necessary. I'm sorry if I didn't tip you enough. I was figuring things out. It was the middle of the night. I was stressed and exhausted—"

Somehow Rocco feels certain that the guy is telling the truth. He also senses that this is about something besides money. No Mexican would risk a scene like this, especially not a guy who depends on tourist business in a tourist town. Ruth must have insulted him. What did Ruth do?

"How much do we owe you?" Rocco asks.

Ruth is staring at Rocco, half annoyed at him for not taking her side, half pleased that he'd said *we.* How much do *we* owe you? He and Ruth are a *we.*

The man mentions a sum. Around seventy-five dollars in pesos.

Ruth still has Rocco's credit card, not that the guy would take it. Luckily, yesterday, Rocco withdrew a hundred dollars from an ATM. He counts out what the man demands, then adds 15 percent as a tip.

He says, "I apologize if there's been a misunderstanding."

"There is no *misunderstanding*," Ruth says. "He's lying. Don't you believe me?"

Mom has waded into the fray. "Rocco's right. Something went wrong. And we're in this man's country. We wouldn't even be here if the conquistadors . . ."

Mom has swung directly into righteous margarita mode. Rocco senses that everyone here knows what a long lecture might be in store.

"Would you like some food?" Mom asks the driver.

"*No gracias.*"

The driver leaves as suddenly as he arrived.

Ten, fifteen minutes go by. Then one by one, couple by couple, the guests approach Mom and hug her and wish her many more happy birthdays. They all need to leave no matter how much they wish they could stay.

Soon the courtyard is empty except for the family and Luz. The tamale and taco vendors pack up their steam tables and fry stations and roll their carts out the door. *Adiós. Gracias.*

"I'm sorry," Ruth says to everyone and no one. "But that guy was wrong. He was putting the squeeze on us. I didn't owe him any money. I don't know why you paid him."

"It hardly matters." Mom shrugs.

In fact it matters a lot. Ruth has ruined her party and will never be forgiven.

When Rocco and Ruth break up, his family will be delighted. It almost makes Rocco want to break up with her on the spot, just to make everyone happy. At the same time, it makes him want to stay with her forever, just to piss everyone off.

Only Daisy seems unbothered. She sits at the table, eating tacos and pasting things in her book. She'd taken up a collection from the guests: business cards, sales receipts. A few people gave her small bills that she glued onto one of the pages, and now she's trying to make a coin stick to the paper.

Charlotte asks Mom if she's tired, if she wants to lie down. Her mother turns on her, enraged. Charlotte must have forgotten that solicitous care is not the way to Mom's heart.

Mom says, "If I lie down, I'll vomit," and no one says anything for a while.

They begin straightening up the patio, throwing out plastic cups and plates, scraps of napkins and food, mopping up slicks of tequila and beer.

"We didn't get to do the piñata," says Eli, and they look up and see Bart Simpson hanging from a high rope, still waiting to be beaten to death by a blindfolded child.

Charlotte says, "There weren't enough kids here to make it fun. Daisy hates piñatas anyway, don't you, Daisy?"

"I guess so," Daisy says.

Rocco thinks she probably likes them. Or at least she likes the candy.

Just then the doorbell rings, and Luz goes to answer it.

She reappears with four men and a boy of about twelve, all in black mariachi suits and white sombreros bordered with black. They're carrying musical instrument cases.

The mariachis seem bewildered. Why is no one here except a gringo family and a maid cleaning up? The men look at their watches. The boy checks the phone he wrests from the pocket of his tight vaquero trousers. No, they haven't gotten the time wrong.

The tallest, the one with the violin case, looks around. Who's in charge here? It's the elderly gringa's birthday. The maid has told them that. But the lady is obviously in no shape to sort things out.

Rocco should do something. But the party has exhausted him. First the worrying about where Ruth was, then her showing up, then the tension between Ruth and Reyna, and last but not least the shit show with the driver.

He hasn't spoken to Ruth since then. Something happened with that guy, but Rocco doesn't know what. It's an effort *not to ask* Ruth.

Thank God he stopped drinking. Who knows what he would do then . . .

Let someone else deal with the mariachis.

Luz says she's sorry. No, the musicians aren't late. Early, even. It's nobody's fault. The guests have gone home.

"*Nosotros te pagaremos*," someone says. "We will pay you."

It takes Rocco a moment to realize it's Mom, who says to Luz, "Tell them we will pay them what we would have paid them for playing."

The head mariachi protests. "Señora, please. Maybe . . . half."

Mom shakes her head. "You don't need to play."

"Why not?" It's Ruth who's spoken up. "We totally love your music."

She's gone over the heads of the hostess and the family—straight to the mariachis. "You're here, you're getting paid anyway, so couldn't you play a couple of songs for us? We would love it so much."

Ruth has cojones, that's for sure. Rocco has to give her credit. And he finds her nerve—the hard nut of toughness under that fragile shell—surprisingly sexy.

The mariachi leader looks to Luz to make sure he understands. He nods at the rest of the band, and they nod back. They seem pleased. The lady has just told them she loves their music.

Rocco is lucky to have Ruth in his life, even if she isn't always 100 percent truthful. Well, who is? What's the point of being honest in a world full of liars?

Charlotte applauds, then Eli, then Mom and Luz. Finally Daisy joins in, clapping louder than the rest. She stops when the mariachis look at her, then edges over and clings to Charlotte.

The head mariachi bows to Daisy. Your wish is my command. *"Mucho gusto, princesa."*

Daisy looks around to make sure that her family has seen that the nice man with the violin recognizes her as the princess she is.

The high percussive notes of the trumpets dare Rocco not to cheer up. The trills and swoops are irresistible, and now the violin comes in, singing around the brass, but sweeter, adding a vibrato of longing to the joy. The musicians take turns singing. The head mariachi croons a heartbroken ballad about his love for a Mexican girl.

Rocco wishes it didn't make him think that he will never feel that way about Ruth—or about anyone. The little boy takes the lead, with a song about how happy he is to be a mariachi, about having a musician's access to beautiful music, tequila, and women. Tequila? Women? Rocco and Luz and the other musicians laugh.

Rocco's feeling a lot better when Ruth ruins his good mood by skipping over to him with her arms out-stretched. Asking him to dance. No way he's going to let her make a spectacle of him. He shakes his head. She doesn't seem fazed, but goes over to Charlotte and asks *her* to dance. It's no surprise to anyone—except Ruth, maybe—when Charlotte refuses.

Before Ruth can approach her, Mom makes the sign of the cross, as if to ward off a vampire. Ruth doesn't ask Eli, which might have irritated Charlotte, and she's not about to ask Luz. Rocco would have despised Ruth for adding dancing to the tasks that Luz has been hired to perform.

There's no one left but Daisy.

Everyone waits for Daisy to dive under Charlotte's skirt, but the little girl holds out her hands, and Ruth bends down so they can join in a demented polka.

Ruth and Daisy whirl and dip. Rocco's never seen his niece look so carefree. Her eyes are half closed, her head thrown back. Daisy giggles and slides her feet in time to whatever Ruth is doing. Dancing with Daisy changes Ruth, until she begins to resemble a child, and the spectacle takes on the charm of two little girls dancing. Or almost.

Rocco worries that he's misjudged Ruth. If she's capable of bringing his shy, solemn niece so much joy, she must be a better person than he'd thought.

The mariachis play two more songs, each livelier than the next. Then they conclude with a blast of horns and a flourish of strings. Ruth and Daisy hold hands and bow. Everyone applauds.

Rocco looks over at Charlotte. The set of her jaw reminds him of the stone heads on Easter Island.

Charlotte has never said so, but he knows she dislikes and distrusts Ruth. And though Rocco would never admit it, he thinks, despite everything—despite even the magic that Ruth has worked on Daisy—that his sister may be right.

Something is wrong with his girlfriend.

He wishes he knew what it was.

18

Charlotte

Mom wanted the musicians to play for her party, but this is better. It's like having their personal mariachi band. The boy and his dad sing, in harmony, a ballad about the soul. Charlotte longs to stay in this moment forever. They won't have to leave Mexico, go home, deal with all the problems and responsibilities. Daisy will stay this age forever and never grow up and leave them.

And Daisy will never have to find out what Ruth knows—or doesn't know—about her. Charlotte watches Ruth ask Rocco to dance. Ruth knows Charlotte will refuse but asks anyway. When Ruth moves on to Daisy, Charlotte can't stop her.

Charlotte watches her daughter beaming, twirling,

shaking her hands in the air, jumping and spinning. She knows that she should find it heartwarming, but Charlotte feels sickened, queasy.

She *really* wants Ruth to stay away from her daughter.

Charlotte doesn't trust Ruth, who has begun to scare her. First one thing, then another.

The story about the beggar children. Her claiming that Eli isn't Daisy's father. Chef Basil saying she'd never worked for the baroness. The incident with the driver.

What had so enraged the driver that he'd risk bursting into a party full of expats? They could have had him arrested. Surely he must have known that. But no one here calls the police.

Now Ruth has cast her unwholesome spell on Daisy, whom she's whirling around in a way that Charlotte never could. Charlotte could never be that wild and free. The mariachis are so enchanted that their professional smiles have become genuine.

Charlotte can't grab her daughter and put a stop to her dance. Why would she? She doesn't suspect that Ruth means Daisy any harm. Yet something about Ruth seems . . . what? Charlotte has drunk too many margaritas to think of the right word.

Maybe Charlotte is just jealous. Resentful of Daisy's affection for Ruth. Maybe it's that simple. That shameful.

The mariachis swing into a rousing finale. "Happy

Birthday." In English, for the gringos. Everyone sings along.

Happy birthday to you. Happy birthday to you. Happy birthday, dear Mom, dear Grandma, dear Sally, dear Señora Sally. Happy birthday to you. The musicians finish with a blast of brass.

Ruth bows to Daisy, who giggles and bows back. Charlotte applauds with the others, and the mariachis bow too. Then Charlotte pours herself another margarita from the pitcher.

Mom whispers to Luz, who produces an envelope she gives the head mariachi. Once more he bows, and the musicians sweep off their sombreros and place them over their hearts. They pack up their instruments and leave.

Mom and Rocco and Ruth congratulate themselves and one another on how well everything has worked out. Charlotte is helping Luz clean up the patio when she hears a familiar sound—

How long has Daisy been wheezing?

"Jesus Christ. Where's Eli?"

Luz says, "He just went off to sleep."

Charlotte tells herself: Relax. She's dealt with this, or something like this, so many times before. She just needs to get Daisy calm enough to be able to use her inhaler.

Her inhaler! Did Charlotte remember to pack it? Of course she must have. The margaritas and the tension of the party have fogged her brain. She needs to concentrate; she needs—

Daisy's eyes widen in panic; then she closes them to conserve effort, and Charlotte hears herself, as if from a distance, begin to whimper.

Ruth says, "Find your phone. Use the app, Charlotte. Thank God your mother has Wi-Fi."

Charlotte finds her phone in her purse. She's cradling Daisy's head as her daughter struggles to breathe. Her own breath is nearly as labored and ragged as Daisy's.

"*You* find the app, Ruth," Charlotte says. "Find the fucking inhaler."

Ruth scrolls through Charlotte's apps and taps her phone. And after a moment—an eternity—the cartoon bunny bounces on the screen. Ruth hurries off toward the spot where the bunny is. Moments later she hands Charlotte the inhaler.

"It was in your suitcase. I hope you don't mind that I had to root around in your stuff."

"Of course not. Did Eli wake up?" Charlotte puts the inhaler up to Daisy's lips. "Breathe, sweetheart. Breathe."

"Why would he?" Ruth says. "After all, he isn't really—"

Dear God, what is Ruth about to say? Charlotte's terror ramps up her fears for Daisy.

"Breathe!" says Charlotte.

Daisy only has to inhale twice before the fluttering in her chest slows to something less frightening, though not yet normal enough for Charlotte to relax.

"Bingo," says Ruth. "She'll be fine."

How the hell does Ruth know? But why is Charlotte angry at Ruth? Ruth didn't mean to bring on an asthma attack by asking Daisy to dance.

If not for Ruth . . .

It doesn't matter that Eli didn't help. He's always been there for them before. Or almost always.

Anyway, Charlotte handled it. The crisis is over.

"Thank you," she tells Ruth.

"You don't have to thank me," says Ruth. "So . . . are you going to tell Eli?"

"Tell him *what*?" Charlotte's heart is pounding.

"Tell him the truth."

"I'm tired," Daisy says. "I want to sleep in Grandma's room."

Mom's bedroom is big enough for a cot for Daisy. Daisy has told Charlotte that sometimes she and Grandma stay up late talking, though she never re-members, or pretends to forget, what they say.

By the time Charlotte has thanked Luz and said good night to Rocco and Ruth—who's snuggling up against Rocco—Mom has gone to her room. And by the time

Daisy and Charlotte get there, Mom is asleep on top of her blankets, still wearing her clothes. The bedroom is dark except for the glow from Mom's Virgin of Guadalupe night-light. Charlotte can barely see Mom, but she hears her snoring, a plosive pop, followed by a gulp that ends in a honking snort that Charlotte finds maddening.

"Grandma's so *noisy!*" Daisy bursts out laughing.

Charlotte says, "You can sleep with me and Dad. It's quieter."

"I want to stay here," says Daisy. "You and Dad snore too."

Charlotte tries to help Daisy into her pajamas, but Daisy pulls away. Charlotte has forgotten how proud she is of the things she can do herself. Something about the way Daisy clambers under the covers breaks Charlotte's heart.

Charlotte kisses the top of Daisy's head. Within moments Daisy begins to snore, a tender snuffling in rhythmic counterpoint to her grandmother's buzz saw.

Mom's snoring stops, abruptly. Charlotte assumes she's gone into another sleep phase when she sees—by the flicker of the night-light—that her mother is sitting up in bed.

Mom says, "Explain something. What *was* that back there, with Ruth and the driver?"

Charlotte has been avoiding that question. She'll

figure it out when she has time. Maybe tomorrow, on the plane. Maybe she can broach the subject with Rocco or even Ruth . . .

"I don't know," Charlotte says.

Mom says, "And where did she get that evil, *evil* mask?"

Charlotte's surprised. Mom seemed so pleased to get it. She has no idea what her mother's real feelings are. But that's often true.

Charlotte says, "There's a little place not far from the zocalo—"

"Leave me the address," Mom says. "I'm returning it the minute you all leave tomorrow."

"I thought you said you loved it."

Mom shudders. "Do you want it?"

Charlotte doesn't understand why she says no. She loves the mask, but she doesn't want it now. It creeps her out.

"Good. I think it's bad luck," says Mom. "I liked it at first, but the more I looked at it, the more it scared me. There's something wrong with that woman, Ruth. She is right smack in the middle of a very dark time. I saw that right away. Like they say on the cop shows, there's something she's not telling us. Take my word for it, Charlotte. There's something going on there. If we knew, we'd be *terrified*."

Charlotte says, "I think so too."

"She is in *so much* trouble. I can say this with some authority, having been there myself. You have a lucky life, Charlotte, knock on wood. Faithful husband, beautiful daughter, work, home. As for Rocco . . . not so much, but his story's not over yet. But this woman . . . Ruth . . . she's barely treading water, and she can't hold out. And I don't want to see your brother going under with her."

"You . . . tried to kill him. Maybe that's why he has a little . . . problem with women."

None of them have ever said this before. Charlotte waits for the world to come crashing down, but it doesn't.

"Strictly speaking, I didn't try anything of the sort," says Mom. "And later he tried to kill me. So I guess you could say we're even."

"Have you told Rocco how you feel about Ruth?" asks Charlotte.

"If I did, he'd marry her tomorrow. I feel sorry for her. As someone who has been in bad shape myself, I can sympathize with a person who has shattered in pieces and is missing some of the fragments she needs to put herself back together. Let's hope her problems are temporary."

How strange that Mom, who has never shown much sympathy for anyone but herself, should pity Ruth.

Maybe her sympathy for Ruth is just a disguised manifestation of her sympathy for herself.

Charlotte says, "Can I ask you something?"

"Ask away."

"When you . . . when there was that fire . . . did you know that Rocco was home?"

"Of course not!" says Mom. "Do you think I would put your brother in danger? I was just trying to get your father's attention. Anyway, I didn't set anything. I was a careless smoker."

Where would Charlotte begin to get at the truth about that? And nothing's going to change her mother, or her mother's story. Better stick to trying to fix what can still be fixed.

"What should we do about Ruth?"

Mom says, "'We'? I'm sixty years old, I'm tired. I'm going to sleep. If you want to do something, you have to do it."

"Good night," Charlotte says. "Happy birthday." She crosses the room to give her mother a last birthday hug.

Mom stiffens in Charlotte's embrace. "The birthday is over, thank God." Then she rolls away and faces the opposite wall.

"Sleep tight. Don't let the scorpions bite," Mom murmurs.

"Scorpions?" Charlotte says, but her mother is already asleep.

Charlotte stands in the doorway. What Mom's said about Ruth has confirmed her own suspicions, and worse, everything seems . . . real. Something is very wrong. There *is* something Ruth's not telling them. But what? Charlotte needs to find out. They all do.

Crossing the courtyard, she hears the front door slam. Has someone come in? She stands still, listening. But there are no other sounds. No footsteps, no motion, nothing.

Someone must have gone out. Probably Luz, finally going home after cleaning up the last of the mess. Unless Rocco or Ruth—or Rocco *and* Ruth—has gone for a walk. But it's late, and they'd seemed as tired as Charlotte.

Charlotte finds Eli in their bed, snoring, louder than Daisy, not as loud as Mom. Charlotte's still angry at him for being passed out when she and Daisy needed him. But she decides not to wake him. They're leaving tomorrow. She's glad to be going home.

Eli's awake before Charlotte, complaining of a headache, which annoys her. A headache! She tells him Daisy had an asthma attack last night. She lets the word *attack* linger until she adds that Daisy is okay. They got through it *without him.*

Eli says, "I'm sorry."

Before Charlotte met Eli, she'd been surprised by how many men found it impossible to apologize. How easy it is to say I'm sorry, how little it costs, how effectively it smooths everything over. Or almost everything.

Charlotte isn't angry now. She's listening.

Someone is screaming. A woman. Then another woman.

Mom and Luz. Charlotte runs into the kitchen.

Daisy!

Mom and Luz are talking streams of English mixed with Spanish, peppered with words, in both languages, for violence, injury, damage.

"Where is she? Where's Daisy?"

"Huh?" says Mom. "Daisy? Last time I looked, she's sleeping in her bed."

"What's going on?"

Mom says, "Reyna got beaten up last night. In the park. Right beneath the statue of Porfirio Díaz. They think she's going to be okay, but she's in the hospital, drifting in and out of consciousness."

"By the boyfriend?" Charlotte asks. "The crazy abusive boyfriend?"

"Her mom thinks so," Mom says. "But no one

knows. The doctors say she got hit on the head from behind."

By now Eli, Rocco, and Ruth have come into the kitchen.

Ruth says, "That is the worst thing ever."

Rocco gives her a funny look.

Of course. She'd been upset when she'd caught him talking to Reyna. But now she seems on the edge of tears.

"Should we go see her?" Rocco says.

Eli says, "We're leaving today, remember?"

"You wouldn't be much use here," says Mom.

They've been dismissed. Charlotte had expected a moment like this. Mom's known for her frosty good-byes. She gets argumentative, sulky. Charlotte likes to imagine that Mom's sad when they leave, but she suspects she's relieved. Her real life can continue without her annoying children.

Daisy stumbles into the kitchen, still in pajamas, rubbing her eyes. Charlotte's weak-kneed with relief. She feels that familiar sense of having survived a near escape, though no one in her family has been in danger.

Poor Reyna. Poor Reyna's daughter. Poor Reyna's mom.

Charlotte kneels and hugs Daisy.

"Good morning, love of my life."

"Good morning, Mom. Good morning, Dad, Grandma, Uncle Rocco, Ruth. Good morning, Luz."

"How are you feeling?" says Mom.

"Fine," Daisy says. "Why are you asking?"

Charlotte doesn't want Daisy to hear about Reyna. "Come on, Daisy. Let me give you a bath and finish packing."

"I'm hungry," Daisy says.

"I'll make breakfast," says Luz.

"Pancakes?"

"Certainly," says Luz.

Rocco says, "I could go check on Reyna . . ."

Everyone notices that he's said *I*, not *we*. He hasn't included Ruth.

"Paco's driving," says Mom. "You're all going in the same van. And there's nothing you can do to help Reyna."

Charlotte says, "Let's all meet here in the kitchen at nine. Mom, can you tell Paco to come at nine fifteen?"

"I can tell him," says Luz. "He'll be waiting for you outside."

19

Ruth

All the time I was in Mexico, I felt like one of those teensy animals we studied in high school biology, those creatures writhing on the glass slides as we peered at them under the microscope. That was how Rocco's family studied me, wondering what it would take to remove me forever from Rocco's life.

No one believed me about the driver who steered me into that swarm of starving kids. Why would I make that up?

Rocco's mother disliked me. Probably she hated me before I even got there.

It was like working at the start-up: frustrating and useless. You can't make people stop seeing the person they *think* you are. I hate being misunderstood, maybe because some childish part of me assumes (wrong!) that people will understand me the way my grandparents do.

When Rocco's mom arranged for us to visit Chef Basil, I knew she was just getting me out of the house. I felt sorry for the old guy, losing his memory—and his business. And I hated how Charlotte treated him, like a total loser.

The driver confirmed Charlotte's worst impression of me. She hates the fact that Daisy thinks I'm fun. It isn't fair that Daisy belongs to Charlotte just because she gave birth to her.

I *see* Daisy. I see her more clearly than her parents do. And I know I'm the only one who can really help her become the amazing little person she could become. Daisy's life would be so much better if she were my daughter.

I'm the only one who knows the truth about Charlotte. Maybe I shouldn't have hinted that I know. Charlotte *really* hates me now.

When I saw how Charlotte reacted to that creepy mask, I saw what her mother didn't like about her. Which also meant that I saw her. I knew what Charlotte's mother wanted her to be. I knew what her mother wanted. And I knew what I had to do.

I told Rocco we'd split the cost.

I spent so long trying to get a break from the old

man in the antiques shop that I was late for the party. Which was a huge mistake. I put the mask on Rocco's card. We'd work the details out later.

I was stressed by the time I got to his mom's. The party was going full blast. I found my boyfriend deep— *deep*—in conversation with the hottest woman there. That was my reward after all I'd gone through, all that bargaining, turning on all my charm, pretending I didn't understand when the pervy antiques-store guy said he'd half the price if I blew him in the back of the shop.

The old freak! I was trembling when I left the store, but I had the mask under my arm.

When I saw Rocco talking to that woman, I didn't trust myself. I didn't know what I was going to do. I counted backwards from ten. I told myself: Nothing is going to happen between Rocco and a woman in Oaxaca. Neither of them is going anywhere. She isn't a threat. She's no one—nothing—I have to worry about. Or *do anything* about.

Or is she?

I could tell that Rocco's mom loved the mask. But she wouldn't keep it, not if it came from me.

I saved their asses with the mariachis, and I saved their asses again when I found Daisy's inhaler. In the meantime, our dance made Daisy the happiest she'd been since she got to Mexico.

Did any of them thank me? Quite the opposite.

By the time we went to bed, Rocco wouldn't look at me. I assumed he was angry at me for interrupting his intimate chat with his mom's friend. Or maybe he blamed me for that awkwardness with the driver, which wasn't my fault.

It really wasn't my fault.

Rocco was in the shower when the driver texted me.

Any normal person would have gotten suspicious when the driver texted (in bad English) that he was sorry. He'd lied about the money. He wanted to return it. Would I meet him in the park?

Any normal person would have assumed he meant to rob me or worse. So maybe I'm not normal. Stupid me, always wanting to think the best of people. I believed that he meant what he said. Because it was true: He *did* lie. He *should* return the money.

Besides, I needed cash. If the driver returned what he'd squeezed out of Rocco, I could repay Rocco for half the price of the mask. Also it was a good excuse for a walk. A reason to get out of the house. I couldn't sleep. When I closed my eyes, I saw Charlotte's face— her jealousy and rage—when she watched me dance with Daisy. Poor Charlotte! Imagine how it feels to realize that your daughter is having more fun with someone else than she ever has with you.

I told Rocco I'd gotten my period early. I had to go get tampons. He asked if it couldn't wait.

I said, "Not unless you want your mom's bed looking like a crime scene."

He offered to come with me, but I said I wanted to be alone, and besides, he didn't mean it. It wasn't very gentlemanly, but he wanted some alone time. Sure. I understood. The party had been stressful.

The driver was waiting by the Porfirio Díaz statue, just where he said he would be. He gave me back the money from Rocco. He said he was sorry.

I said, "Don't worry, it's nothing," which wasn't true. It wasn't nothing. I was glad to have the money.

I hate when people lie. So many times I would like to lie, because it would be so much easier than telling the truth. But I don't lie. I'm an honest person.

It was smart of me to take Rocco's keys. All the houses on his mother's block are locked behind wrought iron cages. Maybe they should wonder if that means no one wants them here. Didn't Chef Basil notice that his staff was figuring out the best place to stick his fancy Japanese knife in him when they rose up and took back the house?

Sometimes I wonder what it would be like to stab someone. Who would I stab first? Charlotte? Rocco's mom?

Rocco was asleep when I got back. I nicked my finger

with a razor blade and bled a few drops onto a tampon (I'd brought some from New York) and wrapped it in toilet paper and threw it on top of the trash in the bathroom. I had to take an Ambien *and* a Klonopin so I wouldn't be lying there with my eyes wide-open watching headlights sweep by on the wall.

That's why I was a little groggy when I heard the uproar in the kitchen and Rocco jumped out of bed.

The girl Rocco had been flirting with at the party had been beaten up by her boyfriend. Terrible! We'd seen her the night before. Rocco and I had just talked to her. And now she was . . . I couldn't bear to picture that pretty face . . .

I got a creepy feeling when I heard it happened in the park, because that was where I met the driver. I knew I was being absurd. How many men were out that night? And why would a guy who wanted to clear his conscience by returning our money go out and attack a woman?

A coincidence, that was all.

It was painful watching Rocco and Charlotte say good-bye to their mother. She couldn't wait for them to leave. When Rocco tried to hug her, he reminded me of a boy embracing a store-window mannequin. I couldn't watch. I'd never loved Rocco so much. I wanted to protect him, the way my grandparents protected me from my mother.

Rocco's mother knelt in front of Daisy and hugged her. Daisy was in tears as her grandmother, also in tears, promised she'd visit soon.

I was overjoyed to see Paco's van. I felt like an innocent prisoner getting out of jail after a long and unfair sentence.

Charlotte climbed into the back of the van, because she's such a martyr. I had to slide in beside her, to show that I was as unselfish as she was, and also because neither Eli nor Rocco was about to go back there.

"We girls always get the back of the bus," I whispered to Charlotte. She didn't crack a smile.

I wasn't thrilled to sit next to her on the way to the airport. It wasn't a very long trip. But Charlotte's chilly presence made the ride seem endless.

The thing I never saw coming was that Charlotte would steal my passport.

By the time we got to the ticket counter, my passport was gone. Gone! I knew I'd put it in my purse before I left. I'd put it in the special compartment where I always keep it.

No one but Charlotte could have taken it.

When I placed my purse on the seat between us was the only time my passport left my hand.

20

Rocco

There's blood on the sink. Blood on the soap and on Ruth's hands.

Ruth said she'd gotten her period, so when he woke up, that's what he thought. Even when he heard about Reyna. Even then.

When he got back to their room from the kitchen, where he heard about Reyna, he checked his phone for the time and any messages. A pointless reflex. No one was trying to reach him here.

That's when he saw the outgoing text.

From him—that is, it *seemed* to be from him—to Reyna.

Meet me in the park. I need to talk to you.

Could he have sent it? No.

Things like that used to happen when he was drinking. He'd had blackouts, memory gaps. But he hadn't drunk anything last night. He hadn't, so how . . . ?

Ruth.

It had to be Ruth.

She'd taken his phone while he was in the shower. She'd texted Reyna, pretending to be him. Texted Reyna from his phone.

He was going to be sick. He needed *not* to be sick. He had to stay calm. He had to think.

He couldn't look at his phone. He made himself look.

Reyna had texted back:

Half an hour. By the Diaz statue.

That's where the attack had occurred. Someone hit Reyna from behind.

Ruth. It was Ruth who attacked her. Ruth had blood on her hands.

Rocco's head feels like it's full of foul water. Where is he? Okay. He's sitting on the edge of his bed. In Mom's house in Oaxaca. Ruth is looking at him, her face pale and pinched with concern.

"Rocco, is something wrong?"

How innocent. How bright and perky and clear-eyed. She's washed the blood off her hands. Lady Macbeth. She'd played Lady Macbeth. Or so she'd said.

"Stomach," he mumbles, and runs into the bathroom and locks the door.

He's never fainted, but this is how it must feel, just before you go under. His heart shouldn't be beating this fast. He sits on the edge of the tub and puts his head between his knees. He needs to do something . . . but what? He needs to tell someone . . . but who?

No one calls the police down here. No one. Ever. No matter what.

The text came from his phone. Reyna answered *him*. She arranged to meet him. How could he prove he didn't do it? That he and Ruth aren't in this together? That he isn't in this alone?

He's been sleeping next to—sleeping with—a woman who could do this. Who could lie and lie and lie and lie—and almost kill an innocent person.

Everything else—the start-up that never was, the driver, the beggar children, the inconsistencies in her stories—they were nothing compared to this.

How could he not know who she is? And what does he do now? He's a little afraid to break up with her. He's *very* afraid to stay with her.

He needs to tell someone. He can't. Things would

only get more complex. He can solve this by himself. Somehow he can make it go away. He's broken up with crazy women—but not as crazy as Ruth.

He needs to get home. Back to the US. Then he'll figure it out.

He flushes the toilet. Unlocks the door.

"Feeling better?" Ruth says sweetly.

What did she do with her bloody clothes?

"Much better," Rocco says.

He stays as far away from Ruth as he can until it's time to leave. They all convene for goodbyes. When Rocco tries to hug his mother, she pulls away.

Charlotte says, "We're so glad we got to celebrate your birthday, Mom."

Mom says, "Me too. Absolutely. For sure."

Rocco stands back and lets Charlotte and Ruth climb into the back of the van. He doesn't want to sit next to Ruth. He and Eli sit on the bench seat behind Paco, with Daisy belted between them.

Ruth whispers something to Charlotte that Rocco doesn't hear. Otherwise, no one talks. Charlotte says, "Mom seems well; she seems to like her life here." No one answers.

It's unusual that Ruth can let one second of silence exist without stuffing it full of chatter.

But even Ruth is silent now. What could she be thinking?

When they get back to New York, he'll break up with her.

What he'll do is: He'll make her want to break up with him. Slowly, slowly—no rushing it—he'll turn into the Bad Boyfriend. He's been that so many times before—it'll be easy. No effort required. She'll get tired of him. Sick of him not being there for her, not paying attention. She'll get tired of him complaining. Not calling when he's supposed to. He's done it before. He's an expert.

But it never before seemed like a matter of life and death. He's never broken up with someone who attacked a woman he talked to at a party.

The Oaxaca airport is small, manageable. Charlotte urges Daisy and Eli ahead of Rocco and Ruth, who let the little family check in before them. The guy at the counter smiles at Daisy, who hides behind her dad. Charlotte collects their boarding passes, and the three of them step aside and wait for Rocco and Ruth to check in.

Some vestigial gallantry inspires Rocco to let Ruth go first. A mistake, as it turns out.

Later, he wishes he'd checked in before her and refused to intercede when there was a problem with her ticket.

But the problem isn't her ticket. The problem is that Ruth has no passport.

Frantic, she kneels and dumps her purse on the floor, right in front of the counter, despite the line of passengers behind them. Rocco hears grumbling, but most people look away as Ruth paws through coins, old tissues, tampons, keys, and lipstick tubes. She stuffs it all back in her purse, then dumps it out again, as if the second time will do the trick. It does not do the trick.

Ruth begins to wail. "My passport! What happened to it? Someone must have stolen it."

"You probably left it at my mother's," Charlotte says. "I can call her, have them look for it. We might have time for Paco to drive back and get it and bring it back."

"That's not possible," says Ruth. "I definitely remember putting it in my purse this morning. I had it in the car. I checked. Charlotte, did you see it? Rocco, do you think Paco—"

"I didn't see it," Charlotte says, and at the same time Rocco says, "You cannot talk shit about Paco. He's been with my mom since she got here."

"Excuse *me*," Ruth says.

Rocco hates how Ruth thinks that every Mexican

with a driver's license is out to steal her money. She's making Rocco ashamed of being a gringo, and shame leads, as it often does with him, directly to anger.

"Where the fuck did you leave your passport?" he says.

Ruth bursts into tears. "I don't know. I swear. Someone took it."

"Who the hell could have taken it?"

"I don't know," Ruth repeats.

"Fuck it. I'm getting on this flight," Rocco says. "I'm going home. I've got work. I've got responsibilities. You lost your passport, you deal with it."

"I didn't lose it. Someone took it," Ruth cries.

"No one took it," says Rocco.

This could be just what he's looking for. A godsend. He could leave Ruth here and clear his stuff out of her apartment by the time she gets back. Disappear from her life forever.

What if she comes after him? He'll deal with that when it happens.

The airline clerk looks dismayed, and Rocco senses a seismic rumble of impatience from the passengers behind them.

"You can't leave Ruth here," says Charlotte. "You need to stay and help her. I don't think you—"

Rocco is so hurt and angry that he has to fight tears

of outrage welling in his eyes. Since when is Charlotte worried about Ruth? His sister never liked her. Charlotte's supposed to have *his* back. So why is she taking Ruth's side?

If only he could tell her *why* he needs to get away. If he explained about Ruth and Reyna. Charlotte would make him tell Mom . . . or someone . . . and then the trouble would begin. He'd be the one the police questioned first.

"She can stay with Mom," says Rocco. "Mom and Luz will help her replace her passport."

"You can't do that," says Eli. "You can't leave her here."

Then they are shocked into silence by Daisy's voice.

"You have to help Ruth, Tío Rocco." Her clarity— her pure certainty—stops them cold. Even the waiting passengers behind them quit grumbling and pay attention.

A little child shall lead them. Rocco is not a religious person, but hearing Daisy seems, at that moment, like God's command.

"All right," says Rocco. "I'll stay. Because you said so, Daisy."

"Bravo," Charlotte says. Rocco glares at her.

"What should we do?" he asks the airline clerk.

The clerk, a slim handsome man around Rocco's age

with an expensive haircut and a wedding ring, says, "Señor, I assure you. This has happened before."

"It has?" Ruth's so overeager that the agent recoils, though maybe Rocco is projecting.

"Not often," the agent backtracks, "but yes. A tourist misplaces a passport. Most often backpackers who—"

"We know what backpackers do, blah blah," says Ruth. "And I didn't do any of that."

The clerk smiles placatingly at Ruth. "Of course. You will need to go to the American consul. Take a taxi. You can get an emergency temporary passport and possibly be out on the later flight."

"Wait!" cries Ruth. "Hold on, señor. I photocopied my passport, I have a copy in this book. My grandpa told me to do that. In case I lost it. Very old-school but smart. *¿Mi abuelo?*" She smooths a crumpled sheet of paper: "My passport!"

Rocco doesn't think this will work. But stranger things have happened. He allows himself to hope.

They can still make it home. *Then* he needs to leave Ruth. He never wants to see her again. She tried to kill an innocent woman.

"I can't," says the agent. "I'm sorry. Not with this . . . paper, señora. I can't let you board with a copy. You understand."

"We understand," says Rocco. A nasty scene will make everything worse. Not even Ruth wants him to make one. What if someone asks to look at his phone and connects him with the attack on Reyna? Would they have heard about that, at the airport? Unlikely, really unlikely. But you never know.

He'd have to prove his innocence. Mexican jails. Mexican lawyers.

None of this makes any sense. Nothing like this is going to happen. But he can't stop thinking about it. And it's making it hard to think about anything else. He's so scared that he feels as if he's turned into Charlotte.

The agent types and stares into the screen. "There's a chance you could make it out of Mexico City later today. The flight is wide-open." He gets no pleasure from Rocco's distress. He's trying to sound as if this isn't so bad.

"Jesus Christ," says Rocco. This is hell, and he's brought it on himself. So many people have it worse. But the thought of how fortunate he is compared to so many others—a thought that's usually so useful in restoring his perspective—doesn't help.

"Now, if you two would please step aside, I can process the other passengers and reissue your tickets. It won't take long, I promise."

Charlotte looks haggard. Perhaps only now does she

truly understand that she's leaving her brother behind in Mexico. With Ruth.

"We'll be fine," Rocco says. "We'll be home by midnight. I'll text you on the way."

Does Charlotte know how worried he is? He doesn't want her to know.

"Mom's here in Oaxaca," says Charlotte. "She'll help you. She knows everyone here."

"Does that make things better or worse?" Rocco says.

Charlotte laughs. "Please text me when you get back. Stay safe."

"I promise," Rocco says.

Charlotte, then Eli, then Daisy hugs Rocco. Only Daisy hugs Ruth. Charlotte and Eli don't speak to Ruth; they don't even look at her, except when Charlotte pulls Daisy away from Ruth in mid-hug.

Looking steadily back at Rocco as if they are afraid he'll vanish if they lose sight of him, they head for the shuttle bus waiting to take them to the plane.

Rocco would give anything to be going with them. He is supposed to be on that plane. With his family. Not with this crazy murderous stranger.

Goodbye, Charlotte and Eli. Goodbye, Daisy. Goodbye forever. Wait. He is overreacting. A mistake is being corrected. Not *his* mistake, but whatever. And it *is* his mistake. No one put a gun to his head and forced him to carry ten pounds of kale to Ruth's nonexistent office. No one made him ask her out. No one made him sleep with her. No one made him overlook her casual relationship to the truth.

The door to the airfield closes, with Rocco on the wrong side.

The agent looks at him, tilting his head at an angle meant to signal sympathy and willingness to help. Within reason. He squints at his monitor and types.

It's never a good thing when a gate agent frowns and types again and frowns and types again and keeps frowning.

"I'm sorry to tell you"—the agent seems genuinely sorry—"the change fee will be two hundred dollars per person."

"Four hundred *dollars*?" The sob of grief in Rocco's voice is humiliating.

"I'm sorry," the agent says.

"I have money. Three hundred dollars in pesos!" Ruth reaches under the neck of her T-shirt and hands a wad of bills to the agent. "Rocco, all you need to do is put a hundred on your card. And I will pay you back, I swear. This is my fault."

"Where did you get that? You said all your money was gone."

He wonders if Reyna was also robbed. If so, no one mentioned it.

"I took it out from the ATM," Ruth says. "I thought I might need it."

"Where did the ATM get the money?"

"My grandma and grandpa's account," says Ruth. "They gave me their bank card for emergencies."

"An emergency in advance," Rocco says.

"Señor?" They'd forgotten the gate agent, and now they turn, surprised.

"Take it." Rocco hears how rude he sounds. Too bad. "And put the other hundred on my card. Can you do that?"

"I'll call my manager. But yes, I think so. As long as a credit card is on file."

"There will be," says Ruth.

They spend the day running. Running to get a cab, running to the consulate. Rocco wishes he were running away from Ruth.

Outside the consulate, two marines, one tall and one very tall, stand upright as toy soldiers. They hardly even bend as they wand Rocco's and Ruth's suitcases and scrabble through their bags. They let them through only when Rocco explains the problem. Twice.

"My wife did the same thing in Cabo," says one of

the marines, shooting Rocco a discreet man-to-man thumbs-up. "Some Mexican lady with my wife's name is probably packing chicken in the Midwest."

She's probably your kid's nanny, Rocco thinks but doesn't say.

They wait in a large room with dozens of Mexican families who are not going to get visas, except possibly the two wealthy-looking couples. What if Rocco never gets out? What if he has to live here with his mother? That's not going to happen. What if someone finds out what Ruth did—and blames him?

Ruth is called into the consul's office ahead of the Mexicans. Rocco asks if he can go with her, and the marine whose wife lost her passport in Cabo rolls his eyes (women!) and waves him through.

It's true what the airport agent said. The consul has seen it before. A woman of fifty with harlequin glasses and improbably orange hair swept Elvis-style up from her forehead, she's bored with them even before they explain their problem. This time, Ruth's photocopy makes things easier. The consul's shoulders inch down from her earlobes. She gives Ruth a stack of papers and asks her to swear that the statements she's signing are true.

"I solemnly swear," Ruth says to Rocco, who looks away as Ruth grabs the papers from the consul before he can see them.

The bad part comes when they're back at the airport.

By then the first clerk has gone off duty, as has the supervisor who approved their payment. What the computer says has changed. Their tickets are no longer valid and can't be rebooked—the computer can't be reasoned with. They have to buy new tickets. The airline is sorry, but it's not their fault. It's . . . regulations. The man on duty this morning, sadly, he made a small mistake.

"Deal with it," Rocco hisses at Ruth.

"Call your boss," Ruth tells the agent. She argues with the desk clerk and makes Rocco show his receipt from this morning, but the airline won't budge.

"This can't be right," says Rocco.

"*Lo siento, señora,*" the agent tells Ruth.

"All right," Rocco says. "Two tickets." He'll do anything to get home. He'll mortgage his house if he has to. He'll sort it out later. He hands over his card.

Either the clerk feels sorry for him, or perhaps he's decided that they need to be isolated for the sake of the other passengers, but it works in their favor. He gives them two seats by themselves, right across from the alcove where the flight attendants get drinks.

No matter what is going on, it's a blessing to get a good seat on a plane.

As soon as Rocco buckles his seat belt, he is filled with a mysterious gratitude. They've done it; they've passed through the fire. They're going home.

They have been through an ordeal. Something bad has happened. But he'll deal with it.

One step at a time.

He and Ruth don't have to talk until they land in Mexico City. Right now it's as if Ruth doesn't exist. Or that's what Rocco tells himself.

When the drinks cart comes around, Rocco says, "A scotch, please."

Or, anyway, someone says it. Someone who sounds exactly like him. Someone with his exact voice. The funny thing is, he'd known he was going to say it, and he told himself not to say it, and he said it anyway.

Several different voices and opinions weigh in on those three words, and all those voices and opinions seem to be his.

Your girlfriend assaulted an innocent woman. You got hijacked into staying in Mexico and taken for the cost of two one-way tickets. You deserve a drink.

"Make that a double," he tells the flight attendant. It doesn't mean that he's drinking again. It's strictly a onetime thing.

He can feel Ruth's eyes boring into him. Fuck her. It's her fault.

"And you, miss?" the flight attendant asks.

Rocco communicates to Ruth, without a word, that Miss is not putting one more thing on his credit card.

"Just water, please," says Ruth. "No ice. If it's not too much trouble."

But then an unexpected thing happens. After Rocco finishes the double, and is ordering another, he asks Ruth if she wants a drink.

Maybe things aren't as bad as they seem. Maybe there's something he's missing. Maybe he's not seeing clearly.

Ruth says something funny that he forgets as soon as she says it. But it makes him laugh. Then she says that she's not going to judge him about falling off the wagon.

But his sister and brother-in-law and his mother will judge him, she says. He needs to know that. He already knows. Ruth means: It's us against them. Us against the world.

Ruth says, "It's our secret." He doesn't want to have a secret with Ruth, but now he does.

A big secret. More than one. This secret and a bigger one. A serious one. Actually, several big secrets.

Ruth upends the last of her drink and sets it on the tray table. She leans her head on Rocco's chest and presses her chin into his clavicle so hard it hurts.

"You know what would be crazy?" she says.

"What?"

"If we got married."

"That *would* be crazy," Rocco says. "Clinically insane. Certifiably insane. One more round?"

He should stop now. He had a tiny bit of trouble pronouncing *certifiably.*

"Totally," says Ruth. "When does the crew cut us off?"

"Not yet," Rocco says. "And we've got some time in the Mexico City airport. I'll bet we can find a great bar."

"Here's to us," says Ruth.

21
Charlotte

Charlotte didn't mean to steal Ruth's passport. She's never stolen anything. She never even shoplifted as a kid, when everybody does. She has never done anything like that in her life. She is not a person who does things like this. She doesn't believe she did it.

She probably wouldn't have done it if Ruth, who can't tolerate one split second of silence, hadn't turned to her in the van and said, "I'm sort of glad we're going home, aren't you? Don't you think we'll all have to have some, like, totally honest conversations?"

Charlotte nodded. What did Ruth mean by *like, totally honest conversations*?

Something about it felt threatening. They both

knew what she meant. She meant a totally honest conversation about Daisy.

It was as if Charlotte were someone else. Having an
out-of-body experience.

When she saw the passport sticking out of Ruth's
purse, and when Ruth was staring out the window, oblivious, Charlotte realized that Ruth losing her passport
would solve a lot of problems. Or at least it would give
Charlotte extra time to think about how to solve one.

Ruth knows something that Charlotte doesn't want
her to know. Something Charlotte herself can't bear to
think about or call by name. Or admit.

Ruth figured it out. Charlotte doesn't know how. And
if Ruth tells someone, anyone—Rocco, Eli, *anyone*—
the damage will be major.

Besides, what sane person carries her passport
sticking out of her purse?

Charlotte's not a thief. She's furious at herself for
doing this. Humiliated.

But she's feeling a little desperate. More than a little
desperate.

She needs to be home. She needs to be able to think.
She needs to figure out what she'll say if . . .

She takes the passport from Ruth's purse and slips it
into her own purse.

There. It's done. No going back now.

She could always say she found it on the floor and give it back to Ruth. But she doesn't.

She's guilty and horrified at herself, but when she and Eli and Daisy get on the plane without Rocco and Ruth, relief instantly overpowers her guilt and shame.

Charlotte hates thinking of Rocco stranded with Ruth in Mexico. She feels awful for leaving him, for being glad that Rocco and Ruth aren't traveling with them. But she's grateful for the few hours she'll have to decompress before they get home. And doubly grateful for the chance to sort things out.

As soon as they find their seats on the plane, she feels free. Safe. As if she's escaped with her life. But her life was never in danger, so what has she escaped? Mom? Oaxaca? She loves Oaxaca, and despite everything, she loves her mother. She admires her. She respects the life Mom's made for herself, though it's easier to admire her from a distance.

The airplane light seems golden as they prepare their little nest in the bulkhead seats they've been assigned as a reward for traveling with a child.

It's a short flight from Mexico City, but even so, they take out Daisy's books and stuffed giraffe, and slip off their shoes. Daisy claims both armrests, which she can do only because she's sitting between people who love her.

The drinks cart has no tequila. They might as well have crossed the border. That's probably just as well. They were drinking too much in Mexico; they'll cut back when they get home. It's noon; they should probably hold off.

But right now they're celebrating, and they order vodka tonics.

At their mother's, Charlotte had been impressed—no, amazed—by how Rocco stayed sober with everyone gulping down delicious margaritas.

Thinking about her brother will only undo the good effects of the vodka.

Rocco will be fine. If he can transport a truckload of perfect organic tomatoes from upstate to Union Square, he can get Ruth a temporary passport and fly from Oaxaca to JFK.

Daisy asks if she can have a Coke. It feels good to say yes. Even if they'd refused, Daisy would have been fine with it. She's happy to be with her parents, happy to be going home. She had a good time with her grandmother in Oaxaca, and she's glad it's over.

"Sweetheart," Charlotte says, "you promised."

"Promised what?"

"You promised to show me your notebook. *Our Mexican Adventure.*"

"It's in my backpack," Daisy says.

"Should we look at it together?" Charlotte's tone is irritating, even to Charlotte. She's already turning back into a stifling New York parent. Maybe that's why she agrees when Daisy says, "How about you look at the book—and I'll watch a movie on Dad's computer?"

She's seen *Moana* countless times, but Charlotte's so eager to see the book she'll agree to anything.

She opens to the first page. It's less of a diary than a collage of images that caught Daisy's eye. The pyramid at Chichen Itza. Bananas in a market. She's cut them from a magazine. Credit card receipts, food packages, wrappers. Small bills, pages stuck together. Random stuff she'd gotten from guests at Mom's party. Business cards from Chef Basil and a landscaper, cough drop wrappers and matchbook covers, even some puffs of lint.

Charlotte's about to close the book when she feels a hard rectangle beneath several sheets of notebook paper.

Pasted onto the center of the page is a photo of Daisy and Ruth taken at one of those photo booths you don't see anymore in New York but must still exist in Oaxaca. Did Daisy go out with Ruth when Charlotte thought she was with Mom? The thought of Daisy and Ruth on the streets of a foreign city is terrifying, or would be, if Daisy weren't safe beside her.

Charlotte has Ruth's passport.

Breathe in, breathe out.

Charlotte pantomimes to Daisy: Take off the headphones!

"Where did *this* come from?"

Daisy looks guilty but confused about what she did wrong.

"It's me and Auntie Ruth—"

"She's not *Auntie* Ruth," Charlotte says. "She's not your fucking auntie."

"Language," Daisy says. Then she starts to cry.

What's gotten into Charlotte? Ruth has turned her into a thief and a terrible mother.

She hugs her daughter and whispers, "I am so sorry."

"Why do you hate her?" Daisy's voice wobbles.

"I don't hate her," Charlotte lies. But it's true. She doesn't hate Ruth. She just wishes that Ruth weren't her brother's girlfriend. She wishes she'd never met Ruth. She wishes that Rocco had never brought Ruth into their lives.

Stealing her passport was an impulse. She wanted to keep Ruth away forever. But it won't work. She knows that.

"Where was this taken, Daisy? You and—" She can't even say Ruth's name.

"I don't remember."

In the photo, Daisy and Ruth gaze calmly into the camera, not bugging their eyes and grinning goofily like people do in photo booths. They don't look alike—you would never think they were related.

But Daisy doesn't look like Charlotte, either.

She looks like Eli. Everyone thinks she looks like Eli. Everyone but Ruth.

"Where?" Charlotte's voice is so cold it scares her. How frightened her daughter must be.

Still crying, Daisy says, "The circus. When I went with her and Tío Rocco. I found the picture with my stuff, so I put it in the book."

"Why?"

"Because Auntie Ruth was with us at Granny's. She was part of our Mexican adventure."

Daisy has never called Mom *Granny* before.

Granny is what Ruth calls the grandmother she talks about all the time.

Granny Edith. Just the word freaks Charlotte out.

Now Charlotte has the full-on chills. For the first time she wonders if her daughter is lying. If Ruth is teaching her how to lie.

When they get home, Charlotte decides, she will do whatever she has to do to keep Ruth away from Daisy. Ruth and Daisy will never be in the same room together again.

PART THREE

April 19

22
Charlotte

As Charlotte runs to meet Rocco at Ruth's apartment, the smell of hot bread and cinnamon stops her. Looking in the window of what seems to be an old-fashioned Polish bakery, Charlotte pauses to catch her breath again.

Her daughter is missing and she's looking at cake. No. Charlotte is being guided.

Had the driver found Ruth's building, had Charlotte come from another direction, she wouldn't have passed the bakery and stopped to look at the trays of sticky buns. Had the bakery been closed, she wouldn't have seen the icing on the pastry: the sun with the eight rays and eight mini-explosions that Ruth said were her grandmother's trademark.

Does Ruth's grandmother work here? Does she own the place? Is that why Ruth lives nearby?

Ruth's grandparents live in Hoboken. She made such a point of it. Her granny baked the sticky buns for Ruth in her Hoboken kitchen.

For protection, Ruth said.

Granny Edith.

Is it a coincidence that Ruth lives next door to a bakery that sells a pastry with the same frosting design that her grandmother uses? Or did the pastry come from here? Was Ruth lying even about that? Has she lied from that very first evening? How many warnings did Charlotte miss?

Why didn't Charlotte tell Rocco what Chef Basil reported about Ruth and the baroness? Why didn't she question Ruth more closely about the swarm of children and the driver? They had missed so many chances to cut her out of their lives, to protect themselves.

To protect Daisy. What has Ruth done with Daisy?

It's only a sticky bun. A pastry in a bakery window.

Evidence, in a way.

A lie has been told, then another lie. A crime is being committed. Daisy is missing.

And part of Charlotte still believes (*has* to believe) that everything will be all right.

A bell clangs as Charlotte walks into the steamy, yeasty-smelling bakery. Two women—both blond, both young—stand behind the counter. Charlotte glimpses two Latino guys stacking trays in a back room.

It's all extremely old-fashioned. Not faux vintage but truly old-school. *Time travel* is how Ruth described her grandparents' house.

"Can I help you?" one of the women says.

Charlotte points to the sticky buns. "Those look delicious. Do you bake them here?"

"I don't bake," says the woman. "I just work here."

"Do they bake them in back, or are they shipped in—?"

The woman eyes Charlotte warily. Is she from the health department? Do the guys in back have immigration issues? She glances at her coworker. Now they both look suspicious.

Charlotte has been trying to act like an ordinary customer, chatting about the pastry. But she's not good at it. She isn't fooling anyone. She's in hell.

The woman sees that and takes pity.

"Not much is baked on-site. Most of it comes from this mega-factory in the Bronx. Don't you love that crazy thing they do with the icing? What genius invented a machine that can do that?"

Charlotte says, "I'll take a dozen."

She should taste one. But if she does, she'll be sick. She holds the bag at arm's length.

Ruth's name on the buzzer seems like a good sign. Ruth exists. She has an apartment to which she might still return with Daisy.

That would be too good to be true.

Charlottes buzzes more forcefully than she has to, and when someone—Rocco?—buzzes her in, she runs up the two flights of stairs. She's out of breath, and yet she finds the strength to pound on the door like a cop on TV. She imagines the door swinging open and there will be Daisy, sipping hot chocolate with Rocco and Ruth at a kitchen table.

Charlotte will forgive Ruth. She'll chalk it up to a misunderstanding. She will never say a mean word or have a negative thought about anyone. Not even Ruth.

Rocco opens the door. He's wearing a T-shirt and jeans. He's newly showered, his hair is wet, a shaving cut on his chin is sending up a trickle of pinkish blood.

He looks terrible. His face has a yellowish cast, and spider veins have turned the whites of his eyes a hideous sunset pink. She'd know that face anywhere. It's the face of the guy who held a knife to their mother's throat. Charlotte flinches when he steps forward to hug her. He smells of alcohol.

Poor Rocco! Charlotte blames herself. She stole Ruth's passport. If he'd been on the plane with them, he would have stayed sober. *Anyone* would need a drink after being stuck in Mexico with Ruth.

But still, how could he do this? How could he make all those years of sobriety count for nothing?

It's Charlotte's fault. It's Rocco's fault. It's no one's fault. He's her brother. She loves him.

It's Ruth's fault.

Hugging her brother is comforting. Charlotte wishes she could stay like that, with his arms around her, until her panic subsides. But she needs to pull away and look past him for what she knows she's not going to see.

Daisy. Ruth. Where are they?

Ruth's place is tiny, but everything is unexpectedly chic, furnished with good mid-century modern pieces—Ruth mentioned getting furniture from her grandparents—mixed in with knickknacks that are whimsical without being cloyingly cute. A brace of pens sticks up from the back of a ceramic pig. A pagoda and pines trees are carved on a large abalone shell, propped on a stand.

"That was her grandpa's," says Rocco. "From Okinawa."

Why would Charlotte care? Rocco is telling her what he found interesting about Ruth: a grandpa who served in Okinawa. *Does he not understand what's happened?*

"Where are Ruth and Daisy? Where's my daughter?"

"I don't know." Rocco looks at Charlotte. His eyes are half closed, and he's teetering slightly, like someone not quite recovered from a long illness.

"This is fucked," he says. "I'm sorry."

You should be, Charlotte thinks.

In the center of the living room is a large brown couch on which Rocco has staked out his corner of Ruth's kingdom. Charlotte senses that he's straightened up the place since he got her text, but he must have missed the beer bottle signaling, from under the coffee table, its own version of the story of what happened between Rocco and Ruth.

Ruth's home looks like Barbie's dream castle after Ken has gone on a weeklong bender. In the kitchen, bottles bulge like a bodybuilder's muscles under the shiny white skin of the trash bags.

How could he—*anyone*—have drunk this much since they got home last night?

Was Ruth drinking with him? Did she purposely get him trashed enough to pass out and stay passed out while she stole Daisy?

The impulse, which Charlotte restrains, is to smash the bag of pastry into her brother's face.

Calm down. Rocco is on her side. But if he was on her side, why did he let Ruth go anywhere near Daisy? Why didn't he say something as soon as he realized that the sticky buns didn't come from her grandmother's? He's not the most observant guy, but he would have seen it in the shop downstairs. *Everyone* looks in bakery windows, besides which it's one of the few businesses on the block. The icing is distinctive, and Ruth made such a fuss about it.

He must have figured that one out early on.

Charlotte says, "They make those sticky buns in the bakery down the block. It's not from her granny's kitchen. Wasn't that a red fucking flag right there? The first time you saw it in the window downstairs, it must have crossed your mind that something was a little off. A *lot* off."

"I didn't notice," says Rocco. "I swear I didn't see them in the window. I don't even like sticky buns. I thought she was getting them from her grandmother."

Charlotte says, "You're lying. And she's a liar. She never worked for the baroness. Her granny never made sticky buns—"

Rocco says, "Could you forget about the fucking sticky buns? I need to tell you something."

Charlotte yanks the pastries out of the bag, stuffs some in her mouth and then in Rocco's. He gags, but she doesn't care. It's the closest thing to a physical fight they've had since they were kids.

"Taste familiar? What else did she lie about?"

He says, "She attacked Reyna. I'm pretty sure it was Ruth. No. Actually . . . I'm sure it was Ruth."

"Oh my God. You're joking."

"I wish," Rocco says.

"And you didn't do anything? You didn't tell anyone?"

"What was I supposed to do? Call the Mexican police? The Federales? She'd have made it look like I was the one who did it. Ruth texted Reyna on my phone, pretending to be me. That's how she got her to come to the park where Ruth attacked her."

"You and Reyna must have made quite a connection at Mom's party for her to want to come and meet you later that night. But why would anyone think that *you* would hurt Reyna?"

"Believe me, Ruth would have thought of a reason."

Charlotte throws her arms around her brother again. Tears seep down her cheeks.

Only now does she understand what Ruth is capable of. The truth dawns on her in stages. A murderer—an attempted murderer—is out there in the city. Disappeared. With her child, her daughter. With Daisy.

"Does Ruth know that you know she attacked Reyna?"

"I told her this morning. When she was leaving. I was half awake and pretty out of it. I said we had to talk. And when she asked me about what, I said, About what you did to Reyna. I'm pretty sure I said that. Or anyway something like that."

"What did she say to that?"

"She asked what I thought she did to Reyna—and when could she have done it. I said, Our last night in Oaxaca, after the party, when she went out. She insisted that she met the driver she stiffed for the fare from Mexico City. She claimed he'd wanted to give her money back."

"That makes no sense," says Charlotte.

"None. That was when I told Ruth that she and I needed to take a break. That actually . . . well, actually . . . I just didn't think that I could be with her anymore."

"And then?"

"And then she stormed out of the house. And I passed out again. I think."

"God help us," Charlotte says.

"She'll come back here. I'm sure of it."

She? Why doesn't Rocco say *they*? *They'll* come back. Does he mean Ruth and Daisy? Or just Ruth? Can he not imagine the two of them returning safely? Does he wonder if Ruth took Daisy as revenge for him saying they needed to break up? Charlotte can tell from the catch in his voice that he isn't sure of anything. Still it's nice not to be alone. And it helps to cry openly, without holding back.

"You've got to quit drinking," she says. "You know that."

"I already quit," says Rocco. "Drinking."

"When?"

"Just now. When you texted."

"Great. You've earned your twenty-minute sobriety chip."

"Almost an hour," says Rocco.

Has it been an hour?

"I called in sick to work," he says. "I can get up to the country tomorrow—or as soon as this . . . thing gets settled."

Daisy's gone, and Rocco is calling it *this thing*? And he imagines that *this thing* will be settled by tomorrow? Charlotte almost shouts, What if it's *not* settled by tomorrow? What if it's never settled? What if they *never* find Daisy?

If only she hadn't stolen Ruth's passport. Maybe none of this would have happened. Or maybe it would have. Who knows how long Ruth has been planning this?

Where did she put Ruth's passport? In the midst of everything, Charlotte panics about that. In her sock drawer, where Eli never looks. She'll get rid of it tomorrow.

She checks her phone. If Eli had good news, he would call or text. Have the police shown up? Ruth was on the school pickup list! Don't those frightening Amber Alert signs light up even when a child has been abducted by a noncustodial parent? And Ruth isn't even a parent. She's the crazy, violent girlfriend of the kidnap victim's uncle.

The kidnap victim. Ruth assaulted Reyna. And now she has Daisy.

Somewhere out there. The city has never seemed so big!

Charlotte just wants to hear Eli's voice, so she calls him. He says he has phoned the police again, who have promised to stop by—

"Stop by?"

"Let's be glad they're responding at all. Ruth was authorized to pick her up. Apparently the school called too. They're covering their asses."

Eli is trying to stay strong, for her, and Charlotte

loves him for it. But the hoarseness in his voice signals sheer terror, and it makes her even more afraid.

"All right," says Eli. "We can do this. We'll find Daisy. I know it."

Charlotte says, "Find the book that Daisy made in Mexico. *Our Mexican Adventure.* There's a photo of Daisy and Ruth that Daisy pasted in it. You can give that to the police."

"That might work against us," Eli says. "A picture of them being happy together."

"Okay, forget it," Charlotte says.

"Probably the cops will want to know what Daisy was wearing."

There's a long silence.

"I'm pretty sure it was her purple jacket. But I don't remember. I thought I did, but I don't. How could I *not* remember? Oh, Eli, how could I not remember?"

Another silence. Eli says, "I don't remember, either. I think she was wearing the purple jacket. But I'm not sure, either. It's the stress fogging our brains—that's why we can't remember. Okay, let's talk again in a little while."

"I love you," Charlotte says.

But Eli's already hung up, and Charlotte turns back to her brother.

"Rocco . . . you need to think. Do you have any idea where Ruth might go? Where she goes when she feels threatened? Her fucking happy place."

"Her grandparents'. Obviously. Right? She's always calling their house her reset button. Her spa, her yoga retreat, her . . ."

Charlotte knew that. Of course.

"She never took you there?"

"Several times we almost went. But something always came up. She's probably got her phone with her. But let me see if she's got their address or phone number somewhere—"

Rocco goes into the next room.

"Don't," he says when Charlotte tries to follow, and she has to obey. She can't go into Ruth's bedroom—*their* bedroom—uninvited. Not unless Rocco asks. Even when her child's been stolen, some boundaries still exist. She hears Rocco opening drawers. Something is knocked over and shatters.

Rocco says, "Oops!" Charlotte checks her phone.

The inhaler tracker app still isn't working.

When Rocco comes back into the living room, he sits down on the edge of the couch and buries his face in his hands.

Charlotte can't breathe. "What's wrong?"

"Good news. And bad news. I can't tell which. She left her phone on the nightstand."

"What does *that* mean? She doesn't want to get in touch with us. Or anyone. And she doesn't want to be found."

"That's the bad news. Speaking of being found, have you tried that app that lets you locate Daisy's inhaler? Crazy as Ruth is, I'm positive that she's taken the inhaler with them. I don't expect you to believe me, but I'm sure she won't harm Daisy. She cares about Daisy, or anyway, as much as . . ."

He can't finish the sentence.

"I just tried," says Charlotte. "It's not working. It keeps loading."

"Try again." Charlotte does what Rocco says. As if the result will be different when he's here with her.

The same spinning wheel. The same Oops! The same urge to throw the phone at the wall. Charlotte shows the phone to Rocco.

"She's probably figured out some way to disable it. I always thought Ruth was extremely tech-savvy for such a flake. It was one—only one—of the many things that didn't add up about her. Did you know she could speak Spanish?"

"It didn't seem like it, in Mexico."

"Well, she does. She hid it. Who knows what else

she was hiding? I have no idea who she is, or how her mind works. That's the shocking part."

"I don't understand," says Charlotte. "How can you live with someone and—"

Charlotte's ringtone sounds: It's Eli. He says, "The cops are here now. I'll call you when they leave."

She says, "Call me *before* they leave."

When she turns back to Rocco, he says, "Don't you want to hear the good news?"

"I really do," says Charlotte. "I want to hear *any* good news you can think of."

"The strange thing is, it's the same as the bad news. Her phone is here. Her contact list. We can call around and try to find her. I'll bet we can find out where her grandparents live. Maybe she's there, maybe they know where she is. That's where I'd start."

Rocco turns Ruth's phone on. He knows her passcode.

"Jesus Christ. You may not want to look at this."

Charlotte forces herself to look. The wallpaper on Ruth's phone is a photo of Ruth and Daisy, in an old-fashioned photo booth. It's from the same series as the picture that Daisy pasted in her book.

The expressions on Daisy's and Ruth's faces are goofier than in the photo in *Our Mexican Adventure*. Daisy's grinning so hard that her face must hurt, and she's bugging out her eyes. Charlotte has never seen that face before. The stabbing pain in her chest is so intense that she gasps.

Rocco takes Ruth's phone from Charlotte and scrolls through Ruth's recent calls.

"No." His voice is hushed. "This makes no sense. I don't get it. Unless she's trying to get me fired—"

"What? What is it?"

"The last half dozen calls she made were to Andrew John's office. Last night and early this morning. Maybe she wanted to lie about me."

"Maybe," Charlotte murmurs.

But somehow she knows that's not the reason that Ruth is calling Andrew John.

23

Seven Years Before

Charlotte

It had been the most beautiful summer day, the kind of day you live the rest of the year for, the kind of day you remember all winter.

This was before Daisy was born.

Eli was in Panama for a month, visiting his family. Buddenbrooks and Gladiola hadn't yet expanded. The business was still just the flower shop, and Alma was Charlotte's only employee. How happy they felt to come to work every day! How simple everything was!

Charlotte had no way of knowing that she would never again—or certainly not for a long time—feel so free, so unburdened.

That day, her only worry was about Rocco, who was

scheduled to get out of rehab in a few weeks. And she had no idea where he would live, where he would work, what he would do.

She'd hoped that Matt and Holly, her friends who ran the flower farm where she bought most of her stock, might find work for him. It would be good for him to be in the country. He would be happier than he would be in the city. It would be harder for him to get into trouble. Not so many bars and girls, not so much temptation.

Luckily, it was time for her annual trip to the farm. And during the wonderful annual lunch, Charlotte had asked Matt and Holly—she'd tried to sound casual and relaxed—if they knew of a job that Rocco might have. Maybe he could do something on their farm.

Matt and Holly were sorry, they couldn't. They themselves were just getting by.

Then Matt said, "What about Andrew John? I hear he's hiring. All the stuff he's been doing to restore the soil and plant cover crops and make the farm organic is finally done. This year he's planted his first market crops."

"Wouldn't it be awkward for you?" Holly asked. "I mean, it was *your* family farm, and now—"

"I don't know," Charlotte said. "Rocco might be

okay with it. All of that seems so far in the past. The old house is gone, so there wouldn't be that—"

Holly still looked dubious, but Matt said, "Think about it."

Charlotte did think about it. She thought about it so hard that she was distracted all through lunch.

She didn't really know Andrew John. In fact she didn't know him at all. The only time she'd met him was at the office during the real estate closing.

That day he'd been very gracious and smiled warmly when they were introduced. Then he'd sat more or less silently as his lawyer and Charlotte's lawyer arranged the transfer of the farm. Charlotte remembers the words *dazzlingly handsome* occurring to her. She'd been embarrassed even to *think* a cliché like that.

Now she had no idea how to get in touch with him. She could call or email his Manhattan office, but what were the chances of getting through? If she left it up to Rocco, it would never happen. Rocco would give up when the first unfriendly receptionist blew him off, or the first out-of-office reply email bounced back and discouraged him from going further.

Charlotte drank three glasses of wine at lunch with Matt and Holly. She probably shouldn't have been driving, but she felt okay. In fact she felt an infusion of courage, as if she'd been dosed with some intense shot of bravery that didn't feel like her natural state.

The force of her need to help Rocco made her turn off the road just past where her childhood home used to be. She headed up the long driveway to where she knew Andrew John lived.

She'd expected men with machine guns to come charging out of the bushes. But that didn't happen. She assumed that at least there would be a locked gate where you had to speak into a box or press a code. But there wasn't even that.

There was one car—a Range Rover—parked in front of the impossibly stylish, rectangular glass structure.

Andrew John answered the door. She explained who she was.

He smiled and said, "Of course. I remember you from the closing." He invited her in.

From the moment she stepped into the house, they both knew what was going to happen. It was *on.* Just like that. Eli, Andrew John's wife and children, their lives before and after this afternoon. None of that existed—or anyway, it had temporarily ceased to exist.

She was painfully self-conscious, aware of him watching her as she moved through the sleek, transparent box in which he lived, as close to nature as you could be without actually being outdoors. He watched her admire the view. He came and stood beside her.

It was as if she were observing herself from a distance—moving, speaking, listening, responding. Nothing she did was remotely like anything she would normally say or do. She wasn't walking the way she normally walked. She couldn't. He was watching.

She was prowling the edges of his house. And Andrew John watched her prowl.

The fact that she couldn't look at him was a sign of . . . what? Of how tall he was, how handsome he was, and (she had to admit) how rich and powerful he was. She'd never cared about any of that before. Now she finally understood the appeal.

She almost forgot why she was there—how desperately she wanted him to hire her brother.

He asked if she wanted a glass of wine. She nodded. He filled her glass, which almost immediately seemed to be empty, though she couldn't remember drinking it. He filled it again.

After the second glass she blurted out, "My brother, Rocco, needs a job. He can do a lot of things. He's very capable. He should work for you."

Andrew John said, "Sure. If it wouldn't be awkward . . ."

Charlotte said, "That would be up to you."

Just watching him *think* was exciting.

"Fine," he said. "I'll tell my assistant. Tell your brother to call my office."

After a while he asked if she would like to see the rest of the house.

He took her hand as they walked down the hall. Neither of them had any doubts about the fact that this wasn't your neutral, ordinary house tour.

He would have hired Rocco even if she hadn't slept with him. This wasn't a quid pro quo business deal. The only thing exchanged between them was pleasure and how good it felt.

They never mentioned Eli, or the Argentine wife and two children she'd seen on the internet. That would have spoiled everything. Neither wanted anything more. Neither wanted to see the other like this again; neither wanted whatever this was to go any further.

In the morning they kissed goodbye. A friendly, affectionate kiss. Charlotte turned her phone back on. She hadn't even realized that she'd turned it off.

Eli called on her drive back to the city. She said she'd slept over at Matt and Holly's farm. Sometimes she did that. He'd never check.

She was good at repressing things. She had—she still

has—a talent for not thinking about what she doesn't want to think about.

Driving back to the city from Andrew John's, she wondered when she would stop thinking about him. Soon, she decided. What had happened in his glass house would begin to seem unreal, almost as if it never occurred.

The memory was already beginning to fade by the time she got to the FDR Drive.

She assumed that Andrew John wouldn't think about her, either. He had a wife and kids and a mega-farm to run.

And she *would* have forgotten about it. Well, maybe not forgotten, but chalked it up as one of those things that happen . . . except that three months later she found out that she was pregnant.

Eli had been home from Panama for only two months. She waited another month to tell him.

She'd never lied to Eli before or after. Only that one time. She began to have trouble sleeping, until the pregnancy hormones kicked in and she slept all the time.

Eli never did the math. He had no reason to doubt her. Of course he thought the baby was his. Who else's could it possibly be?

It was lucky, in a way, that the one time she cheated on him had been with a man who looked a little like Eli. Not exactly. But close enough. Eli chose not to notice the differences between himself and Daisy. If he had, he might have said that some Panamanian great-grandma was showing up generations later.

Did the truth occur to Andrew John when he and Rocco chatted about their families and Rocco mentioned his niece? Andrew John worked with numbers. But it was not in his interest to calculate precisely when his employee's niece was born.

Charlotte and Eli and Daisy were happy. Their lives were peaceful and loving. It wasn't that she kept silent because she wanted to lie to Eli, or even to protect herself.

She was protecting Daisy. The fallout from Charlotte's confessing the truth would have been like a bomb blowing up their happy home, like an act of violence directed at the baby. Not that Eli would have been violent. But their lives would have exploded. And as the youngest and most vulnerable, Daisy would have suffered the most. Charlotte had often thought that Daisy's asthma was Charlotte's punishment for what she'd done. She knew it was irrational, but she couldn't help it. And it was something she'd have to live with.

Charlotte told no one but her therapist. And no one else ever knew.

But now, it seems, Ruth knows. Somehow she guessed. Or found out. Ted said that disturbed, unhappy people often have superior powers of intuition. They pick up on signals.

Was that why Ruth called Andrew John? To say that she has his daughter? That she is holding his daughter hostage? To blackmail him in some way? Unless it's what Rocco suggested: that Ruth is planning to lie about Rocco as revenge for his breaking up with her.

Ruth assaulted Reyna. She's capable of violence.

It's too late for good manners. Charlotte pushes past Rocco into the bedroom. The room is girly in a hippie sort of way, with a Persian scarf over the lampshade casting everything in a red glow. But it stinks of whiskey and sweat and sleep. Charlotte holds her breath.

In the corner is a small desk, and on it a stack of photos. Who prints out photos anymore? Everyone keeps them on their phone or on their Instagram accounts.

Except for people who want other people to find a certain picture.

Some gravity draws Charlotte over to the photos.

And there on the top of the pile is a picture of her therapist.

Ted.

He's sitting at a restaurant. He has a glass of wine in his hands. He's toasting the person taking the picture. He looks besotted; his mouth is slack with desire. Charlotte has never seen that expression on his face. She has to look hard to be sure it's him.

How did Ruth find out his name? Then Charlotte remembers. That very first time, when Ruth showed up at the shop and they went out for coffee. Ruth claimed she used to date a therapist named Ted. She just had the tenses wrong. She *was going to* sleep with a therapist named Ted. She would hunt him down and seduce him to find out about Charlotte and Rocco.

Charlotte feels as if she's been punched.

She runs back into the living room and thrusts the picture at Rocco, like an accusation.

"Who's that?"

He scrutinizes the photo.

"Oh, that guy. He's a friend of her grandma and grandpa's. I think she slept with him a couple of times. She used to do kinky stuff like that. Sleep with old guys. Before we met."

"*After* you met," says Charlotte. "While she was

with you. That's Ted. My therapist. That's why she sought him out and fucked him. Because he's my therapist. Because he knows things about us that she wanted to know."

"*That* Ted?"

How did Ruth get to Ted? Seduce him, is how it looks. Plied him with wine and sex. How could Ted be so unprofessional? He's been Charlotte's therapist for nearly a decade. She trusted him more than anyone in the world. What did Ruth have? Some way to make an older man feel that he was still young and hot.

Trust no one, Charlotte thinks now.

She stole Ruth's passport. Which means that she isn't exactly trustworthy herself. Why should she expect it from others?

Rocco sinks onto the couch. "That's the thing with Ruth. Every second with her is like falling down the rabbit hole."

Charlotte thinks of those last phone conversations with Ted. Why did he bother telling her that a woman had called asking for information about her childhood? Was he trying to warn her about Ruth? Why did he say her name was Naomi? Was that the name Ruth gave him? Why did he tell Charlotte to be careful? Because he'd already slept with Ruth or Naomi or whoever she is and revealed Charlotte's secret? How did Ruth get it out of him? Charlotte may never know. Doctors can be sued for doing things like this.

First things first. She needs to find Daisy.

She phones Ted. The calls goes to voice mail. Of course.

"Call Andrew John," she tells Rocco.

"Why?"

"Just because. Call him!"

Rocco calls Andrew John's office number and after a brief conversation tells Charlotte, "Actually, he's in Argentina."

"Do you have his number there?"

"Yes . . . but I'm only supposed to use it in case of an extreme emergency."

"This is an extreme emergency. Call him." The big sister's giving an order, and she half expects Rocco to rebel. But it's too late for that. He's too guilty.

"I never call him at home," says Rocco. "I've never done anything like that. I wouldn't—"

"Now you are," says Charlotte. "Your niece is missing, and the kidnapper has been calling him."

Rocco goes into the bedroom. Charlotte can hear him through the open door.

"I'm sorry . . . I know . . . I wouldn't. I don't, except I need to ask you one question. Do you know a woman named Ruth Seagram? Yes, that's right. My girlfriend. My ex-girlfriend. Have you ever met her?

"Okay," Rocco says at last. "I thought so."

He notices Charlotte watching from the doorway, and he shakes his head.

Charlotte says, "Ask him if he knows a Naomi."

Rocco listens. Then he says, "He says that he's heard that a woman named Naomi has been calling his office and saying it's urgent. He gets a lot of trolls and cranks and stalkers. His staff assumed it was one of those, though they always report the calls to him, so he can be on guard, just in case."

24

Ruth

In Catholic school we learned about the seven deadly
sins. The nuns said the worst is pride. But I think
it's envy. Envy hurts the most. I used to envy kids with
nicer houses, better clothes, more money. I envied every
kid whose mother didn't leave them with their grandparents and run off to Arizona the way my mother did.

And now I envy Charlotte. Why does she get the
beautiful loft, the cute husband, the brilliant daughter?
Why does she get paid for fooling around with flowers? Why does her mom get to live in a cool house in
Mexico with a servant and tons of friends? Why does
everyone get everything, and I get a dark apartment
over a superfund site in Greenpoint and a job at a start-
up that never started up?

Oh, and I forgot. I get an alcoholic fiancé who is breaking off our engagement.

Envy is a disease. Your sick soul tells you that you want to have what that other person has.

I don't want to *take* Daisy. That's not what I mean to do. She loves her parents. She thinks Eli is her real dad, which is probably better for her. She loves and needs her mom and dad. But I don't see why I can't borrow her for a while. I don't understand why I can't just spend a day with her as if she were my daughter, why I can't have some fun with her, just for a day . . .

I'd been thinking about it. About taking her without asking Charlotte, who would never let me do it.

But I wasn't planning to do it today. And maybe I wouldn't have if Rocco hadn't said we were breaking up. If he hadn't accused me of hurting Reyna. Which I would never *ever* do. It's true I texted her, pretending to be Rocco. But I only wanted to talk to her, to tell her to stay away from Rocco, who was so obviously attracted to her.

I wouldn't have taken Daisy today if things hadn't lined up so perfectly. One thing led to another so smoothly—it would have been stupid not to make this day the special day I get to hang out with Daisy. And I knew that if Rocco and I do break up, I might never get another chance.

Rocco started drinking again on the plane. It was late when we got home. He was acting weird. I understood why he'd had to quit drinking. He grabbed me by the arm, which he'd never done before. He'd never done anything like it.

He said he knew I had a bottle of something stashed away, that I was only pretending not to drink when he was around.

"Busted," I said. "Whatever." I got the scotch from the back of the closet, the wine from under the bed. I retrieved the six-pack from my laundry basket and put it in the fridge.

He drank everything I had, and then he passed out. I kept checking to see if he was still breathing.

This morning he woke up just long enough to tell me that we were breaking up. He's leaving me. He isn't even sorry.

He accused me of attacking Reyna. Which I never did. I told Rocco that I'd gone out and met the driver in the park near where Reyna got hurt. I said that the driver had lied, and that his conscience had started to bother him, and he wanted to give us back the money.

Rocco was in no shape for me to start an argument. We'd deal with all that later. We should probably have a serious talk about what happened in Mexico, especially if we're going to start telling his family that we're engaged.

For now I just want my passport back. That's why I'm going to Charlotte's. I know she has it. She took it. It was in my purse in the van—and then it wasn't. I wasn't imagining things. I don't make mistakes like that.

There's only one explanation. She did it to keep me in Mexico, so I wouldn't come home and blow the whistle on her. So I wouldn't tell her charming husband what I'd heard from her horny therapist, Ted.

Getting the truth out of Ted was the easiest thing I ever did. Basically all it took was one "session" in his office, during which he told me that he couldn't "treat" me since he was already "treating" Charlotte. I was dying to go through his files and find the notes on his sessions with Charlotte, but he didn't leave me alone long enough. So I had to find another way.

"Okay, Doc," I said. "How about if I 'treat' you?"

Two bottles of wine at a bar, and he was so loaded he didn't even know I was taking his picture so I could show Charlotte someday. Then we had our sleepover at his place; then he told me everything I wanted to know. He was supposed to be a professional. Maybe he was losing it. Maybe he wanted out of the "profession." I was lucky enough to be in the right place at the right time. He told me exactly what I needed.

The sexiest thing—the *only* sexy thing—about our hookup was knowing that Charlotte had paid this guy a fortune over the years, and all it took was one medium-good old-guy orgasm (and one fake orgasm on my part) for him to tell me the very last thing Charlotte wanted me to know.

I knew Charlotte would never answer her phone if I called. Even if she was worried about Rocco, which she probably was, she'd be even more worried about me ruining her life. Telling her husband about Andrew John—and telling everyone that she stole my passport.

She was probably sleeping in late. She and Eli and Daisy got home just before Rocco and I did. Their flight was delayed. I checked their arrival time online.

I decided: I'll go to her house and confront her. She'll hand over the passport, if she still has it. If she hasn't ditched it somewhere. Not that it will do me any good now. I reported it lost in Mexico, and they had to cancel it, so I have to apply for a new one. But I want her to admit it. I want to see how scared she is about what I can tell her husband.

Eli, I hate to be the bearer of bad news, but your wife stole my passport. Oh, and by the way, your daughter's not your daughter.

It takes me a while to get dressed, tiptoeing around passed-out Rocco and deciding on my look. Business-like, no nonsense. I dig out one of the power suits I used to wear to the start-up. I even wear little heels and the fuzzy Prada vest I bought at the resale shop on East 11th.

I take the train to her house. It's around two when I get there. I ring and ring her doorbell. She knows it's me, and she isn't answering. I ring a few more times.

Finally a man walks out of the front door.

My first thought is: How can this greasy creep live in a building where the lofts cost $4 million? Maybe he's a famous actor who plays the pervy killer on TV crime shows.

He says, "Are you the fucking idiot who's ringing and ringing? They're not home, and my mother and I can hear the bell through the ceiling, and it's driving us nuts."

He is *not* an actor. He's the downstairs neighbor whom Charlotte and Eli feel so superior to and complain about.

"They're all gone?"

"They left this morning. I saw them from my

window. First the bitch, and then her bitch husband with the little girl, off to school."

"There's been some kind of mix-up," I say. "I couldn't reach Charlotte or Eli, so I decided to show up and—"

"Who the fuck are you?"

I take a deep breath. He's never seen me, he couldn't know—

"I'm Daisy's nanny. Who are *you*?" I ask, though I'm pretty sure I already know.

"I'm Drew. Their downstairs neighbor. How come I never saw you?"

"She hired me two weeks ago," I say. "Just before they left for Mexico."

He seems to know they went to Mexico. Maybe Eli told him. My having this information seems to make my story more credible.

It's as if a voice is telling me what to say. It happens every so often, and I can only step back and admire that force speaking through me. Speaking through the person Naomi has become. Through Ruth.

"I need you to do me a favor." I look at him in a way that worked on Rocco and even worked on Charlotte's therapist. A look that works on most men, I've discovered.

"What would that favor be?" he says warily.

"I have to pick up Daisy at school. But I'm feeling really sick. I need someone to watch her in case I have some kind of emergency." I gaze into the beady eyes behind his filthy glasses. I'm improvising now. I'm not sure that I even want him along, except that I know that Charlotte will be *really* scared if the school tells her that I was with someone fitting Drew's description. Or if Drew tells her that I asked him to go with me.

"How long will this take?" he asks. As if he's got somewhere important to be.

"Two hours, I promise. No more."

It's the most interesting offer he's had in a while.

"I'm in," he says.

That's when the whole plan locks in. I don't know exactly how, but it does. That's when I *really* decide— today will be the day.

I'd much rather have Daisy than confront her mother about my passport.

The next thing I know, I'm on the subway with creepy Drew. Going to pick up Daisy. My heart is beating so hard I'm afraid even Drew can hear it over the roar of the train.

Helicopter Charlotte would never allow it. But I can be creative. I can think for myself. I don't need anyone's permission.

I can pick Daisy up from school and take her to

Hoboken to meet Grandpa Frank and Granny Edith. They would love meeting Daisy. And Daisy will always remember the funny old people in their time-travel house.

I'm nervous, picking up Daisy. What if some nosy teacher insists on calling Charlotte? But all my anxiety disappears when Daisy is so obviously happy to see me. That settles it. I'm not doing anything wrong. We'll just have a little fun, and then I'll return her, unharmed.

"Auntie Ruth!" she cries, running toward me across the gym, proving our closeness and my trustworthiness, credentials even better than my name on the pickup list, where it's been since Rocco and I took her to the circus. I'd taken a risk, since Charlotte could have crossed off my name. But she must have forgotten. She must have been too busy with her fabulous life.

Daisy's delighted to see me. Drew not so much.

She shrinks away from him when he tries to pat her head.

The after-school teachers can't help noticing, but I smile at them and put my finger to my lips, as if that will keep Drew from hearing me whisper, "My cousin." And I give them a little eye roll, meaning: Not quite right in the head.

Not that it matters. I'm on the list.

The kindly women who oversee the after-school

program ask for my ID, and one of them writes down my name. But they never doubt that Daisy's mom approved this. I'm doing the family a favor. I sign Daisy out with a casual flourish. I write: *Ruth Seagram.* Why not?

Daisy doesn't seem surprised. She doesn't ask questions, doesn't ask if something's wrong, doesn't ask why I'm there and not Mommy.

I kneel and zip up Daisy's cute bright purple quilted jacket. That's the hard part—so far. The zipper sticks, and I have to try not to seem impatient or afraid that I will never be able to do it. Finally, success! After that, we're coasting. We find her backpack, and as we head out, I locate her inhaler.

Daisy watches me flip the switch that disables the tracking device.

She asks, "Why are you doing that?"

"We don't want the batteries running low." A reasonable, grown-up answer. Everyone has a right to privacy—even a child and her favorite aunt.

Daisy and I will be free. That's why I left my phone at home. Even if I turn it off, someone can tell where I am, and probably listen to what I'm saying. Now we can spend an afternoon having fun without Electronic Mom tracking our every move. If Daisy has an asthma attack, which she won't, I won't need an app to find her inhaler. Which is more than you can say for her parents.

I was just going to confront Charlotte about my passport. But intuition is a funny thing. Somehow I must have known that, by the end of the day, my plans would include Daisy.

Otherwise why would I have left my phone at home?

In that moment I'm conscious of a possible mistake. I should have wiped my contacts list. If Rocco finds my phone . . .

There's no time to worry about that. Whatever happens, happens. For the moment I'm happy. We're free.

Hand in hand, Daisy and I exit the gym.

I hardly notice Drew tagging after us.

He says, "I thought you said you was her nanny. But I just heard you say that you're her aunt."

"In fact I'm a little of both. Thanks for everything." I grab Daisy's hand, and we ditch Drew the moment we get outside.

"What happened to that guy?" Daisy asks. "Isn't he that bad guy downstairs in our building who smokes?"

"Nothing happened to him," I say. "He left. He didn't want to play with us. He went home."

Another mistake. Maybe.

"Should we go home?" Daisy asks.

"Later. Let's go. Ready? We're going to have fun."

"Did Mom send you?" Brilliant Daisy waited until there's no official busybody around to listen.

"Sure. Your mom told me, Aunt Ruth, could you please pick up Daisy and go out on a fantastic fun adventure?"

"What kind of adventure?"

"It's a secret. I can't tell. Except that it involves candy."

"Cool," Daisy says. "Let's go."

This is what Charlotte gets to enjoy every day. I can't help wanting what she has. Who could blame me? I want it too. I want a beautiful, brilliant little daughter to pick up after school.

Just once.

25

Charlotte

Rocco scrolls through Ruth's contact list.

"Bingo!" he says. "Here's 'Mom.' Let's start with her. Whom I've also never met or spoken to. You call her, Charlotte. It's better if a woman calls, looking for her friend. Not some guy who's stalking her, some old boyfriend or worse. Who knows what her mother's heard about me, if she's heard about me at all. How many pissed-off guys Ruth has on her trail, or men she's scammed, or whatever—"

How long has it been since Ruth took Daisy? Where did they go? The pressure of wanting to turn back the clock feels like a fist pressing into Charlotte's sternum, a bully not wanting to hurt her but just scare her. Scare her a lot.

She says, "If I dial from Ruth's phone, maybe her mother will think it's her and pick up."

"Knowing Ruth, maybe her mother will think it's her—and *not* pick up. But it's worth a try. If the mother doesn't answer, we can wait awhile and call back on your phone."

"We don't have a while," Charlotte says.

Rocco presses the number with the Arizona area code and hands the phone to his sister.

A woman says hello. No regional accent, no obvious age. Purified of anything that might distinguish her from her neighbors.

"Hello, Naomi," she says. Her voice is cold. "What do you want now?"

Very slowly and, she hopes, unthreateningly, Charlotte says, "Actually, I'm a friend of your daughter, Ruth. Not a very close friend—I don't know her that well. We went out for dinner yesterday evening, and she left her phone on the table in the restaurant. I can't remember her address, and I'm trying to get in touch with her, so I took the liberty of trying the number that said 'Mom.' I'm trying to figure out where she lives so I can—"

The woman (Mom) says, "She told you her name is Ruth? That's what she tells everybody. Her name is Naomi. I should know. I named her. But as soon as she was old enough to read the Bible, she began to say I'd named her after the wrong person in that story. She said, Naomi's the one who *has* to go to another country, Ruth's the one who *chooses* to go with her. My daughter was determined that she was the one who was going to do the choosing. She changed her name to Ruth as soon as she was old enough. But her real name is Naomi, and she knows it. Naomi always had a chip on her shoulder. You know she lies. She hasn't said one true word since she learned to talk. She doesn't know the difference between telling the truth and lying."

Rocco registers Charlotte's astonishment. He mouths the words: "What's she saying?" Charlotte could put Ruth's mother on speakerphone, but she's afraid of an echo. She pantomimes writing, and when Rocco brings her his phone, open to the memo app, she types in, Ruth's name = Naomi.

It's difficult listening and writing—*and* conducting a deeply unnerving conversation. But Charlotte will do whatever she has to do in order to find Daisy.

"Holy shit," Rocco says. The woman hears a male voice, though not, Charlotte hopes, what it says, and she audibly tenses: a thread just slightly pulled.

They were right to have Charlotte call. Ruth's mother might not have spoken to Rocco.

"I assume you know the Bible story," Ruth's mother

says. "Ruth's mother-in-law—Naomi—loses her husband and sons and has to go back where she comes from. Ruth insists on going with her. They meet this rich man, Boaz, who owns the land they're harvesting, and Ruth puts on her nicest clothes and perfume and slips into Boaz's tent and sleeps at his feet, and he's so impressed he marries her. That's the one, the ambitious one, the nervy one, the one my daughter wanted to be—"

Charlotte thinks she's going mad. Her daughter is missing, and this woman is telling her Bible stories. But she can't explain why she has no time to chat, why this is so urgent. A kidnapped daughter is an emergency. Wanting to return a misplaced cell phone is not.

Charlotte is lying to Ruth's mother. Ruth's a liar, and now she's turned Charlotte into one too.

The woman says, "Wait. Is everything okay? Has something happened to Naomi?" She must have heard an off note in Charlotte's voice.

"No, not at all." Charlotte's proud of how quickly she's thinking. "She's fine. She said she was going to her grandparents' house in Hoboken, and I'm going to be passing right near there today. I could just swing by and drop off her phone. We live in Montclair, which isn't far away."

Her knowledge of New Jersey must be coming from

God. Charlotte has no idea if Hoboken is anywhere near Montclair. "I know how inconvenient it is, trying to function without your phone. Ruth—I mean, Naomi—must be having a hard time—"

The silence lasts so long that Charlotte says, "Hello? Are you there?"

"Are you *sure* you're friends with her? How *good* a friend?"

"Pretty good?" Why does that sound like a question?

"Because the truth is: Naomi's grandparents have been dead for ten years. She told you they were alive? How typical."

Charlotte's hand is shaking as she types: Grandparents dead 10 yrs.

Rocco's grown alarmingly pale, but Charlotte needs to focus.

"Let me guess. I'll bet she's told you that her grandparents are angels who treated her like the princess she is. I bet she told you that they're totally responsible for her health and happiness. Her sanity. That they saved her from her cruel witch of a mother who abandoned her. Am I right?"

Charlotte has a bad feeling about where this is heading, but she has to tell the truth. Or whatever version of the truth she knows.

"She speaks about her grandparents so lovingly—"

"My parents were monsters from hell, both of them. One summer, I made the mistake of leaving Naomi with them because I was having some personal problems. And when I returned to collect my daughter in the fall, I learned that every time she'd talked back or annoyed them in any way, every time they caught her in a tiny white lie, they'd lock her in the basement, which—or so Naomi told me—was crawling with enormous wolf spiders.

"By then I'd learned not to believe her, but my parents said she was telling the truth. About the spiders, anyway. My parents weren't even the tiniest bit embarrassed. They said they'd been trying to teach her a lesson, to make her behave like a lady. A little lady, they said. Sometimes they starved her for days until she begged for food and water. My father drowned her cat, and I'm pretty certain he made her watch the cat die. And my God, the way my parents died—"

"I'm so sorry. I don't mean to pry, but how—"

"It's no secret. It was in all the papers. My father dragged my mother down into the basement and locked them in. He shot her and then he shot himself. He died instantly, but it took her longer."

"That's terrible," says Charlotte. "I'm so sorry."

"Then you must be sorrier than I am. The terrible part was that it made it damn hard to sell the house. At least Naomi got some of the money when they finally closed. Some payback for what she went through."

"I must have misunderstood," says Charlotte. "She always talks about going to their house. She says she still goes there all the time—"

"Oh, no," says the woman. "I hope not. *Not again*."

"Not *what* again?"

"My parents' house sat on the market for a *very* long time. Given how hot that neighborhood suddenly was, it should have sold in a flash. Or so the real estate agents kept telling me. That neighborhood being 'hot' was beyond *my* imagination. But anyway, a murder-suicide house is a tough sell."

Charlotte's daughter is missing, and this woman has shifted from Bible stories to real estate.

"During the time the place sat empty, Naomi was picked up by the cops for loitering near the house. The real estate agents had to change the locks. Supposedly she harassed—or threatened or *something*—some people renovating one of the brownstones down the block. The neighbors got nervous. Naomi called me from the police station. That's what it took to make her get in touch with me. I think she blamed me for her grandparents' deaths, just like she blamed me for everything. But of course I had nothing to do with it."

It crosses Charlotte's mind that maybe the woman

isn't telling the truth about any of this, that maybe Ruth learned to lie from her mother. But somehow Charlotte believes her.

"The police let Naomi go, with a slap on the wrist, and without even a restraining order. The grief-stricken granddaughter, et cetera. Even in New Jersey, people have a heart."

Charlotte says, "Do you know the address? The house where your parents' lived?"

She's actively praying now. Please make this work.

"You're asking me if I know my own parents' address? How could I forget something like that? It's 129 South High Street, Hoboken."

"Thanks for your help," Charlotte says. "I'll give . . . Naomi your regards."

"Giving her the phone will be enough. And do please tell her to call me. But . . . maybe it would probably be better if you don't let her know I told you any of this. She tends to lash out when she feels threatened."

Charlotte had thought she couldn't feel more terrified than she already was. But now she does. She's shaking so hard she nearly drops the phone when she hands it back to Rocco.

When the line goes dead, Rocco says, "Can we keep calling her Ruth?"

"I think we have to," says Charlotte. "Ruth is the person we know."

"We didn't even know her fucking name," Rocco says. "She pretends to go out to Hoboken. She pretends to visit the dead. Can you believe that?"

"I do," says Charlotte. "I actually do."

"Call Eli one more time," Rocco says. "I'll go get the van. Let's drive out to Hoboken. I have a feeling that her grandparents' house is the first place we should look."

"They don't live there anymore," Charlotte says. "They don't live anywhere anymore."

"Please," Rocco says. "I got us into this mess, and I'll get us out."

It's a cliché, but Charlotte clings to it, like a drowning person clings to a hunk of driftwood.

"It's worth a try, I guess." Not for one moment does she think it will work, that they'll find Daisy at the house where Ruth's grandparents died horribly, a decade ago.

"I'll make it right," promises Rocco.

More than anything in the world, Charlotte wants to believe her brother. For just an instant, the terror subsides, and then it rolls back in again, like an icy wave with a murderous undertow.

26

Ruth

First stop is the candy store in Union Square, the place where Daisy's mom is least likely to take her, where we're least likely to run into Charlotte. Candy is sold by the pound, and the fun part is letting the candy out of giant funnels, sort of like lab equipment, from which the Technicolor sugary bits pour and rattle into paper bags. It's all you can eat, more than you can eat, more candy than a child with the biggest sweet tooth can imagine. It's a cosmos of candy, created for children, a world that grown-ups can only observe from the sidelines.

Daisy runs from funnel to funnel. At first I help her, but she quickly gets the knack of operating the stops that release and shut off the floods of candy.

"Is there some kind of candy *you* want, Auntie Ruth?" Daisy pauses to ask, though only after she has almost filled her bag.

"No," I say. "Have a little more. Make sure we have plenty for later. And we'll have to eat it all, because you know what your mom will say if we bring all this candy home, or even if we tell her how much we ate."

"All of it?" says Daisy. "We have to eat it all?"

"Every piece," I say.

Daisy nods solemnly. A pact has been made: Whatever happens this afternoon will be kept secret from her mother. What happens in the candy store stays in the candy store.

"What's so funny?" asks Daisy.

"Nothing," I say. "Just thinking."

"Are you *sure* that this is okay with my mom?"

"Sure I'm sure. I mean, I'm probably sure."

"You said 'sure' three times," says Daisy.

I'm a little surprised by how quickly Daisy agrees to lie (though we won't call it that) to her mother. But when candy and kids are involved, the normal rules don't apply, and the truth is endlessly elastic.

Daisy scrupulously avoids sampling the merchandise, unlike the other children stuffing their mouths, all over the store. The sugar will come in handy for the energy we'll need to get through the day and bring Daisy home—and face the music.

The young woman (blue hair, nose ring) at the checkout counter weighs the candy—two outrageous sugary pounds!—and asks Daisy if she plans to eat it all herself. The question throws Daisy into a panic. What grown-up will allow that? But she has no one to share the loot with, no siblings, no cousins, and, as far as I can tell, no friends. Except me. Daisy looks down and grabs my hand.

What would Charlotte do in this situation? Charlotte would never *be* in this situation. Charlotte would never let her daughter buy two pounds of candy.

That's the good thing about dropping in and out of Daisy's life. Everyday reality is not an issue. This might be my last day with Daisy. It almost surely is. Two pounds of candy, thank you very much.

To rescue Daisy from the overfriendly checkout person, and put a stop to my own gloomy fears about possibly going to jail for kidnapping and certainly never seeing Daisy again, I say, a little too brightly, "We're bringing it to share with her great-grandparents in New Jersey."

I have the checkout girl at *great-grandparents*. She doesn't stop to wonder: Who brings an elderly couple two pounds of obscenely bright, sweet candy?

"Great-grandparents!" She crosses herself—a strange thing for a punked-out girl to do. "God bless them."

"Totally." I pay in cash—I've borrowed a little from Rocco—and we sail out into the crowded Union Square afternoon.

The bag is so heavy that Daisy can't carry it and eat at the same time, so she hands it to me, and we walk west on 14th Street, sharing sweets. Until then I'd never believed that sugar was a rush. I'd thought it was the fantasy of parents worried about dental bills. But it's definitely a high. It turns up the volume, the color, the speed. No wonder children crave it.

All around us are moms and kids, dads and kids, nannies and kids, kids being walked home from school. It's a city—a world—full of children. For the first time, maybe ever, I don't feel sick with envy. For the first time I have a child of my own.

Daisy and I are happier than these strangers could possibly be. This is our once-in-a-lifetime special day. We appreciate it more, and we have enough sweets to sustain us, however long our adventure lasts.

On the PATH, it's rush hour 24/7, so the crowd is no surprise. But it's surprising that a child works like a magic charm to protect you from the wolves and monsters underground. Or that's how it seems today.

The wolves and monsters get up to give us seats on the train.

Daisy's looking around, delighted. She's fallen down the rabbit hole into a wonderland beneath the city. It's as if she's a feral child who's wandered into civilization, an outer space alien landed on Earth, or a mermaid washed up on land. All this is new to her, or almost new, and the thrill of newness is contagious. Everyone in the train catches her excitement. They must think we're from out of town.

"Do you take the train much, Daisy?"

It's an unfair question. I already know the answer.

"Some. Not much. Mostly taxis."

"The train's a lot more fun," I say.

"Really fun," says Daisy.

27

Vanessa

Vanessa should be at work, but she longs—the way she might long for a lover—to go to Hoboken and check on the renovation. The house *is* like a lover. It was love at first sight. She fell in love the moment she saw it. It's the place where she and Brian were destined to raise the kids.

They were shocked that they could afford it, but the real estate agent was honest about the reason for the bargain price. She had to be, by law. A crime had been committed here, a decade ago. A very old couple had lived and died here: a murder-suicide in the basement. It was awful, but Vanessa thinks it's the *only* serious crime she can sort of understand. She and Brian are going to grow old together, and if one of them was in horrible pain, or end-stage dementia, and didn't want to live . . . she can imagine. You pray it never happens. But it does.

The house sat on the market for ages. The old couple's granddaughter tried to buy it, but they hadn't left a will, and by the time things were sorted out, the granddaughter got a chunk of cash from the estate but not enough to buy the house. Or she couldn't get a mortgage. Or something.

Someone—an investor—bought it and never lived here, never intended to. The developer lost interest or went out of business—the real estate agent wasn't sure—and the house fell into disrepair. All that time, it was waiting for Vanessa and Brian and their kids, for buyers with the courage and energy to show the house the love it needs.

The house is the first thing Vanessa thinks about when she wakes up in the morning and the last thing before she falls asleep at night. It *is* like a love affair. She can't wait to move in, to furnish it, to have a kitchen and a dining room and—

She reminds herself to be patient. But still, she can't help going to the house, more often than she probably should, just to see what's happening, how things are coming along.

Of course, it's never going as fast as she hopes.

Everyone says: Renovations take twice as long and cost three times as much as you expect. But every tiny sign of progress fills Vanessa with joy.

Today she arrives to find more cracked paint removed from the staircase, exposing the beautiful wood underneath. An incremental improvement, but a step in the right direction. The house smells awful. It's full of toxic fumes from the industrial-strength paint remover.

But the woodwork is beautiful. And she loves it.

Vanessa tells herself she'll only stay a little while and then go back to work. Brian will feed the kids and put them to bed if he has to. He'll understand. He knows how much she loves the house.

She walks from room to room, then sits on the bottom step of the staircase that leads from the front hall. It's not the most comfortable place, but it's the only spot there is to sit.

That's when she hears the doorbell ring—amazing!

She didn't know the bell worked.

She looks up to see a woman and a very pretty little girl in a bright purple jacket.

They're standing on the top step.

Staring at her, through the window.

28

Ruth

Granny Edith and Grandpa Frank's neighbors never liked me. They still eye me with suspicion. No matter how often they see me with my grandparents, they act as if I'm a stranger come to steal their money. So Daisy and I are careful to walk on the other side of the street.

I can see my grandparents' brownstone from the corner the way you might notice a cool guy at a party. Not necessarily the handsomest guy, but the one you want to see.

At last we're across from the house. Does Daisy sense my happiness? She can't help it.

My feet know the front steps, their height and depth. I could climb them blindfolded, but climbing stairs with your eyes shut isn't something I want to teach Daisy. Plus I would miss seeing the banisters and the stone urns in which Granny plants pansies and nasturtiums every spring.

The front door has a decorative pattern of cast iron over glass, so you could say there are bars on the door, like Rocco's mom has in Mexico. But these never seem like bars. They're more like a maze through which I can always find my way.

I've forgotten my key, which is strange. I never do. I need it for when I come in late at night. When my grandparents are watching TV, they don't always hear me ring the bell. And they've finally begun to listen to me about keeping the door locked, for safety.

But today it's early, so they'll be closer to the front of the house, though Granny Edith may have the vacuum running, which she does so often that it's a wonder the house ever gets dirty enough to clean.

I ring the bell. It's hard to see through the windows, which are always dusty, no matter how much I tell Granny Edith to hire someone who can get to the places she can't reach.

If I move to the edge of the steps and lean over as far as I can, I can just see inside. There's a ladder and tarps on the floor and all the way up the stairs. Could my grandparents have started renovating without me? A shiver of . . . something . . . icy cold travels from one shoulder blade to another.

At last a young woman answers. She's wearing jeans and a sweater, the kind of sporty clothes that have that infuriating way of signaling that her outfit may look casual but really it's expensive. It's a look I aim for and can pull off pretty well, but never as well as this woman does. I aim for the look of the weekend guest heading out to Montauk, but women like her *own* the Montauk house. They're the hostesses who invited me—but only for the weekend! Come Sunday night, I crawl right back into the hole I crawled out of.

The woman looks like Charlotte. That is, she has Charlotte's vibe. The loving, confident mother. Today's hip, stylish young mom. The lady of the manor. The woman whom everyone is supposed to envy. And I do. Oh, I do. Envy breaks out in a light film of sweat on my forehead. I hate this woman already, though none of this is her fault. She's just being who she is. She's probably snagged the sort of rich husband who would never even buy me a drink if I hit on him in a bar.

"I'm looking for my grandparents, Edith and Frank Sloane."

She's obviously puzzled. But she smiles at Daisy, as

if to reassure herself that we're not home invaders about to tie her up, duct-tape her mouth, and pistol-whip her into giving us the keys to the safe.

What have we got in that bag? Candy! Again, it's a good thing I'm nicely dressed. We're not selling anything. Not even Girl Scout cookies, though a "homeowner" might find that charming. Nor are we Jehovah's Witnesses, the most likely possibility when a strange woman appears on your doorstep with a child.

There's a funny look on her face, though, as if my grandparents' names are ringing a bell—and it's not a bell she likes the sound of.

"I'm not sure . . . maybe they were the owners before the owner we bought it from. Before the owners before that—" She laughs, but Daisy and I don't think it's funny.

"They probably were!" I can play along if she wants to pretend that she lives here. Something about me must be alarming, though, because I can watch her decide that she's not going to be helpful.

That's going to be a problem for her, though she doesn't know it yet. How could she?

"I'm sorry, you must have the wrong house." She really believes what she's saying.

But we don't have the wrong house. This is the right house.

I'm stunned by a flash of understanding. Shocking, but probably true: She must have done something to my grandparents. *She's* the home invader holding them prisoner. *How could anyone do that to two sweet old people?*

She doesn't look like a criminal, but everyone knows that the worst offenders wear the most innocent disguises.

And then I know. That bad thing I always imagined happening in my grandparents' basement . . . well, now it's happened. And I wasn't here to stop it. I wasn't here to protect Granny Edith and Grandpa Frank. I was far from home, trying to enter a filthy disgusting world that doesn't want me.

I was always terrified of my grandparents' basement. Only now do I understand why.

I thought it was about spiders. But the truth is: I was seeing the future. I foresaw that they'd be locked up in the basement where—the thought makes my chest hurt—they might be suffering and dying right now, as I stand on the doorstep, unable to hear their dear little voices crying weakly for help.

I say, "I'm wondering . . . if we could just *look* at the house . . . it's where my grandparents used to live. I have such fond memories of it . . . such a sentimental attachment . . . I so want to show my daughter . . ."

The woman isn't stupid. Why am I asking to see the house where my grandparents used to live when a moment ago I was telling her that they still live there? Something doesn't compute. Can she tell that Daisy is not my daughter? Does Daisy wonder: Why is Auntie Ruth lying?

The flicker of disquiet that crosses the woman's pretty face lets me know that she's all alone in the house. It's a tell, like gamblers say. Okay, fine. Her face has told me something I need to know.

No, she's sorry, she's terribly busy. She's not going to be here long. Her husband is going to meet her here soon.

That part about the husband isn't true. He's not coming out here.

Liars know when someone is lying.

She's really scared of us. And she has reason to be. She's in my house.

This is my house, not hers. My grandparents left it to me.

Then Daisy—my wing girl—says, "Could I *please* use the bathroom?"

Daisy must be desperate. Normally, I bet, she'd rather pee her pants than ask that of a stranger. I should have thought of her bathroom needs sooner, as any *real mother* would.

No decent human being could say no, and the woman resigns herself to whatever is going to happen. Probably nothing. We're probably innocent. Honest. Just a little strange. Anyway, harmless. Who would bring such a dear little child along on a robbery-murder? I feel a mix of conflicting desires—to push past her, to hurt her, to warn her about what I might do.

Or just beg her to set my grandparents free and stop this cruel charade.

She says, "You'll have to excuse us. We're in the midst of a renovation. Your grandparents had a lovely house. But the investor who bought it let things run down. The house turned out to require an almost total gut job."

What could be crueler than telling someone you're "gutting" their childhood? Sheetrocking over your memories? This woman deserves whatever she gets, though I don't yet know what that will be. But a part of me already knows. It's as if I've lived through this before. As if I've been here and seen this. As if I've done what I'm about to do.

The sane part of me holding Daisy's hand doesn't want to listen to the crazed part of me that can see into the near future.

It's not pretty, I want to say, except that she (meaning the sane part of myself) knows that already.

The woman is still talking. About something. Nothing. "Once the systems needed updating, one thing led to another. The plumbing, the electricity, the—"

I don't know how anything leads to anything, at least not in my grandparents' house.

"The minute the contractors came on board, we had to dumpster what was left."

Since when is *dumpster* a verb?

The woman is talking nervously, filling the silence with random words. "It's like that TV show, where the couple's house is being fixed up, and the designer says, 'I have a not-very-nice surprise for you.' Well, renovating a house is one very not-very-nice surprise after another."

All this time I'm thinking that she may be about to have the *most* not-very-nice surprise of her life. I squeeze Daisy's hand to make my thoughts stop racing like a hamster on a wheel.

"Help," says Daisy. "The bathroom." She's dancing from foot to foot.

"Oh! Excuse me! This way."

I look past the woman onto a desert of plaster dust, paint-speckled tarps, ladders rising like oil rigs from the wasteland they've made of the only place where I was ever happy.

What has she done with my grandparents? Where are they? What must I do to find them?

Suddenly I'm conscious of holding a huge bag of candy. The candy I used to lure Daisy here.

"I'm Vanessa," says the woman.

"I'm Ruth," I say. "And this is my daughter, Daisy."

No reason to not give our real names. In a few moments none of that will matter.

Is Daisy looking to see why I lied? I can't look her in the eye. I can't let her solve the mystery that she might see in my face.

"The downstairs bathroom is useless," the woman—Vanessa—says. "The plumbers shut off the water. But the one upstairs still functions. Be careful not to trip on the steps. The tarp's—"

"Can you come with me?" Daisy, my heroine, asks me. "Can you keep me company? This house is sort of scary."

I look at the woman for permission. Permission to move through my own home.

"Go ahead," she says. "I promise, dear, that it won't be the least bit scary by the time we fix it up. It will feel comfy and safe and nice. The bathroom is at the top of the stairs. I'll walk you up."

Daisy has no idea what this woman is saying. She

literally can't hear. The only voice she's hearing is saying: I need to pee!

Do I really need this *stranger*, this *intruder*, to tell *me* that Daisy and I can go upstairs? On the second floor, unless she's destroyed it, is my old room stuffed with memories of my childhood successes. With memories from when I was Daisy's age and the sun hadn't turned its back on me in order to shine on the lucky. That room is probably empty, if it exists at all. The walls have probably been knocked down.

The stairs are covered with white canvas, and chemical fumes sting the back of my throat.

Wherever she's got my grandparents, they are inhaling this.

Daisy sneezes.

"Bless you," Vanessa says.

We let Daisy precede us toward the bathroom at the head of the stairs. Daisy rushes in and closes the door.

Then I turn around and push the woman—Vanessa—as hard as I can.

I push her down the steps.

It doesn't feel like violence. It doesn't feel like anything. It's just something that I have to do.

Once I was crossing 23rd Street and a bicycle messenger turned the corner and came *that* close to running me over. I had to push him as hard as I could. I wasn't hurt; he wasn't hurt. We were breathless and upset.

This feels a little like that. Except that the woman at the bottom of the stairs isn't cursing me out and shooting me a dirty look and getting back on her bike and riding off.

She isn't moving.

Daisy must have heard the scream and the shockingly loud *thunks* as the woman's head hit each step, and the final heavy thud when she landed at the bottom.

I stay at the top of the stairs waiting for Daisy. I try to arrange my features to look as if nothing unusual happened while she was in the bathroom.

Finally I hear the toilet flush.

Daisy reappears.

"What was that noise?" she says.

"The nice woman," I say. "Vanessa. She had an accident."

Daisy looks beyond me and sees the woman at the base of the stairs.

"Don't look," I say, and she buries her head in my side. Did she notice that the woman's head is at a terrifying angle? Clearly her neck's been broken, but Daisy can't know that.

Daisy says, "The lady who lives here is bleeding. From her head." Daisy has seen more than I did.

I say, "She *doesn't* live here."

The woman has opened a gash in her forehead, and dark liquid—like maple syrup—is seeping onto the tarp. Now I remember what happened and what the liquid is.

"Is that real blood?" Daisy says.

She wants to hear that it isn't. But for once—at this moment, of all moments—I can't bring myself to lie.

"Don't be scared," I say. "She fell. She had an accident. She'll be fine. We need to call a doctor. I promise. She'll be fine."

I hit reset and I fake a 9-1-1 call on a nonexistent phone. I don't like lying to Daisy, but you can't expect kids to handle the truth.

I wish I weren't thinking of Charlotte. I wish I weren't wondering how to persuade Daisy not to tell her parents what we did today, starting with the candy and ending with the dead woman at the base of the stairs.

I steer Daisy around the woman. I can't stop myself from bending down and moving the dead woman's head so that it doesn't look so skewed and awful.

And so no one can see her from the window.

Does she have a husband? I feel sorry for whoever finds her. I hope it's the carpenters or the painters, and not a loved one or a child.

Daisy says, "You've got blood on you."

I wipe it on my skirt.

I'm not worried about fingerprints. No one's going to wonder what happened. Our homeowner tripped on the sloppy tarp. The contractors will be lucky if they don't get slapped with a lawsuit. There's no forced entry. No sign of a struggle. No one's going to check for DNA, besides which Daisy and I obviously aren't in the system, as they say on TV.

I can't ask Daisy to stay here while I search the house to see what this woman did with Granny Edith and Grandpa Frank. I'll have to rescue them later.

I'll bring Daisy home and come back. I hope I can get back before the police get here. If my grandparents have survived this long, they can hold out a few more hours . . .

I call down toward the basement.

"Grandpa! Granny! Are you down there?"

All I get is a blast of mildew.

Maybe I don't want to know what happened to them. Maybe their remains got thrown into the dumpster with the drywall and all the beautiful wallpaper. I can't let myself think about what the house used to be. If I start to remember, I'll crawl into a corner and stay there until someone finds me and Daisy and . . . the dead woman. Vanessa.

I can't do that to Daisy.

I hate the sight of blood. Why am I thinking of Eli? Lady Macbeth. I told a little lie about playing Lady Macbeth in high school. Out, out damned spot, all the perfumes in Arabia . . . Who cares if that bloodstained queen wasn't me? I played one of the witches. I was typecast. Underestimated. Like always.

I say, "We'll get cleaned up later."

What does *later* mean? What will we do after this? I can't think that far ahead.

I'd imagined the nice meal Daisy would have. Granny Edith's delicious cooking. Fried chicken, mashed potatoes, coleslaw. Then I would bring Daisy home. That was as far as I got.

Vanessa spoiled all that.

Recalibrate. Reconsider. I need a new plan.

Maybe Granny Edith and Grandpa Frank are still watching out for me, wherever they are. Because there, in the hall, not far from Vanessa's head, is a little table—exactly where the table was when my grandparents lived here. And on the table are car keys and the garage keys, just like they always were back then.

It's a message from my grandparents. They're taking care of me, still.

Thank you, Grandpa Frank!

I know where the garage is. I take the keys, grab Daisy's hand, and go around back of the house.

One key unlocks the garage door. I almost expect to see Grandpa's Caddy. But these new people have gotten rid of that along with the evidence of their crime.

They have a fancy but sensible family car, a Volvo SUV. A Volvo is way safer for Daisy than a vintage Caddy. I have their keys.

"Get in," I tell Daisy. "Road trip."

"Are we going home?" Her voice is shaky again. I wish she weren't frightened, but given what she's seen, I can't really blame her.

"The long way home," I tell her. "You'll be home before bedtime. I promise."

29

Rocco

Rocco's head aches. Pain knuckles between his forehead and at the back of his neck, like two fists so strong they can hold him suspended in their grip.

He's woken from a long dream to find himself in a room he knows and doesn't know, as familiar and strange as a place in a dream. Ruth's apartment looks different. Everything that used to seem charming or cool now seems sinister and mocking, like a nasty joke she's playing on him even when she isn't there. Especially when she isn't there.

His niece is missing. Ruth took Daisy.

His sister's eyes are scarlet and raw. And it's all his fault.

What did he see in Ruth? Who would believe him, who would care, if he told them about the nights when he woke from troubling dreams—and Ruth, always a light sleeper, woke the same moment he did? Her dreams were just like his. He dreamed of a house; she dreamed of a house. He dreamed of a plane; so did she. Did she ever tell him her dreams first? How easy it must have been to lie about her dreams if she lied about everything else. He'd thought they were so connected that they communicated even in their sleep.

They shared the same dreams, had the same thoughts. Finished each other's sentences. But he didn't even know her name.

Naomi? Who *is* that? And who is Ruth? That person—Ruth—never existed.

He should have left her in Mexico. Maybe she wouldn't have gotten back to New York in time to kidnap Daisy. But probably she'd be back by now, like the evil dead in zombie films.

There were so many signs. Not just whispers but shouts. The nonexistent start-up. The beggar children in Oaxaca. The missing passport. The pastry from downstairs! The job with the baroness! If someone told him about a guy who stayed with a woman after all that, he would think the guy was insane or very, very stupid. Of course Rocco always really knew the truth. And by the time they got back from Mexico, he most *certainly* knew.

Ruth assaulted Reyna. And now she has taken his niece.

When he realized that the pastry she'd brought Charlotte was from downstairs and not baked by her granny, that's when he should have bailed. He was so embarrassed about that, he'd lied to Charlotte. Worse, he'd lied to himself. Is anyone *not* lying? Probably Daisy. Where is she? Now his niece is missing, because he is lazy and passive, and because he likes getting laid on a regular basis.

The first time he'd seen the pastry in the bakery window, he and Ruth were passing it together. Ruth gave his arm a squeeze. It was their fun little secret, their joke on Charlotte, whom Ruth had convinced that her granny baked it. In that conspiratorial moment, Rocco-and-Ruth-against-the-world went upstairs to Ruth's bed and had amazing sex.

Granny Edith didn't bake those sticky buns. Now it turns out that Ruth's grandparents are dead. The truth is that they have been dead for years.

Where was she getting her money? Maybe he'll never know, no more than he'll know what happened to her passport.

Her stories were always so detailed. Who could invent lies like that? He'd wanted to believe her.

Now he's paying the price. He'd always known that a reckoning would come.

He's never been happier to see his van, parked where he left it on Nassau, not towed away overnight. Patient old friend, his vehicle, waiting for him, no matter what.

He pulls away from the curb and rounds the block. Charlotte has come downstairs. So far, so good.

As his sister buckles herself in, she turns and looks at the nest of discarded jackets, cables, wooden farm crates in the back of his van. The part of her that expects to find Daisy—the part that coexists with the terrified part that thinks her daughter is gone forever—says that the back seat is not a safe place for a child to ride home when they find her.

Rocco says, "We'll work it out." The mess in the back is the least of their problems.

"Okay," Charlotte says.

He sets Waze for the Hoboken address and puts his phone in the holder on the dashboard.

All he wants is to get where they're going and not hit anyone. All he wants is to find Daisy. He's always been good at finding things. He was that person in his family. The finder. He'd found his mother's favorite soup ladle, slid behind the stove. Once, Charlotte lost a diamond ring she'd inherited from their aunt, and he'd found it in a pile of autumn leaves. Something had led him to it. Now something will lead him to Daisy. Once, he'd found Ruth's lost earring in their bed. Ruth—or whoever she is.

He has no idea what Charlotte's thinking. All he needs to do is follow the cheerful electronic voice. Let's take the Williamsburg Bridge. Exit left for the Lincoln Tunnel.

He's never been to Hoboken. These days, that doesn't matter. The GPS will get them through. In that way, it's a great time to be alive. But for him and Charlotte—and Daisy—this is the worst time ever.

A mustard-colored Saturn cuts him off, and Rocco brakes, not hard, but hard enough so that Charlotte jolts forward.

"Watch it," she says. "I taught you to drive."

He can't even be annoyed at her. Everything is his fault.

In his fantasies, they find Daisy. He imagines Ruth and Daisy sitting on the steps of the grandparents'—the *dead* grandparents'—brownstone. Or maybe they're hiding behind the bushes.

It will be fine with him if Ruth and Daisy have been

picked up by police. Scary for Daisy, but at least they'll be warm and safe.

Somehow he knows they'll be at the Hoboken address. Maybe he didn't figure out some important things about Ruth—Naomi—whoever she is. But he knows her well enough to predict where she'd go if she stole a child and was feeling insecure.

He has to keep reminding himself that her grandparents are dead.

It's a brownstone just like all the others on the block, except that it's on the corner, with a sliver of garden around the side.

All that Rocco and Charlotte see is absence: Ruth and Daisy aren't there.

Rocco says, "We'll find her. I have a feeling—"

Charlotte says, "You didn't know your fiancée's name, and now you're psychic?"

"She wasn't my fiancée," says Rocco. "And if I'm wrong this time, it's on me."

"It already is," says Charlotte.

"I'll ring the bell. See if anyone's there. Then we'll figure out what to do next."

"Ring the doorbell. It's worth a try. I'll wait in the van." Charlotte seems to have slipped into a trance. Borderline catatonic. Rocco wishes Eli were here to help him with his sister.

Maybe it's just that Charlotte doesn't know what to do after this. If Ruth and Daisy aren't here. The trouble is, he doesn't know what they'll do, either.

No one answers the doorbell. Inside, the lights are off, except in a back room, maybe a kitchen. Or maybe the TV room. That's how Ruth described it.

Light shines weakly into the foyer, onto a tangle of paint cans and tarps.

Otherwise he sees nothing.

Charlotte is yelling at him from the van.

"I've got a signal!"

There's nothing to see here. He runs back to the van.

Charlotte has checked the asthma-inhaler locator app. The bunny bounces on the map.

"Look. Does this mean anything?"

Rocco stares at it for a while.

"Wait. I just thought of something. Ruth used to talk about this picnic spot where her grandparents used to go. It's around where the light's blinking. Not all that far from where we are. Just up the Hudson."

If everything Ruth said was a lie, why should she have told the truth about her grandparents' picnic spot? Because Rocco believes that it's true. Because he sees the evidence on the map. The bunny, bouncing.

Charlotte calls Eli and tells him to meet them there—

with the police, if he can. If Daisy isn't there, at least her inhaler is.

Rocco says, "One thing I know about Ruth. She would never ditch Daisy's inhaler."

Charlotte says, "You know nothing about her. Her name is Naomi."

Rocco fiddles with Charlotte's phone till he finds the spot on the map where the bunny jitters.

"Let's give it a try," he says.

30
Ruth

You never know when your worst trauma will be the thing that saves you. All those times I was terrified out of my wits, in the back seat of the Caddy while Grandpa Frank rampaged through Hoboken and somehow got us to the picnic spot, I'd stare out the window, wondering: Should I beg Grandpa to let me drive or shut up and save his pride? I memorized every landmark between their house and the riverside clearing in case I had to take over and drive them home.

That's why I can find the picnic spot even though it's growing dark and Daisy is getting upset.

Such a polite little person! She doesn't complain or ask questions, but I can feel the anxiety seeping from her as she sits securely seat-belted into the front seat beside me.

Charlotte would never let her ride up front. I probably shouldn't, either, but Daisy seems to love it. She's a tiny bit anxious about missing Mommy and Daddy, but otherwise she's enjoying every minute. We could be on a motorcycle—that's how wild and free she feels.

She's already forgotten the dead woman in my grandparents' house.

"I want my mommy," Daisy whines.

I try to reassure her. "Hey, little pal. Would you like me to drive faster?"

No one's ever asked her that before.

"Yes," she says. "Can you go *really* fast?"

As I floor the Volvo, it's as if I'm *becoming* my grandpa.

Am I me or Grandpa Frank? That's an interesting question. Grandpa Frank didn't kill a woman lying dead in Hoboken.

My grandparents should have killed her when she came to steal their house.

Daisy's saying something in a twittery voice that sounds like Granny Edith's annoying chirping.

I can't hear her. I don't want to. I need to concentrate.

I find the turnoff, then the picnic spot. Thank you! It's still there!

I can't remember how long it's been. You always worry that a place will be changed beyond recognition. I was afraid that the clearing would have been turned into riverfront condos. But unlike the Hoboken brownstone, the spot matches my memory precisely.

I know that I will find them here, waiting for me and Daisy.

The willow tree leans into the water. The remains of the apple orchard, older but even more beautiful, say, Ruthie, you're back! Welcome home!

It isn't the tree's voice. It isn't my Granny Edith's voice.

It's someone else. A child. Daisy.

"What are we doing here?"

"Having a picnic. Like I promised."

"What are we eating?"

"Fried chicken. Coleslaw. Potato salad. Lemonade."

I show her the picnic hamper.

"That's a bag of candy."

Am I joking or serious? She doesn't know whether to laugh.

Moments like this, I see myself as a child.

I never knew what was funny. That's what Grandpa Frank used to say. Sometimes he would hit me when I didn't get the joke.

Granny Edith unpacks the picnic basket, its metal

sides printed with green-and-white plaid. She unwraps the fried chicken, opens the tubs of coleslaw and potato salad, the lemonade in the thermos she gives a vigorous shake.

I help Daisy to the chicken, the sides, the lemonade.

"How is it?" I say.

"I'm getting tired of candy," she says. "I'm starving. I want real food. I'm bored."

"This isn't boring," I say. "It's fun."

"It's boring," Daisy says.

"Have some more chicken," I say.

"It's not chicken, it's candy," says Daisy. "I'm tired of this game."

We enjoy our picnic in silence. We don't have to speak.

For the first time all day, I think that the business suit and heels were a mistake, a terrible choice for a picnic in the country. I'm cold.

Daisy's busy eating.

Granny Edith and Grandpa Frank are curious about Daisy.

But the four of us have four lifetimes to say what we need to say.

Four concurrent life sentences. Why am I thinking that?

I say, "Do you know any poems?"

"No," Daisy says. "My teacher reads us poems. But I don't know any."

"I know a poem."

I take a deep breath and begin:

James James
Morrison Morrison
Weatherby George Dupree
Took great
Care of his Mother
Though he was only three.
James James
Said to his Mother,
"Mother," he said, said he:
"You must never go down to the end of the town,
*   if you don't go down with me."*

"I don't like that poem," says Daisy.

"Come on," I say. "It's funny. It's sweet. My grandpa used to say it."

James James
Morrison's Mother
Put on a golden gown,
James James
Morrison's Mother

Drove to the end of town.
James James
Morrison's Mother
Said to herself, said she:
"I can get right down to the end of the town and be
  back in time for tea."

King John
Put up a notice,
"Lost or stolen or strayed!
James James
Morrison's Mother
Seems to have been mislaid—"

"I hate that poem," says Daisy. "Stop saying it. Stop it now. I want to go home. I'm hungry and cold. I want my mommy and daddy."

"All right," I say. "The party's over. You're right. It's getting too chilly for a picnic. Let's get in the car, and I'll take you home."

Bye-bye, Grandpa and Granny.

They'll clean up the remains of the picnic.

Daisy and I get into the SUV. I turn the key in the ignition. Nothing happens.

The engine won't start. I try again. Nothing.

I am being punished. Why is it always me? People

do things a million times worse and get rewarded. I get punished for nothing. I'm the one who gets locked in the basement with the spiders.

"What's wrong with your car?" Daisy says.

It's not my car. Has she forgotten what happened in Hoboken?

The woman in the hall.

"Nothing," I say. "We can figure this out. We made it work so far, right?"

Daisy says, "I want my mommy and daddy. Now." She sounds years younger than she did two minutes ago.

I think, Too bad. *I* want my mommy and daddy. Everyone wants their mommy and daddy.

"Okay." I try not to sound stressed. "We're on our way. Hold on. Your auntie Ruth—"

"You're not my aunt," she says. "My uncle's going to break up with you like he did with all his other girl-friends."

"Don't say that," I tell her. "I mean it."

I have a feeling she's crying, but I don't want to see.

I try the key again. Nothing.

I don't know what to do. It's getting colder, darker. Daisy will be scared. She already is. We don't want to be here. There's no way we can walk back to the high-way. It's too far, in the dark. Too dangerous. There's no way we can get help.

We'll have to figure out something. *I* will, anyway.

"Call my mom," says Daisy.

"I forgot my phone," I say. "It was stupid of me not to bring it."

That's more information than a child needs.

"I don't know what I was thinking. Even grown-ups do stupid things sometimes."

Daisy sobs. "I'm freezing."

I say, "Let's turn your inhaler tracker back on. Maybe your mom will check her app."

I can still be brilliant. A survivor. Cool, even at moments like this.

I know Charlotte is checking the app. I know she won't have given up.

For once she'll remember she has it.

Daisy and I *are* the inhaler, and we want her mother to find us.

31

Charlotte

Rocco drives fast and well, and with each mile that passes, he's gradually working his way back into Charlotte's good graces. It's as if they have company, four presences in the van. Rocco, Charlotte, the GPS voice, the cartoon bunny bouncing on her phone. Let Rocco watch the road, she's staring at her screen, never letting it out of her sight, as if the cartoon might vanish.

Rocco's saying it's not far, but it's taking forever. Every red light, every slowdown. She wants to pound the dashboard or slam her fist against the window.

Rocco must feel the tension streaming off her, but he's in no position to criticize or tell her to calm down. He knows it's his fault. But he's wrong.

It's not only Rocco's fault. It's also Charlotte's and Eli's.

They knew something was wrong with Ruth, but they didn't expect this. Charlotte should have been on guard starting when Ruth made them eat those sticky buns. She *was* on guard. Or so she thought.

Rocco says, "Breathe," and Charlotte draws in a rattling croak.

"Suit yourself," he says. "Don't breathe."

After a moment, he says, "Joke."

Charlotte isn't laughing.

The GPS and the bunny cartoon lead them off the road and into a clearing by the river. It's almost dark. There's no one around.

Can your heart literally break? Charlotte feels it might be happening. Something's cracking in her chest, like ice on a pond at the end of winter.

One car—a Volvo SUV—is in the parking area.

How could Ruth be driving a car like that? Did she have an accomplice?

Did a serial murderer leave Daisy's inhaler in that car? Panic destroys the hope beeping at her from the pulsing blue cartoon.

Rocco and Charlotte get out of the van and walk toward the Volvo with its lights off.

"If this was TV, we'd have guns," Rocco says.

"I was thinking that," says Charlotte.

The front passenger door bursts open, and a bright purple creature jumps out and runs in their direction.

Daisy is racing toward them. She's wearing her purple jacket.

Charlotte's shock and joy are so intense that at first she doesn't believe it's really Daisy.

Is she imagining this? Seeing what she wants to see? Please let this be real.

It's only when she's holding Daisy, inhaling the dusty-kid smell of her hair, that she knows it's real. Daisy is here with her. Safe.

Impossible. But already the last few hours are beginning to seem like a bad dream.

"Where were you?" Charlotte says.

"Ruth got me from school. We had a picnic," she says. "But it got cold."

Charlotte wants to ask Daisy if she was scared, but she doesn't. If she wasn't scared, Charlotte doesn't want to make her think that she should have been. Or that she was in danger.

"Ruth said we were eating fried chicken, but it was candy."

"Candy!" Trying to normalize this, Charlotte struggles to sound disapproving. Nothing's worse than candy!

"It was boring," says Daisy.

Charlotte usually tries to keep Daisy from saying that anything is boring. How silly, how trivial she used to be. The only thing in the world that matters is that Daisy is here. Alive and well.

"We went to this old house," says Daisy. "They were fixing it. A lady let me use her bathroom. Then she fell down the stairs and was lying at the bottom of the stairs. And there was blood. Real red blood."

The chill Charlotte feels seems to be coming from some new, freezing-cold place deep inside her. They'll have to take Daisy to see someone, a therapist. Not just any therapist, not one like . . . oh, God. Ted. They'll have to find out how much damage has been done, and then they'll have to fix it.

Daisy's going to be okay . . . It's Ruth who will never . . . *Who was the woman who was bleeding?*

"Where's Ruth?"

On cue, the door on the driver's side opens, and Ruth steps—no, tumbles—out. She's walking half bent over.

"Is Ruth okay?" Charlotte asks Daisy.

Daisy looks bewildered.

Ruth is heading for Rocco. Charlotte has almost forgotten him in her joy at finding Daisy. He'd stepped back and let them have their reunion. He's just the loving uncle.

The only way to help Rocco is to forgive him and hope this mistake is big enough to make an impression. It's not Rocco's fault that Mom was who she was. That Mom is who she *is*. Rocco is Charlotte's brother. That's the bedrock fact of their lives, and Charlotte will never desert him.

Rocco turns his back on Ruth, and Ruth stops cold, then shambles over to Charlotte and Daisy. Charlotte braces herself for Ruth to muscle Daisy into saying they had fun, but Ruth is beyond that.

She hardly notices Daisy. She hardly knows that Daisy's there.

She seems to have collapsed in on herself. The bright, confident young woman whom Rocco brought over to their loft has turned into a shattered wreck, ten years older and sadder than she'd looked only yesterday—*how could it be just yesterday?*—in the Oaxaca airport.

There's dried blood on her hands. She stares at it.

Out, out damned spot. Lady Macbeth. The bad-luck part.

Charlotte passes Daisy over to Rocco, partly to put more distance between Daisy and Ruth. She is operating on instinct now, maternal adrenaline. She's grateful that her brother is here. That Rocco has her back.

Ruth holds out her arms to Charlotte. Surprising

Daisy and Rocco, shocking herself, Charlotte puts her arms around Ruth and gives her a hug.

Poor Ruth!

Despite everything she's done to them, she's a suffering human, in pain. Their happy lives will be happy again. Her sad life is about to get sadder.

Charlotte feels lucky, so blessed that she has compassion to spare. Forgive those who have trespassed against us.

She can forgive Ruth, but the law won't. Charlotte can have it both ways. Forgiveness and revenge.

Ruth is shaking from cold and fear. It's unpleasant, holding a broken person who has done something so awful to you and your family. Charlotte feels Ruth's terror almost as if it were her own.

"Ruth," Charlotte says.

By the time tonight is over, Charlotte thinks, she and Eli and Daisy will be safe and home. Rocco will spend the night with them, like before.

And what will happen to Ruth? Where did she get that SUV? Who is the woman lying, bloodied, at the base of the stairs? Will Daisy have to give a statement? Will Charlotte be called upon to testify that Ruth isn't responsible for her actions? Ruth belongs in a hospital . . .

Rocco says, "Eli's on his way. Along with the police."

Soon Eli will be here.

Charlotte will wait a few days before she tells him that they have to talk about Daisy.

She'll tell him about Andrew John.

At least part of the story. Like her, Eli will be so happy to have Daisy back that nothing else will matter.

The police will have taken Ruth away. There will be statements, a trial.

"My name is Naomi," Ruth says. "My grandparents are dead."

Charlotte and Ruth stand at the edge of the bank looking down at the river. Charlotte hears Daisy chattering to Rocco, but she can't hear what she's saying.

Night has fallen, and tiny triangles of moonlight glisten on the wave caps puckering the Hudson. A barge floating downriver honks its horn. It echoes into the velvety night, bouncing off the rising fog.

The foghorn is the fog's voice. Charlotte listens to what it is saying.

The voice says, You are one of the lucky ones.

You are safe for now.

About the Author

DARCEY BELL is the author of the *New York Times* bestselling hit *A Simple Favor*, which was adapted into a major motion picture starring Blake Lively and Anna Kendrick. *Something She's Not Telling Us* is her second novel.

HARPER LARGE PRINT

We hope you enjoyed reading
our new, comfortable print size and found it
an experience you would like to repeat.

Well – you're in luck!

Harper Large Print offers the finest in
fiction and nonfiction books in this same larger
print size and paperback format. Light and easy to read,
Harper Large Print paperbacks are for the book lovers
who want to see what they are reading without strain.

For a full listing of titles and
new releases to come, please visit our website:
www.hc.com

HARPER LARGE PRINT